Who had betrayed her?

In Rizal park she saw nothing. No brother and no milling crowds. But the tall Caucasian man about a quarter of a mile away caught Marilyn's attention. When he turned and began to walk toward her, she realized he was FBI. Had Mac told the Bureau about her? Had the agent come all the way from California to arrest her for espionage?

When a second man got out of a taxi and paid the fare, Marilyn's body stiffened in shock. It was Mac himself!

A gamut of confusing emotions made her feel like screaming. If Mac truly loved her, could he betray her? Were the past three days of passion and desire nothing more than lies?

Marilyn refused to believe that Mac's love was just another ruse designed to make her trust him...and yet she knew Mac McDonough was a very clever, cunning man.

ABOUT THE AUTHOR

Vickie York has served as a commissioned officer in both the U.S. Army and U.S. Air Force. After an assignment to the Defense Language Institute in Monterey, California, Vickie served as an intelligence officer for the rest of her military career. She was awarded a Bronze Star for service during the Vietnam conflict. Beginning with the publication of *The Pestilence Plot* in 1982, in hardcover, her novels have been based on her intelligence expertise. Vickie has traveled extensively and now makes her home in Tacoma, Washington, where she was born. She enjoys riding ferries on Puget Sound with special friends, singing in the church choir and taking long walks with her German shepherd.

Books by Vickie York

HARLEQUIN INTRIGUE
43–A TOP SECRET AFFAIR
73–MORE THAN A HUNCH
178–SCHOOL FOR SPIES

Liar's Game

Vickie York

Harlequin Books

TORONTO • NEW YORK • LONDON
AMSTERDAM • PARIS • SYDNEY • HAMBURG
STOCKHOLM • ATHENS • TOKYO • MILAN
MADRID • WARSAW • BUDAPEST • AUCKLAND

For Kathleen
Who, like the heroine of *Liar's Game,*
was also a reluctant double agent

Harlequin Intrigue edition published January 1993

ISBN 0-373-22211-4

LIAR'S GAME

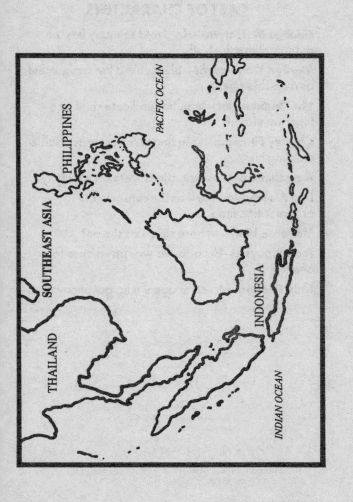

CAST OF CHARACTERS

George MacIntyre—He'd told so many lies, he didn't believe the truth.

Marilyn Wainwright—She flunked her assignment as a double agent.

Van Wainwright—Was he syndicate chief or innocent victim?

Charley Finnegan—MacIntyre's boss was double-crossing him.

Tony Benson—Assassinations were his specialty.

Dan Moschella—He was the consummate organization man.

Madame Vinh—Whose side was she on?

Toan Nguyen—His address was listed once too often.

Thuy Phoung—A secret agent who got uncovered.

Chapter One

Flipping the file folder closed before he was half finished scanning the papers inside, George MacIntyre shoved it across the table toward his boss, Charles Finnegan.

"Sure you got the right party here, Charley?" he asked, in his best New York City accent.

Whenever Mac sensed an emerging difficulty with his superiors, he spoke with enough nasal sounds to remind them of his rough-and-tumble origins on Manhattan's lower east side. The fact that he had a law degree didn't mean he reserved his bare-knuckle fights for adversaries outside the FBI's Washington headquarters.

Tilting his chair back as far as it would go, he clasped both hands behind his head. "The lady in this folder sounds more like a candidate for a convent than *our* tender attentions. There's nothing she could've done that's worth the time and money this sting's gonna cost."

The paunchy balding man across the table smiled with the bureaucratic self-confidence of one privy to special information. "That's where you're wrong, Mac," he said. "Ms. Marilyn Wainwright's been stealing secrets for a Vietnamese syndicate headed by her brother. They're peddling them to the highest bidder." He paused.

Mac knew Finnegan was waiting for him to ask how the bureau had found out. Since security regulations prevented his boss from revealing the source of his information, there wasn't much point in asking—other than to give Finnegan a chance to flaunt his already considerable authority. Grinning, Mac remained silent.

With no questions forthcoming, Finnegan frowned. "Our analysts figured out the information's being stolen from the Wakefield Aircraft Corporation in San Diego. They've pinpointed this woman as the spy."

Mac's eyebrows, a couple of shades lighter than his wavy copper-red hair, rose at his boss's words. "Are you saying the little librarian described in this folder—" he began "—this paragon of virtue who's the darlin' of her neighbors—this loving daughter who's footing the nursing-home bill for her sick mother—" He paused dramatically. "Faith now, Mr. Finnegan, you can't be telling me this little lady's a loathsome spy."

From his boss's chuckle, Mac could tell that Finnegan appreciated his quick switch in accents. Mac could change personalities almost as easily—one of the reasons he was the bureau's best undercover agent. A wiry man just under six feet tall, he exuded the dangerous charm of a playful tiger.

"We're almost one-hundred percent sure she's the one we're after, Mac."

"But not absolutely positive." This time Mac used no accent of any kind.

Finnegan responded with a sound that was more of a grunt than the sarcastic laugh he probably intended. "C'mon now, Mac, if we were one-hundred percent sure, she'd be on her way to court." He rubbed his pawlike hands together. "Don't worry. She's the one, all right. The others with unlimited access at Wakefield are clean, and the information started leaking about the time she was cleared for the vault."

"Which was?"

"Look for yourself. It's right there in the folder. Do us both a favor and spend five minutes going through it."

Reluctantly Mac reached for the folder again. The endless paperwork that seemed to go along with every operation aggravated him. Quickly he scanned the information on each page, memorizing pertinent facts, retaining a sharp impression of the rest.

The suspected spy was Marilyn Wainwright: twenty-six years old, five-foot-three, slender build. Graduate of the University of California at San Diego in library science. Good grades in college. Good credit ratings. Favorable comments from the neighbors questioned about her during the background investigation for her Category five security clearance. It was granted three months ago.

Mac sighed. If the info in this folder was any indication, Marilyn Wainwright had all the dash and excitement of a plate of cottage cheese. At least she probably wasn't a virgin. The neighbors reported a long-term relationship with a navy lieutenant who was "just as nice as she is," in the words of one of them.

He looked up after reading their comments.

"What do you think, Charley? This boyfriend going to be any trouble?"

Across the table, Finnegan smiled happily, obviously pleased at Mac's show of interest. "The boyfriend's kaput," he said. "We've had a bug on her phone the past few days. She dumped the lieutenant the last time he shipped out of San Diego. He's called a few times since he got back in town, but she keeps turning him down."

"Good," Mac said. "I'll be able to get more time with her." To himself he thought: *Maybe she fooled him just like she fooled all the neighbors.* Well, she wouldn't fool George MacIntyre. He could spot a phony female no matter how convincing she was.

He returned to the folder, this time studying the black-and-white head-and-shoulders picture fastened to the inside front cover. Round plastic-rimmed glasses dominated her face. That told him something, first crack off the bat. Most women took their glasses off for a photo, but not Ms. Marilyn Wainwright. *Typical librarian,* he thought, *high-necked blouse and all.* She wore her dark hair pulled away from her face, probably up in a roll of some kind on the back of her head. A wave drooped above her right eyebrow, softening her already delicate features.

Too bad she's not a big blonde, he thought. *That'd liven up this assignment considerably.* At least in San Diego he'd be able to log some beach time, and that counted for a lot in Mac's book. He glanced at his boss again. "What about the brother? How the hell did he get tangled up with these gangs of Vietnamese thugs?"

Finnegan leaned a pudgy elbow on the table. "He's half Vietnamese, Mac, four years older than the sister. Their father brought him to this country in the sixties, when he found out he'd fathered a son while he was over there in the early part of the conflict."

Mac whistled. "Mrs. Wainwright must be one hell of an understanding wife."

"They weren't married when he was in Vietnam. He already had the boy with him by the time they got together."

"Then the kid—what's his name?" Mac checked the file. "Van—grew up right along with Marilyn?"

Finnegan nodded. "It's all there in the record. They got along well together, even as kids. Didn't seem to make any difference that he was a half brother."

"What the record doesn't say is how she got a Category five clearance when her brother runs a crime syndicate. Any fool knows a person with a family connection like that should be turned down for a top-level clearance."

Studying his superior's face, Mac caught a flicker of hesitation. For the first time it occurred to him that there was more to this case than he was being told. Uneasily he stood up and paced back and forth along the length of the table, his black oxfords making no sound on the carpeted floor.

"The truth is, Mac," Finnegan said, "the San Diego office just alerted us to the brother's connection to the syndicate. We've decided to nail them both."

Mac didn't like what he was hearing. Eyes narrowed, he paused and leaned toward his boss, resting his forearms on the chair he'd just vacated. "We don't have much of a case, do we, Charley? You're expecting me to work some kind of miracle with this sting operation? Well, what if she doesn't bite? After all the taxpayers' money that's going into this, somebody's going to want your head on a silver platter if she guesses what we're up to. Just make sure mine's not on it, too."

"She'll bite," Finnegan soothed. "She won't be able to resist your charms. I'm betting you'll have this whole thing wrapped up by Christmas."

"In two weeks? Don't get your hopes up, Charley my boy." Mac unbuttoned his suit coat and started pacing again. The trouble with being the bureau's boy wonder was that his success was taken for granted. No matter how many operations went like clockwork, George MacIntyre never took success for granted. He ran lean fingers through his red hair, leaving it in boyish disarray.

His boss leaned toward him. "For this job, you're George McDonough, buying secrets about the British for the Irish Republican Army. With your coloring, the IRA cover's a natural. As soon as she agrees to steal classified info for you, we've got her."

"And how do I arrange to meet this virtuous-looking traitor?" Mac asked, returning to his chair.

"She's running a situation-wanted ad in the local paper. Says she's a librarian who wants to do part-time research. All you have to do is answer the ad and turn on that famous Scottish charm of yours."

Mac flipped the folder shut again and shoved it toward his boss. "If she's getting paid for all this juicy information her brother and his syndicate are peddling, why's she advertising for extra work?" His hazel eyes lanced Finnegan's.

Finnegan didn't look away. "Because she's a smart cookie, Mac. Based on her profile, the analysts downstairs say she's not likely to change her life-style until she's made her pile. That way nobody's the wiser about what she and her brother are up to."

Mac knew a spy with any smarts avoided spending his profits to increase his standard of living or make changes in his normal routine. Apparently Miss Librarian fit into the "smart spy" category.

"It's possible they use the ad to contact potential customers," Finnegan added.

That makes sense, too, Mac thought. The relaxed, congenial expression left his face. It was replaced by a tense alertness, the kind of alertness a man needs to stay alive under fire. "Then they've caught themselves a mighty big fish," he said.

San Diego

FADING LATE-AFTERNOON sunshine filtered through the open doors near the Hotel del Coronado's registration desk. The hotel was the crown jewel on Coronado, a strip of expensive real estate connected to San Diego by a mile-long bridge. Inside the hotel's dark, wood-paneled lobby, guests drank apple cider flavored with cinnamon sticks while they listened to holiday songs played on an ebony grand piano.

Seated on a comfortable couch near the fifteen-foot-high, old-fashioned Christmas tree, Marilyn Wainwright checked her wristwatch for at least the tenth time in the last forty minutes.

Why couldn't people be on time? she wondered, feeling irritated. She'd left work half an hour early to make it by four-thirty. Now here she sat, waiting for somebody who probably had no intention of showing up.

She should have known! That brogue he'd affected on the telephone last night should have given her a clue. Nobody this side of the British Isles spoke with an accent that thick. Obviously somebody was kidding her. Even if he wasn't, Marilyn wasn't sure she wanted to work for a person as undependable as this man was turning out to be, no matter how much he paid or how much she needed the money.

Twisting her head, she searched the lobby for a red-haired man about six feet tall in jeans and a dark sweater. That's how he'd described himself.

Nobody. Apparently he wasn't coming. Picking up her black leather briefcase and bulky knit sweater, she stood to go.

Almost as though he'd been waiting for her to move, an auburn-haired man appeared from behind the Christmas tree.

With his square tanned face, sinewy six-foot frame, and burnished hair the color of an Irish setter's, he looked like somebody out of *Sports Illustrated*—not the least bit like a man who needed a researcher. In addition to the jeans and dark sweater, he wore the most charming smile she'd ever seen.

Marilyn didn't smile back. It was best to be all business until she found out what he was up to. Since she'd been advertising for extra work, she'd had a couple of calls from out-of-towners more interested in a dating service than research. On the phone, this man, too, had sounded as though he had an ulterior motive, despite his entirely legitimate questions about her work.

Deciding she was reacting to his strong accent, Marilyn had chided herself for being prejudiced. She'd agreed to meet him here in the hotel lobby. Now, looking at his roguish smile, she wondered if she shouldn't have trusted her intuition.

"Marilyn Wainwright? I'm George McDonough." His voice was confident, but she detected a thread of tension underlying the easy tones. Beneath the charming smile was a coiled spring, ready to snap loose with minimum provocation.

"I'm Ms. Wainwright, Mr. McDonough." She didn't offer him her hand. Neither did he, his. *Good,* she thought. Marilyn believed in shaking hands after agreements were made, not before.

She watched his eyes course down her high-necked, long-sleeved cotton blouse to her pleated, gray wool skirt, to her nylon-clad legs and to her sensible low-heeled black pumps. Suddenly, Marilyn wished she'd worn something a little more colorful to work that morning. After all, it was the Christmas season.

"My friends call me Mac." His voice was smooth, its range somewhere between tenor and baritone.

"We're not friends, Mr. McDonough," she returned. "We're not even business associates yet." Might as well get him squared away right from the start.

His smile broadened. "I hope we soon will be, Ms. Wainwright. Both friends and business associates." His hazel eyes reflected the confidence in his smile. "Would you care to discuss our working arrangements here in the lobby? Or, since this isn't very private, perhaps upstairs in my room?"

She studied his face. He had the air of a man offering to do her a big favor, a favor probably unconnected with the research he'd called her about. She was tempted to walk away, but something *different* in his manner held her. Whether it was his accent, or his alert bearing, or simply the way he was standing—a little closer than new acquaintances normally stood—he was the most out-of-the-ordinary person she'd met in a long time.

She nodded toward the couch.

"We can talk here," she said, sitting down on the spot she'd just left. Two elderly women next to her squeezed closer together to make room for him at the other end. They beamed when he thanked them.

Without sitting down, he leaned over Marilyn, so close she caught a whiff of spearmint toothpaste. His hair appeared slightly damp. Apparently he'd cleaned up just before meeting her. *What was he doing the rest of the day?* she wondered and was annoyed with herself for caring.

"Sure you don't want to reconsider my offer?" he asked. Marilyn didn't have to glance at the two women beside her to realize they were listening to his every word with rapt attention.

"Positive!" she snapped. "But you're right about the privacy, Mr. McDonough." She struggled free of the cushions on the sofa. With unaccustomed perversity her wool skirt, in spite of her efforts to keep it pulled down, seemed determined to cling to the couch upholstery, revealing much of her thigh.

He didn't help her get up, just stood watching with an amused expression, his copper-red hair reflecting the multicolored lights from the Christmas tree. "You don't think I'll be trying to seduce you if you go upstairs with me?" he asked, after she'd regained her equilibrium. They started toward the garden court on the far side of the lobby.

"It doesn't matter what I think," she returned. "What matters is that we're going to discuss our business down here, not up in your room."

Outside, lights had been turned on in the garden court, an expansive green area in the center of the old Victorian hotel. A dramatic display of potted poinsettias surrounded the covered bar near the court's lobby entrance.

Marilyn draped her sweater over her shoulders and led the way to a stone bench near a towering bougainvillea vine loaded with wine-colored blossoms. She sat down carefully so she wouldn't snag her skirt or stockings on the bench, and placed her briefcase flat beside her. It would be a barrier between them.

Grinning, Mac set the case on the sidewalk before sliding his long length onto the bench.

Marilyn ignored his gesture. "So, Mr. McDonough," she began, "last night you said you were writing a book on British military history. That sounds like a subject better suited to libraries in Cambridge or Oxford than San Diego."

He leaned forward, resting his arms on his knees. "That's the certain truth of it."

Now that Marilyn was getting used to his brogue, she found it rather soothing, like a cat's purr.

"So why not get a researcher in England to help?"

"Unfortunately, I need to work closely with my researcher, Ms. Wainwright, and I'm here, not in England."

"Just why *are* you in San Diego, Mr. McDonough?"

It was the question Mac had been waiting for. For the sting to work, Marilyn Wainwright had to believe what he said so she'd agree to work for him. Sometime in the near future, he'd reveal that what he'd told her was a cover for his Irish Republican Army connection. But right now, it was imperative that she believe him.

He grinned convincingly. "Logical question," he said. Years of undercover experience went into his confident answer.

"I'm on a three-month leave of absence from the faculty at Notre Dame to the La Jolla Institute of Geophysical Phenomena. The institute's involved in a project I'm working on at the university, but I'm on a light schedule. In my spare time, I'm hoping to wrap up work on my manuscript."

"Then your book is almost finished?"

She wasn't nearly as impressed as he'd hoped by the educational background the bureau had dreamed up for George McDonough, but at least she didn't seem suspicious that it was all a fabrication.

"I'm on the last phase—the modern British army. That's what we'll be working on." He resisted the temptation to clinch the deal by offering her the exorbitant sum the bureau had suggested. Since she was pretending to be interested in the research project, maybe he could save a few bucks for the U.S. taxpayer by letting her name her own price.

Abruptly she changed the subject. "Why stay here at the old hotel if you're working in La Jolla? That's a good half-hour commute every day."

Her voice, pitched like a soprano's, had an interesting lilt to it. He heard simple curiosity, not suspicion, in her tone. He smiled to himself. *Because you live on Coronado, Marilyn my lovely Miss Librarian.* She lived only about a mile and a half away, as a matter of fact.

Aloud, he recited the answer he'd memorized at the bureau. "This place is famous all over the country. It's not every day a man gets to stay in a shingle-style Victorian hotel designed by Stanford White and used by Marilyn Monroe in one of her motion pictures."

Her eyes narrowed.

"Something be wrong with that?" he asked.

"You don't seem like a man who would pick a hotel because of its architectural design or because it was used as a setting for a movie."

Clever little thing, Mac thought. No wonder she'd been so good at fooling everybody. He'd have to be more careful, a lot more careful.

He grinned. "You've caught me trying to impress you, Ms. Wainwright," he said, improvising on the story he'd just told her. "Actually, I had no choice in the matter. The institute's paying my hotel bill and they get a special rate here. Only this morning I was told about the architect and how he was shot by Evelyn Nesbitt's jealous husband."

She bought that version, he was relieved to see.

"Everybody around here knows the story, but not many tourists. When did you arrive in San Diego, Mr. McDonough? Or is it Dr. McDonough?"

Modestly Mac looked down at the ground. He was very good at feigning modesty when the occasion warranted. It was an attitude most women found irresistible.

"I prefer not to dwell on academic titles," he said. "But it would please me very much if you'd call me Mac."

He stole a sideways look at her face. Unreadable. Too bad the damn woman was so prim and sober. Even though she was too thin for his tastes and those modish round frames on her glasses gave her an owlish look, she had the bone structure most women would give their life savings for. With a pleasant expression and the right incentive to fix herself up, she could be a real beauty. He expected her to make some sort of comment about his educational status, but she didn't.

"I arrived yesterday," he continued. "I called you right after I checked into the hotel." Actually he'd landed at San Diego's Lindberg Airport only a few hours ago. Last night's call had been made from bureau headquarters in Washington.

"What kind of a schedule did you have in mind for the research?" she asked.

At last! he thought triumphantly. "Then you've decided to work with me?"

"For now, let's just say that I haven't decided not to."

"I leave the institute at two and plan to spend the rest of the afternoon and evening working on the book. I assume you have another job since your ad mentioned part-time research?"

She nodded. "I'm a technical librarian at the Wakefield Aircraft Corporation. Like the institute, it's in La Jolla, but I get off at four-thirty, not two."

As she answered the question, Mac crossed another bit of information about her off his mental checklist. From studying her folder, he already knew her background. It was important that he didn't confuse what she'd told him with what he'd found out from her file.

"Then the earliest you could get here would be five o'clock?"

"If I stopped by directly after work, I could meet you here by five and go over the research you wanted me to do that night."

"Good!" Mac's enthusiasm was genuine. She was as good as sold. He had one more hurdle to get her across, but before he approached it, the matter of her pay needed to be settled. With that juicy carrot dangling in front of her, she'd be sure to clear the barrier.

"What kind of wage does a researcher expect in San Diego?" he asked.

She named a figure even higher than the exorbitant sum suggested by the bureau.

Mac whistled softly. "You don't come cheap, do you, Ms. Wainwright?"

"I'm not doing this for my health, Mr. McDonough. I require payment for the first thirty hours in advance. Take it or leave it." Her eyes, behind the owlish glasses, stared levelly into his.

"We'll try it for a week," he said. "Starting tonight."

Standing, she offered her hand. "We have a deal, Mac." When she smiled, the effect was dazzling.

As SOON AS Marilyn reached for her briefcase, she realized that he hadn't asked to see her résumé. A man who knew nothing about her qualifications to do his job had just agreed to pay her a very respectable amount of money in advance. Odd, to say the least.

There was still something a bit out of focus about Mac McDonough, too, the way the world looked without her glasses. Somehow it didn't seem logical for a man with his charm—*yes, Marilyn, he IS charming in a tense, perverse sort of way*—to be spending his afternoons and evenings alone in his hotel room working on a dreary old manuscript about the British army. Especially not in San Diego, where the mild climate and miles of sandy ocean beaches offered innumerable opportunities for doing just about anything outdoors.

Then there was his golden tan. It testified to hours spent either on the beach or in some tanning parlor in South Bend. It didn't go along with his professed Notre Dame faculty credentials.

Don't be prejudiced, she scolded herself. *All tanned men aren't beach bums.* Marilyn herself never tanned and was secretly envious of people who did. Most of her swimming trophies had been won in indoor pools. When she swam outdoors, she invariably ended up with an ugly sunburn, no matter how much sunscreen she lathered on her pale skin.

Beside her, Mac pressed gently on her elbow, guiding her toward the sidewalk. "Let's go inside," he said. "Now that the sun's down, it's chilly out here."

In the lobby, the crowd had changed during the short time they'd been outside. Most of the elderly women were gone, and there were more men, some in business suits. Highballs had replaced the afternoon's apple cider.

Marilyn headed for the couch near the lighted Christmas tree. Before she reached it, Mac stopped her with a hand on her arm.

"Let's get right to work," he said.

"I'll wait here while you get your outline, bibliography, whatever." She wished he wouldn't stand so close. It distracted her resolve.

"I thought you understood that we'd be working upstairs." His roguish look was back, tinged by a fine edge of impatience. That, more than anything else, made Marilyn stand her ground.

"I thought *you* understood that I don't intend to go up to your room."

"It's a suite. You won't be working in my bedroom if that's what's bothering you."

Funny little thing, Mac thought. *She'll steal government secrets for a bunch of Vietnamese bums, but she won't work with a man in his hotel suite.* "At least take a look at my setup, Marilyn. If you decide you don't want to go ahead with my research, all you've lost is the time it takes to go up there."

Marilyn sensed there was more to be lost than time if she agreed to his terms. Congenial though he seemed, there was something not quite right about this charming professor from Notre Dame.

Still, what harm could it do to glance through his door from the hallway? The work promised to be lucrative, and she couldn't afford to turn it down without a good reason.

"All right, Mac," she said, struggling to cast her doubts aside. "I guess it won't hurt to take a look at this project of yours."

He grinned down at her. "I promise you won't be sorry."

Marilyn resisted her urge to turn and walk away. *I wish I were certain of that.* Her heart pounding, she started toward the broad stairs leading to the hotel's upper floors.

Chapter Two

From the doorway Marilyn could see books piled on the coffee table and scattered helter-skelter on the sofa. More were stacked in a corner next to the cardboard boxes they'd been shipped in. A computer and printer sat on a round table near the window. Dr. George McDonough appeared to be doing exactly what he claimed: finishing a manuscript in his spare time.

"See." He waved his hand expansively in the general direction of the room's interior. "It's no den of iniquity."

Marilyn couldn't imagine why she felt so fluttery at the thought of working in his hotel suite with him. She left the door ajar when she stepped inside. "Looks like you've brought your library with you. Are these the books you want me to use as research sources?"

Marilyn's clients usually expected her to locate the reference materials herself. Apparently the professor had done part of the job and saved himself some money in the bargain. An unwelcome flicker of empathy made her lower her guard a notch. If anybody appreciated saving a few dollars by cutting a corner or two, it was Marilyn herself. Between the outrageous rent for her small apartment, the money she loaned her brother for his failing auto repair business, and her mother's expenses in the Good Life Nursing Home, she had to count every penny.

The professor grinned at her in such a charming way that Marilyn began to wonder if she wasn't being a tad para-

noid. With his square chin and laughing hazel eyes, he
seemed as harmless as a golden retriever puppy.

"That's why I suggested we work together here," he said.
"I brought most of the books I'd need along with me."

"I get suspicious when a man asks me to work in his hotel room," Marilyn explained—and immediately kicked
herself for making excuses. She didn't have to explain herself to anybody, certainly not to a client, even one as compelling as George McDonough.

"If you've had bad experiences with some of your customers, I'm surprised you advertise in the classifieds. There
must be a better way to get business."

Marilyn detected a hint of criticism in his comment. It
bothered her. She couldn't imagine why. "If you know a
better way, I'd like to hear it, Dr. McDonough."

He grinned again. "Mac, please. I didn't mean to offend
you, Marilyn. It's only that you seem very distrusting and
that upsets me." His Irish accent sounded less pronounced
than before, but maybe she was getting used to it. "You're
obviously well qualified, but the work will go much more
smoothly if we trust each other."

There it was again: a reference to her qualifications. This
time Marilyn didn't let it pass.

"How can you be so sure of my credentials when you
haven't seen my résumé?" As she asked the question, her
voice cracked. Dismayed, she cleared her throat. Marilyn
had always hated her voice because it sounded squeaky to
her when she was at her most earnest. Fortunately he seemed
too preoccupied with her question to notice. Was she wrong,
or did he hesitate before he answered, as though his mind
were searching, rapid-fire, for exactly the right response?

"Since the matter of your qualifications has come up, I've
got a confession to make." He sat down in a chair next to
the table.

Marilyn noticed that he left the one in front of the computer for her. Instead of sitting there, she crossed to the
sofa, pushing books aside to make room for herself.

Mac saw the curious look on her face. It bordered on suspicion. Damn! Why couldn't he keep his wits about him? Something about Ms. Marilyn Wainwright interrupted his finely honed concentration. He reminded himself that in spite of her fragile appearance and musical voice, this woman was a pro. He'd have to be careful or she'd realize Dr. George McDonough didn't add up.

"I checked you out this afternoon before we met," he lied, watching her closely. It was the only way he could cover his oversight.

Behind her thick lenses, her eyes narrowed. She didn't seem angry, only suspicious. "That's not possible. You didn't have enough information to check me out with anybody." She looked at him like he'd claimed the earth was flat.

Mac thought fast. "On the phone last night you said you had a degree in library science. It seemed logical that you graduated from a local university. It took only one phone call to the La Jolla branch of the University of Southern California to find out I was right."

"You're not interested in my work background since graduation?" Sitting primly on the couch with both feet flat on the floor, she looked closer to sixteen than twenty-six, even with her hair rolled up in back. If Mac hadn't reviewed her file, he'd never have guessed how old she was.

He could see she was still suspicious, but not as much as before. *Too bad she's involved in such a filthy business,* he thought and was immediately aggravated at himself for feeling sympathetic toward a criminal. With her delicate face staring at him, the fact that he was on the side of law and order didn't seem to make much difference. They were both phonies. That was the black and white of it. He couldn't trust her, and she couldn't trust him. The difference was that he knew exactly who and what she was, and she knew nothing about him.

"You told me you're a technical librarian at the Wakefield Aircraft Corporation," he continued. "If the truth be known, I intend to call your personnel office tomorrow to

assure myself that you're who you say you are. Is there any
reason why I shouldn't tell them you're doing part-time
work for me?''

"No reason in the world," she replied.

THE FIRST HOUR they worked together went very well. To
Marilyn's surprise, Mac was able to get her started with a
minimum of confusion. In no time, he was seated across
from her at the table, writing in long hand on a yellow legal-size tablet while she correlated computer notes with his
voluminous outline.

Every so often she'd steal a glance at him. With his copper-red head bent over his tablet, his lean fingers scribbling
an unreadable script, he looked every inch the college professor he claimed to be.

Right from the start, she could tell that his previous re-
searchers hadn't had her experience. The work was appall-
ing, with incomplete references that hadn't been properly
tied in to the outline. The material was so poorly organized
it seemed thrown together by someone who had only the
vaguest notion of how to proceed. Most of it would have to
be done over.

"Are you going to have an index?" she asked, examining one of the notes. When he nodded, she continued,
"Then all these references will have to be rechecked and
cross-filed."

He smiled across the table at her. "That's what you're
here for, Marilyn."

At seven o'clock he stretched. Under his black cotton
sweater, Marilyn could see sinuous muscles rippling down
his arms. He caught her eyeing him and grinned. She
dropped her gaze to the computer screen in front of her.

"Are you hungry?" he asked. "Since you came from
work, you probably didn't have any supper either. We might
as well eat here and save some time."

His suggestion put her on guard again. Eating with the
charming Professor McDonough in his hotel room was a

notch more dangerous than working with him. What would the next step be?

"I can only stay another hour or so, Mac," she said. "Why don't you wait to eat until I leave? Then you can have a good meal downstairs in the hotel restaurant."

"Because I'm hungry right now." There was an impatient edge to his voice. "If you're not, you can continue what you're doing." He dialed room service and ordered sandwiches, salad and coffee—for two, she noticed.

"I'd hoped you could stay until at least nine," he said. "That would give us four hours together every evening."

His face, unsmiling now, looked tense and demanding, as though more than an extra hour's work were hanging in the balance. It was probably because he was hungry. She knew she was.

"Okay, we'll try it tonight and see how it goes," she conceded. "But I may not be able to keep up with your schedule for more than a few days. I get up early."

"We'll play it by ear." He flashed her a smile and returned to his scribbling.

A few minutes later when a bellboy brought their food, he insisted they take a break. "We'll have a chance to get better acquainted while we eat."

Marilyn wished she'd insisted on leaving before the food came. Getting "better acquainted" sounded suspiciously personal.

Not a good idea when we'll be working together in his hotel room. Then it occurred to her that supper was an excellent opportunity to ask him some questions without seeming unduly interested. She waited until he was sitting on the couch with his salad and roast beef sandwich on the coffee table in front of him.

"So tell me, Mac," she began, swinging her chair around so she was facing him. "How long have you been in this country?"

Mac took a big bite of his sandwich, giving himself time to think about what he was saying. Lying was tricky, even for a professional. With a sharp cookie like Marilyn Wainwright, he'd have to remember every word he'd said—plus every bit of background information about her and his own cover persona—or he'd trip himself up. He swallowed before he answered.

"So you guessed I'm not a native?" He did his best to look crestfallen because she'd noticed his accent. "I'm finishing up a two-year exchange program between Notre Dame and Queen's University at Belfast." He put down his sandwich and picked up his salad so he could continue eating if she asked another question. Of course, she did.

"If you're on an exchange program, I'm surprised Notre Dame's willing to grant you a three-month leave of absence to the institute in La Jolla. Isn't that a little strange?"

"Not when you're a physicist, Marilyn." The lie rolled easily off his tongue. "My work at the institute is connected to what I was doing at Notre Dame. The university gets credit for my discoveries whether I'm working here or in one of their labs." Mac wasn't sure that information was accurate, but it didn't much matter. The important thing was not to spook her before he was ready to reveal his identity as an IRA operative who wanted her to steal classified information about British defenses.

Too bad the woman was so damned conservative in her appearance. Studying her face, Mac wondered how she'd look with her glasses off and her hair flowing down her back. Completely untanned, she had the whitest skin he'd ever seen. A typical librarian, he thought, without the interest in the outdoors that Mac himself enjoyed.

"So you're not a historian after all?" she asked, breaking into his thoughts. "I'd have thought that would be your specialty."

Her question caught him off guard. For half a second he scrambled furiously to understand her meaning. "You thought I was a historian because of my book?" he finally said. "I consider it a military treatise."

"You're obviously not a librarian, Mac."

She smiled, a little indulgently, Mac thought. *Good. Anything to get her on my side.*

They spent the next few minutes finishing their sandwiches and talking about the manuscript. Afterward he watched her cross to the coffee table and put her dishes on the tray. She might be short, but she was certainly well proportioned. From where he was sitting, her legs looked as long as any showgirl's. With her slim neck and racehorse lines, she might be mistaken for someone much taller. It was only when he stood right next to her that he realized how truly small and delicate she was.

When Mac returned to his scribbling, he realized she'd skillfully guided the conversation away from herself. It was an indication she was hiding something. That meant she was probably guilty.

Now why did that make him feel mad enough to knock somebody's block off?

AT EXACTLY NINE O'CLOCK, Marilyn stood to go. She put on her sweater and picked up her bag and briefcase. To her surprise, Mac yanked a windbreaker from a closet near the door.

"Where do you live? I'll follow you home."

"You don't have to do that, Mac. My apartment's right here on Coronado, only a couple of miles away."

Shrugging his jacket on, he went out the door with her. "As long as you're working for me at night, I'll be seeing that you get home safely afterward."

She started to protest again, only to have him insist. Finally she sighed. "If you want to waste your time, I won't argue with you, but it's really not necessary."

He winked at her. "If you were living clear across town, I wouldn't insist."

"I won't be able to invite you in," she warned. Might as well get that settled right at the beginning.

"I wouldn't think of such a thing," he said.

So why did she get the notion he had an ulterior motive for wanting to follow her to her apartment?

Mac didn't doubt she'd make it home safely. But he wanted to establish the evening trip together to her place as part of their regular working routine. After tonight he planned to pick her up in his car. That way he'd have a chance to talk to her outside the restrictive atmosphere of his hotel suite.

The Hotel del Coronado's parking lot was between the original shingle-style hotel and a new addition that also fronted on the beach. They crossed through the old-fashioned lobby and went down the stairs to the circular drive at the entrance.

"My car's in the pay lot, too," he said, taking her arm as they crossed the landscaped area at the driveway's center. "Why don't you give me your address, in case I lose you in traffic?"

"This is a waste of time," she protested, but gave him a business card with her address and phone. "It's the Gold Key Apartments. Go down Orange a mile or so and turn right on Second and left on A. You'll see the sign."

Mac pocketed the card. He already knew where the place was located. With the help of a street map, he'd driven there after checking in at the hotel that afternoon.

"I have a bad sense of direction, so keep an eye out for me," he said, pointing out his rental car as they walked past it to her ancient BMW. *I've told her one true thing, at least,* he thought grimly. Mac was one of those people who automatically turned the wrong way at any strange intersection. To compensate, he'd learned to trust maps implicitly and totally ignore his own instincts.

"When you get home, wait for me in your car." He watched while she unlocked her door.

As she climbed in, her wool skirt caught on the seat and bunched under her. She tugged at it and the door at the same time.

Pretending not to notice, Mac helped her slam the door shut. "I'll walk you to your apartment. Then we can talk about something I want you to do for me tomorrow at your office."

He wheeled and started toward his car so that she wouldn't have a chance to respond. He wanted to continue

their conversation at her apartment building, not here in the
hotel parking lot.

MARILYN SWUNG ONTO the drive leading away from the
hotel with the uneasy feeling that the charming Dr. Mc-
Donough was trying to put something over on her. They'd
just spent four hours working together. Why did he wait
until she was on the way home to spring a new requirement
on her? One that needed to be done the very next day at her
office?

   She glanced in her rearview mirror expecting to see the
lights of his car behind her, but he didn't turn out of the
parking area until she was all the way down the long drive,
almost to Orange Avenue. Marilyn didn't slow down. If he
couldn't keep up, he'd just have to stop and ask directions.
She didn't intend to wait for him in her carport, either. His
assignment for the office, whatever it was, would have to
wait until tomorrow night if he missed her.

   A block down Orange Avenue, she checked again to see
if he'd caught up. A car was pulling away from the curb,
headed in her direction. Behind it, she spotted Mac's car
turning out of the hotel driveway.

   She slowed to let the car behind her pass, but it slowed
when she did, maintaining a careful distance a block or so
behind. Curious, she speeded up. So did the car behind her.

   The tiniest suggestion of fear nagged at the fringes of her
consciousness. What reason would anybody have to follow
her? She tried to see the license in her mirror but couldn't
even make out the plate, let alone the numbers. The car appeared to be a late-model full-size sedan in a dark color—
brown or maroon or black. Maybe even green. Marilyn
checked her mirror again and caught a comforting glimpse
of Mac's headlights.

   When she reached her turn, she noticed that the car following her was still a discreet distance behind. It also turned.
But when she swung into her apartment parking lot, it drove
on by. She watched it continue down the street and, finally,
round a corner three blocks away.

Maybe he's going to come back now that he knows where I live. The thought frightened Marilyn enough to keep her locked in her car for the next few minutes, until Mac pulled in beside her.

"Did you know somebody besides me was following you?" he asked, as soon as she got out of the car.

"Then you saw him, too?" Marilyn's voice sounded squeaky to her again.

"That I did. No doubt in my mind he was following you. No doubt at all." His smooth Irish brogue radiated confidence.

Marilyn was so glad to see him, she didn't object when he started up the outside stairs with her to her second-floor apartment. Thanks to the unknown car behind her, Mac had become a trusted ally in the short space of a ten-minute drive.

"Have any idea why somebody would want to follow you?" He studied her face.

She could see his curiosity in the tilt to his eyebrows, which were a couple of shades darker than his copper-red hair.

"No jealous boyfriends lurking about, are there?" he asked.

"Goodness no!" The idea would have been funny if she hadn't been so scared. "Nobody I know would do anything like that."

She stopped midway up the stairs. "You were pretty close behind him. Did you get a look at the driver? Could you tell if it was a man or a woman?"

From his crestfallen expression, she knew the answer before he said anything.

"Sorry, Marilyn. I guess I'm not a very good detective." He mussed his hair by running his fingers through it.

Marilyn took an impatient breath. "I suppose you didn't get the license number, either."

He shrugged. "Sorry, again. It was too dark."

"Or the make of the car?"

He shrugged again. "Like I said, I'm no detective. It might have been blue or green."

"Great." Marilyn resumed her climb up the stairs.

The door to her apartment was off an outside second-floor walkway around the two-story building. When she reached it, she paused with her key in her hand.

"You said you wanted me to check into something for you tomorrow at the office?"

"Glad you reminded me." His tanned face took on a conspiratorial expression. "You wouldn't have access to any government data bases at your library, would you now, Marilyn?"

She set down her briefcase. "You mean U.S. government data bases?" When Mac nodded, she went on. "There are several. But I doubt they'd have any historical information about the British Army."

"Exactly what kind of information would they have?"

It was an odd question, one that seemed unrelated to his manuscript. As though he could read her mind, he explained, "The last section of my book is on current research in weapons. It would be helpful to compare British and American research and development."

"I'll make a list of what's available."

"Good. Why don't I pick you up here tomorrow night at five-thirty? That'll give you a chance to change out of your work clothes."

Marilyn started to say no, but the earnest look on his face stopped her. After being followed tonight, she wasn't sure she wanted to drive her own car home from the hotel tomorrow night, even with him behind her. She hedged her denial to make sure he was serious. "You don't have to bother, Mac. We can get started earlier if I don't come home first."

"It's no bother. The time clock starts ticking at five either way, so you're not losing anything by letting me pick you up."

"That's very generous of you." Marilyn unlocked the door to her apartment and pushed it open. "But I don't want any favors. If we start work half an hour later, we'll quit half an hour later."

"Fine." Mac picked up her briefcase and thrust it inside the door. He made no attempt to enter. "I'll see you tomorrow night at five-thirty then."

"I'll be waiting for you here." Marilyn felt vaguely disappointed when he turned and headed back down the walkway. What had she expected him to do? Storm after her and crush her to his chest? Of course not, she told herself irritably. But that didn't stop her from wondering what she'd have done if he'd tried.

MAC WOULD NEVER HAVE LEFT Marilyn alone if he'd thought she was in danger, but he knew exactly who was following her. Eyes blazing, he drove back to the hotel. Its ground-floor level featured an arcade with fashionable little shops and a plush lounge and restaurant that overlooked the ocean. He made his way to a bank of pay telephones at the far end of the yellow-tiled walkway through the arcade's center.

He dialed a number collect. His boss answered and accepted the charges. Mac didn't identify himself.

"What the hell's going on, Charley?" He didn't try to hide his anger.

"You know what time it is here, buddy?" Finnegan sounded like he had mush in his mouth. "Almost one o'clock."

Mac heard an exasperated sigh.

"Since I'm wide awake, you might as well tell me your problem. But, let me warn you, it better be serious. And you'd better be mighty careful what you say. This isn't a secure phone."

Mac tightened his fist. "You know the case I'm working on? What's the big idea having my lady followed? Either you tell me what's going on or get yourself another boy for this job. Nobody messes around with my cases unless I know about it."

"Simmer down. I don't know what you're talking about."

Mac's mind went into overdrive. If the bureau wasn't having Marilyn followed, then who was? Somebody in her brother's syndicate? But that didn't make sense. He snorted into the receiver. "You lie to me about this, Charley, and I'm outta here."

The silence was just long enough to be noticeable. Then Mac heard the low grunts that meant Finnegan was laughing. Sarcastically.

"Better watch your step, buddy. Sounds to me like this woman's getting to you. Just because you spot a tail is no reason to get me out of bed at one a.m. Why don't you find out who the hell it was?"

"You better be on the level, Charley." Mac felt his anger fading. It was replaced with the nagging fear that something was wrong. He didn't like the feeling. "The car was a late-model green Olds sedan. It had California plates. Here's the number." He spit it out. "Find out who owns it and let me know tomorrow."

After Mac hung up the receiver, he realized his boss hadn't come right out and denied the tail. Was the bureau behind it after all?

Feeling like a fool, he headed back to the Gold Key Apartments and scoured the area. There was no sign of the green Olds or of anything else suspicious. Annoyed, Mac warned himself to settle down. Why was he so damned upset because somebody was following Marilyn Wainwright, a suspected spy?

Chapter Three

The Wakefield Aircraft Corporation where Marilyn worked was located amid rolling hills in La Jolla, about twelve miles north of downtown San Diego on Interstate five. The entrances to the building were guarded by a security staff who checked badges on a twenty-four-hour basis. As she passed the counter at the main entrance, she said good morning to the middle-aged guard. He greeted her with a bigger smile than usual.

Probably because I'm wearing high heels for a change, Marilyn thought, aggravated with herself for going to the trouble. The shoes already hurt her feet, and she'd worn them less than an hour.

A second man in uniform was watching a bank of video monitors trained on the upstairs hallways. Every now and then a human figure passed across one of the screens, fading from view, only to reappear when picked up by another camera.

Usually, seeing the monitors put an extra bounce to Marilyn's step. There was something exciting about working in a high-security area where access was limited to people with special clearances. Wasn't that why she'd changed jobs? To get a little excitement in her life, along with the higher pay that went with it?

This morning, though, the monitors made her feel anxious. Would she be breaching security by getting Mac the information he wanted from the government data bases? In the short time Marilyn had been moonlighting, none of her other employers had asked her to search her computer files. Even though the material wasn't classified, there might be some kind of rule against printing and removing it from the building. Frowning, Marilyn went to the elevators across from the entrance. When the doors closed behind her, she automatically stuck her key card into the horizontal slot below the floor designator buttons and pushed number four, the floor the library was on. Her supervisor, Edgar Knowling, was at his desk when she walked in.

He eyed her up and down. "What's the big occasion, Number One? I must say I approve of your change in uniform."

Like the security guard downstairs, he'd apparently noticed her outfit: a jade-green jacket flecked with gold that matched the gold in her silk blouse. It was the brightest thing she owned.

In his early forties, Edgar was a "Star Trek" fan who entertained the office with glib references to the library as a starship. He was the Captain, Marilyn, Number One, and their secretary, the Chief—short for Chief Engineer. Surprisingly, Wakefield's engineering staff, many of whom used the library's resources on a daily basis, accepted Edgar's fanciful terminology without so much as a raised eyebrow. It took a real oddball to surprise a Californian. Edgar Knowling didn't come close.

"You must have a lunch date with that nice navy lieutenant," he said with a wink. "When did he get back in town?"

Marilyn plunked her briefcase down on her desk, trying not to let her superior's friendly snooping aggravate her. For some reason, she felt as prickly as this morning as a kid stung with nettles. "I don't have a lunch date. I decided to wear something bright today, that's all, Edgar. It *is* the Christmas season, you know."

"Well, it's a big improvement. Really livens up the bridge." He eyed her speculatively. "That lieutenant of yours looked like a good catch to me when I met him last summer. Academy man. Solid. Steady. He'll be an admiral one of these days. Don't let him get away, Number One."

Marilyn dropped her handbag in her desk drawer and slammed it shut. "For your information, I have no interest in him, or in anybody, Edgar. Now, if you don't mind, I'd like to get to work."

"Tut, tut, tut—edgy this morning, aren't we?"

Their secretary, Rosemary, a corpulent woman in her fifties, looked up from the page she was typing. "Don't pester the poor girl, Captain. Can't you see she wants to be left alone?"

"No woman wants to be left alone, Chief. Especially not one as pretty as our Number One, who's all dolled up for— heh, heh—the Christmas season." He reached for the half-empty cup of coffee on his desk.

"Keep pestering her, and you'll never see her in high heels again." Rosemary pointed a finger at Edgar. "Or a skirt, either."

After three months, Marilyn was used to their friendly bantering. It had never bothered her before, but this morning Rosemary's mother-hen cluckings were almost as bad as Edgar's nosiness.

What was the matter with her anyway? Could George McDonough have something to do with this prickly feeling that made her want to bite somebody's head off? Had she worn her brightest outfit for him? *Don't be silly,* she told herself. *The professor doesn't work in this office. He'll never see this outfit.* The thought made her feel even more prickly, mainly because she'd halfway decided to wear it to the hotel that night.

Picking up a writing pad and pencil, Marilyn escaped to the sanctuary of the vault to finish an office project with a late-afternoon deadline. The vault, a room at one end of the library, was constructed like a bank depository to protect the highly sensitive materials it contained. The secure or "dedicated" line to access classified data bases was located in the vault as was the Category five special intelligence information she needed for the project. She spent the next couple of hours there compiling a comprehensive all-source bibliography of guidance technology.

When Marilyn was finished, it was a little after noon. Both Edgar and Rosemary were at lunch. It was a good opportunity to start the work she'd promised Mac. Using her desktop computer, Marilyn checked for the information he wanted. She found three on-line data bases maintained by the Defense Technical Information Center that provided access to piles of scientific and technical information about weapons. The catch was that the material was for the stated use of Department of Defense personnel, DOD contractors, and other U.S. government agencies and their contractors.

Marilyn hesitated, tapping her fingers on the keyboard. As a university instructor, Mac didn't fit into any of those categories. Did that mean he shouldn't have access to it, even though the material was unclassified?

She was dialing Wakefield's Chief of Security to find out when she remembered that Mac was going to call the corporation himself today, to check out her story that she worked here. She hung up the receiver. Before she talked to security, it might be a good idea for *her* to check out *his* story. Feeling apologetic for playing detective, Marilyn called the La Jolla Institute of Geophysical Phenomena and asked for Dr. George McDonough.

There was a long silence. Apparently the woman who answered the phone was having trouble locating him.

"He's new," Marilyn volunteered helpfully. "A professor from Notre Dame who just went to work there a day or two ago."

"We keep complete lists not only of the people working here but of any visitors," the woman said. "He's not on any of them. Are you sure you have the name right?"

"I'm positive." Marilyn frowned. She couldn't believe he wasn't there. "Would you mind checking your list again? I'm doing some research for Dr. McDonough, and it's important that I reach him."

Marilyn heard a man's voice in the background asking
who the call was for. The woman's reply was muffled, as
though her hand were over the receiver. Then she asked,
"May I put you on hold?"

"Yes, you can." Marilyn hardly breathed during the next
few seconds. If Mac wasn't working at the institute, why had
he told her he was? And why did she feel betrayed at the
thought that he'd lied to her? She barely knew the man.

The woman came back on the line. "Sorry, the name was
out of order on my list." The disembodied voice sounded
flustered. "George McDonough's on it all right, but he'll be
gone for the rest of the day. Do you want to leave a message?"

Marilyn let out her breath in a huge sigh. "That won't be
necessary." She thanked the woman and hung up.

*So that's how the professor gets his gorgeous tan, by
leaving work early and spending his afternoons on the beach
or in some tanning parlor.* She was smiling when she redi-
aled the number of Wakefield's Chief of Security.

MAC SPENT THE MORNING parked down the street from the
nondescript building that housed Van Wainwright's modest auto repair business in El Cajon, fifteen miles east of San
Diego. By watching the place for a couple of hours, he
hoped to spot some of the young Vietnamese thugs working for Marilyn's brother. If Finnegan was right about the
brother heading a syndicate, they probably used the garage
as a sort of headquarters.

*He sure doesn't put any of his take back into his busi-
ness,* Mac thought, when he first drove past the place. The
outside of the building was a mess with peeling paint and
cracked windows. Two big double doors were open, and
Mac got a good look inside. Car parts were scattered on
every spare bit of floor space and tools lay everywhere. The
walls and floor were so dirty they looked slippery.

The hours passed slowly. It was stuffy in the car, even
with the windows open. Farther from the ocean than San
Diego, El Cajon was warmer. Figuring he'd be less notice-

able in sportswear than a business suit, Mac had worn shorts and a T-shirt, but he was still overdressed. By eleven o'clock, he was ready to call it quits. Not a single Vietnamese had come near the place, including its proprietor. The two male mechanics were Caucasian.

From his briefings in Washington, Mac knew he'd recognize Van Wainwright. About five foot eight, he was tall for a Vietnamese, and looked more Caucasian than Oriental. Even though he was Marilyn's half brother and from a different race, there was a strong resemblance to the fragile-looking woman Mac had met last night. He found himself wondering again what her silky dark hair would look like flowing down her back, how it would feel if he touched it. He shook his head, aggravated at himself for letting his attention wander.

The two young mechanics obviously enjoyed the absence of their employer. They took frequent smoke breaks, and during the three hours Mac watched, they interrupted their work several times to socialize with friends who stopped by. *The person who said the best fertilizer on any field is the footsteps of the owner sure had it right,* Mac thought cynically.

Recalling that Marilyn's brother lived in El Cajon, he decided to take a look at Van Wainwright's house. After a couple of wrong turns, Mac finally found the place. In a poorer section of town, it was a square wooden structure with a flat roof. A chain-link fence surrounded the parched yard.

With one practiced glance, Mac took in the dead plants beside the front stoop, the neatly edged but yellowed lawn and the coiled garden hose at the house's corner. The door was closed, the curtains drawn. Nobody was home.

Judging from the look of the yard, nobody had been home for quite a while. Why hadn't Finnegan told him about that? The bureau had surely done enough preliminary checking on Van Wainwright to know he was off on a trip, and to find out where.

Mac found a pay phone and dialed his boss at the office. The bureau's outside phone lines were no more secure than those at Finnegan's house so he was careful not to use names.

"Our boy's flown the coop, boss."

"You're kidding!"

Something in the quick way Finnegan responded made Mac suspect he wasn't telling his superior anything the man didn't already know.

"You'd better level with me, boss." There was a harsh, demanding quality to Mac's voice. "If this is old news, talk to me about it."

"I'm as surprised as you are, buddy. Scout's honor. Any idea where he's disappeared to?"

Finnegan sounded tense. Mac heard him try to cover his nervousness with a sarcastic laugh.

"How the hell would I know where he's gone?" Mac asked.

Another sarcastic laugh. "I thought maybe your lady had mentioned it."

Mac felt like banging down the receiver. It was an urge he'd had before when he talked to Charley Finnegan. So far he'd never done it, but each time the urge grew stronger. He scowled. "If that's what I'm supposed to be doing here—finding out where this guy's gone—I'd appreciate knowing about it."

"Look here, buddy, you're the one who said he's gone. We need him to wrap this thing up. If you can find out where he is, we're that much ahead of the game."

Mac still sensed that Finnegan was holding something back, but he didn't pursue it. Conversation had to be restricted on an insecure phone line. "What'd you find out about the car, boss?" Mac glanced up and down the street through the open door of the phone booth but saw nothing unusual.

"Family living in Escondido reported it stolen last week. There doesn't seem to be any connection to your case."

"Mind if I check it out myself?" Mac didn't try to keep the sarcasm out of his voice.

"Be my guest. I'll call the local office on the secure line, and they'll deliver the name tonight to your box at the hotel. Unless you want to pick it up yourself."

"Too risky." Mac never dropped by a local bureau office when he was working on a case. The office's location was no secret since it was listed in the local phone directory. Anybody could be keeping an eye on the place. If one Vietnamese thug spotted him going into the local office and then saw him with Marilyn, the sting would be down the tubes.

"Anything the local boys can do for you?" Finnegan sounded eager to please.

Mac wasn't impressed. "Tell 'em to stay out of my way. If I need help, I'll get in touch."

"As far as they're concerned, you're the original invisible man."

Mac grunted his thanks and hung up. Then, since it was still early in the afternoon, he decided to spend a couple of hours at the beach. If he got lucky, maybe he'd run into a well-developed blonde with a good tan who liked to talk about herself—the kind of woman George MacIntyre was used to.

WHEN MARILYN GOT HOME that afternoon, she wasted precious minutes sorting through the clothes in her closet. Finally, after considering various combinations, she decided not to change out of her work clothes after all. As she'd told Edgar this morning, it was a bright outfit, one worthy of the season. Whether Mac liked it or not was totally irrelevant.

She took her hair down and brushed it thoroughly before rolling it up again. Then, with fifteen minutes left, Marilyn dug out the soft contact lenses she'd bought because Navy Lieutenant Kevin Randall said her glasses made her look too bookish. She'd hoped the darned things might liven their relationship. Of course, they hadn't.

Maintaining them was a bother. But they *did* make her feel as though she could see a little better. And if there was ever a time she needed to see clearly, it was tonight, and all the other nights she'd be working with Mac in his suite. Maybe by seeing his face better, she'd get a clue to what he was thinking. She told herself that was the only reason she wore the contacts. The fact that she did look better without her glasses had nothing to do with it.

The doorbell rang. It was Mac. Marilyn took one look at him and knew he'd been at the beach all day. His skin had a kind of bronze glow that made his hair seem redder and his eyes more green than hazel. He was wearing tan cotton pants and a yellow T-shirt with a reptile on the pocket.

Marilyn groaned inwardly. Why couldn't she tan like that? When she was growing up, she'd won enough swimming trophies to cover one wall of her family's house. But all the trophies in the world couldn't buy her the golden tan she'd always wanted.

Mac eyed her up and down with a critical look. "I thought you were going to get out of your work clothes and into something comfortable."

"I didn't have time. Besides, I'm very comfortable in what I've got on." Unfortunately her left contact lens was fogging up. She blinked a couple of times to clear it.

"I hope you brought your glasses along," he said, obviously noticing her irritated eye. "You won't be able to work if you can't see the computer screen."

Marilyn thrust her chin out. "Don't worry. You'll get your money's worth."

"Then you do have your glasses?"

"I'm wearing contacts."

He grinned. "Well, I must say they're an improvement over those old-maid spectacles you had on last night." His Irish brogue seemed more pronounced than ever.

Grabbing her purse and briefcase, Marilyn slipped out the door. She took a deep breath as they started down the outside stairway. "I can see where you've been all day," she said, going on the offensive. "At the beach."

"You're only partly right. It doesn't take long to get a tan around here, even when the temperature's in the sixties."

Marilyn paused at the bottom of the stairs, an odd wariness coursing through her. "Are you telling me you worked at the institute until two this afternoon?"

Mac heard a suspicious edge to her voice and thought fast. "Somebody at the institute tell you different?"

"The woman who answered the phone said you wouldn't be back until tomorrow." Her level gaze held a hidden challenge.

"Well, she was wrong. I'll have to talk to those people." Mentally, Mac crossed himself in gratitude. Thank God Finnegan had been shrewd enough to clear this part of his cover with the institute.

Mac opened the door of his car for Marilyn. "Did you leave a message at the institute? If you did, I never got it."

She shook her head as she got in.

"Why did you call?" he asked, without closing the door. "Did you have a question about the research for tonight?" Smart little thing. She'd been checking up on him, all right. Would she admit it?

She stared straight up at him. He was struck by the deep blue violet of her eyes. Why hadn't he noticed them before? Because she'd been wearing those absurd glasses, of course. He wondered how she'd managed to pick a style so unbecoming to her delicate face.

"Since you said you were going to call Wakefield to ask about me, I decided to return the favor," she said. There was no hint of apology in her tone. "I didn't leave a message because the only reason I called was to find out if you were on the level."

Mac adopted his favorite hurt-puppy expression. "Faith, Marilyn, my heart aches at your lack of trust in me."

She didn't seem sympathetic. "If that's all it takes to make your heart ache, you're in serious trouble, Professor."

As he shut her door and walked around the car to the driver's side, Mac had the disturbing feeling that she might very well be right.

LATER THAT NIGHT, after Marilyn was safely delivered to her apartment, Mac checked with the desk clerk for messages. The information Finnegan had promised wasn't there. Hadn't Charley said the bureau knew who owned the car that followed Marilyn last night? That the San Diego office would deliver the name to his box at the hotel this evening? Obviously somebody goofed.

Typical bureaucratic bungling, Mac grumbled, taking the stairs to the upper floor two at a time. *The idiots probably brought it to the wrong hotel.*

He smelled cigarette smoke as soon as he opened the door to his room. A lanky dark-haired man wearing immaculate tennis shorts was stretched out on the sofa, his feet propped up on a stack of books on the coffee table.

"What the hell you doing here, Moschella?" Mac's voice was edged with steel. "The last thing I need right now is you guys from the local office nosing around my operation."

The man on the couch grinned, showing even white teeth. His squarish face exuded the phony charm of a used car salesman's. "Well, excuse me, MacIntyre. We sure don't want to foul up your sting." He exaggerated his words so that "sting" came out sound like "stink."

Mac knew he did it on purpose. Dan Moschella had been a radio announcer for a couple of years before joining the bureau. His pronunciation was excellent.

"All the San Diego office wants," Moschella went on, "is to help out a brother in need."

Mac didn't sit down. "Finnegan said you'd deliver the name to my box downstairs."

Moschella put out his cigarette in an ashtray and clasped his hands behind his head. "The woman at the desk knows me—knows I'm with the bureau. I wanted to be sure she didn't connect us."

"Damn it all, man, you should have had somebody else bring it tomorrow." Mac had worked with Dan Moschella a couple of years ago on a drug case. He was a nails-hard agent, almost as good at deception as Mac himself. If anybody knew better than to jeopardize an elaborate operation like this one, it was the man on his sofa.

"Finnegan said you wanted it tonight, Mac. I made sure nobody saw me come up." Moschella's voice had turned mildly apologetic.

Mac examined the other man's face. A too-large nose saved it from being movie-star handsome.

"Plus," Moschella continued, "I checked out the car's owner myself this afternoon. He's legit. The vehicle was stolen a couple of days ago. It hasn't been recovered."

Mac felt his anger fading. If he didn't have to drive to Escondido tomorrow to investigate the stolen car, he could spend the morning at the beach.

"So how's it going, Mac? The fat man thinks you'll wrap this up by Christmas."

"Next time you talk to Finnegan on the secure line, tell him I still think we're wasting our time. My gut tells me the woman's innocent."

Moschella lit up another cigarette and leaned back again, like he wanted to sit around and gab for a while.

It wasn't the way Mac intended to spend what was left of the evening. Dan Moschella would have to wait until the case was over to satisfy his curiosity.

"The sooner you get out of here, the better," Mac said.

Moschella stood. He was taller and broader than Mac and had the muscled legs of an athlete. A phony kind of charisma oozed from him like juice from an overripe peach. "Hey, brother, I did you a favor. Hows about a little gratitude?"

Mac didn't smile. "The gratitude comes when this operation's finished." He didn't offer the other man his hand. "Now get out of here, Moschella. And make sure nobody sees you."

After he'd left, Mac took his fake passport from the dresser drawer, wrinkled some of the pages, and crushed it open to one specific place. Then he put it back in the drawer, facedown, with a book on top of it.

Sometime during the next few days he'd plant the passport where Marilyn would be sure to find it. When she did, he wanted to be sure she couldn't miss seeing that one particular page.

Chapter Four

During the next few days, the work settled into a predictable routine. Mac picked Marilyn up at five-thirty at her apartment, and they worked steadily for an hour or so with minimum conversation.

He seemed totally engrossed in the book, but several times each session she'd glance up unexpectedly and catch him watching her with a quizzical expression that was vaguely disconcerting. There was an air of mystery about him that kept her wondering what he was thinking and feeling.

Marilyn spent most of her time establishing files for the material gleaned from the on-line government data bases at the office. The Chief of Security at Wakefield had approved her use of the material as long as she paid the necessary costs. Edgar agreed to let her do the work during her lunch hour so the way was cleared for her research. She didn't even have to put in extra time to do it. When she told Mac about it, he seemed more interested in how she'd gotten the material than in the material itself.

"I'm surprised you bothered to check with your security people," he'd said, after she'd described the steps she'd taken.

Obviously he didn't understand that she worked in a high security area, so Marilyn had explained about the guards, the monitors and the key card she had to use for the elevator. She'd left out any mention of the vault and the dedicated line to the classified data bases. Since those topics could lead to questions about the highly sensitive material kept in the vault, she avoided them altogether.

At about seven, Mac would order something to eat, and they'd break for supper. Each night the breaks got longer, from fifteen minutes the first night, to almost an hour on the fourth. Marilyn had never met a man with such an interesting background. He told her he'd been raised in Northern Ireland, educated in England, and had traveled extensively in Europe and Africa. Thanks to his travels on the continent, he spoke fluent French and passable Spanish. There seemed to be no subject or place he didn't know something about.

Even more remarkable, Mac acted as though he enjoyed hearing her opinions and listening to her talk about her experiences, mundane as they were. Marilyn found herself telling him things she never dreamed anybody would be interested in: like how it felt to be the daughter of a career air force officer stationed in remote places away from his family. And how hard it had been to lose her father to a heart attack and see her grief-stricken mother paralyzed by a stroke only months later.

Tonight they were enjoying a steak dinner. Two bellhops had set up a table in the middle of the room complete with linen cloth, sterling silver and a single yellow rose in a tall crystal bud vase. The rose matched the new yellow shirt Marilyn was wearing with her brightly printed skirt, which was also new. Both were purchased only that afternoon from a posh little shop on La Jolla's Ocean Boulevard.

"Doesn't your brother help with your mother's expenses?" Mac asked.

Marilyn had told him she had a brother the night before, on the way home. "He's not my mother's son," Marilyn explained now, a little defensively. "Not that it matters. I'm sure Van would help if he could. He's got a little business in El Cajon, but it's not doing well." She'd always felt protective of her brother because he was half Vietnamese. He'd also felt protective of her, but in the way a brother feels responsible for a younger sister.

"Then your father was married before?"

Even though Mac's tone was casual, Marilyn sensed his interest. For the first time since she'd met him in the lobby downstairs, she was again aware of the tense energy inside him, of the coiled spring waiting to snap free.

"No. My brother was illegitimate." Marilyn concentrated on her baked potato so Mac couldn't see her face. She was proud of her father for the way he'd helped Van but not of the fact that he'd fathered the child of a Vietnamese bar girl.

"Sorry. I didn't mean to be nosy." Mac recognized her shame and yearned to reach out to her. God, he knew how she was feeling. He couldn't count the times someone in his family had disappointed him. As one of ten children from New York's lower east side, illegitimate babies, kids running with gangs, a brother dying of an overdose, and a father who was drunk all the time were all part of his growing-up years.

From the tender age of six, Mac had only one thought: escape. If it hadn't been for his mom and oldest sister, he would have left home ten years sooner than he did.

Marilyn's lyrical voice brought him back to the present. "It's all right, Mac," she said. "You had no way of knowing he was illegitimate."

But I did, Mac thought, cutting into his steak. *That's why I brought it up.* When he put the piece of meat in his mouth, it had no taste.

"At least my father did the honorable thing by Van," she said. "He's turned out to be a good brother and a good man."

Sure he is, the damned traitor. Mac swallowed his steak and washed it down with a gulp of coffee. He encouraged her to keep talking about her brother, even though he could see it was bothering her. "Are you still close?"

"We're not close the way we were when we were kids," she replied, "but we still give each other moral support."

Mac pushed his plate away half-finished, his appetite gone. He was starting to feel uncomfortable for what he was doing to her, not just with the questions about her brother, but with everything connected to this operation.

After working with Marilyn Wainwright the past few days, he still doubted the bureau's accusation that she was a spy. Was he ready for her to find his passport, planted in the stack of books on the coffee table where she couldn't miss it? As soon as she took a good look at the page he'd pressed open, she'd know he wasn't a university professor. That would start phase two of his sting. Then she'd probably never trust him again, no matter how the sting turned out.

"You said your brother has a business in El Cajon." Mac forced himself to go on. "Does he live there, too?"

She nodded, a faint flush of pride on her cheeks. "He bought a little house and is fixing it up to sell. He did fairly well with a couple of others. That's how he paid for the auto repair shop. Now that California's real estate boom seems to be over, who knows how he'll do with this one."

Mac examined her face and found no trace of guile. She honestly believed what her brother had told her.

"Sounds like your mother's not the only one in your family who needs financial help," he guessed, watching her closely. Her skin was as soft and white as a young child's.

From the long silence that followed, Mac knew he'd guessed right. In spite of all the money Van Wainwright was making illegally, he still borrowed from his sister. The thought made Mac seethe inside. Her shoulders were too frail for such a heavy load.

Hiding his profits until he can skip the country, Mac hypothesized. *Damn! Maybe that's what's happened to him. There has to be some way to get her to tell me where he is.* He leaned toward her.

"No wonder you have to work so hard, Marilyn." The sympathy in his voice wasn't feigned.

"Van's going to pay me back," she said quickly. He doubted she believed it any more than he did.

"If I were you, I'd get that in writing." The words popped out automatically. Mac saw the look on Marilyn's face, and knew he'd made a mistake. She was loyal to Van and the last thing Mac wanted was an argument pitting himself against her as she defended her brother. It was an argument he couldn't win.

Hastily he pushed his chair away from the table and stood. "If you'll excuse me for a minute, I've got to wash my hands."

Marilyn swallowed her angry retort as he headed down the short hallway to the bathroom. What right did he have to criticize her brother? He didn't know anything about Van, about his being half Vietnamese. She'd deliberately avoided saying anything about Van's mother. It was something she never talked about.

Mac didn't know how hard it was for Van growing up in a privileged American neighborhood during the Vietnam conflict. He knew Marilyn's mother had never liked him; she almost seemed to encourage the other kids' abuses. Their father was gone most of the time, so he was no help.

Still aggravated, Marilyn jumped out of her chair and grabbed a couple of books from the top of the coffee table, intending to take them with her to the computer. She inadvertently knocked the whole stack on the floor. When she bent to pick up the books, she saw Mac's passport, its pages open and crumpled.

Stupid man, she fumed. *Why doesn't he keep his passport in the bedroom like everybody else?* She picked it up. As she smoothed the wrinkled pages, she couldn't help noticing the date he'd entered the United States. It was in November, less than a month ago.

Stunned, Marilyn stared at the date. There had to be some mistake. If he'd been teaching at Notre Dame for two years, he couldn't possibly have entered the United States only last month.

Maybe the passport wasn't his. With trembling fingers she flipped through the document.

It was his all right. His hazel eyes, flashing with secret amusement, stared back at her from the photo. His face wore a half smile. Something of his cynical sense of humor came through, but there was a bittersweet quality to his expression as though, this time, the joke was on him.

Frantically Marilyn's mind searched for a logical reason for the November entry date on the U.S. visa, a reason that would explain what he'd told her. She drew a blank. There was no way she could avoid the obvious answer. Mac was lying to her about how long he'd been in the United States. There was no other explanation. And if he'd been lying to her about that, was everything else he'd told her a lie, too? What kind of cat-and-mouse game was this man playing with her?

Damn him and his book! Marilyn fought her angry tears. Still holding the passport, she clenched her hands into fists and swallowed hard to dislodge the lump in her throat. *I should have listened to mom when she said never to trust an attractive man. God knows, mom sure couldn't trust dad. Why did I let myself have feelings for Mac when I hardly know him?*

Marilyn heard the toilet flush and the bathroom door open. Then Mac was striding down the hall toward her, his steps lithe and confident, his copper-red hair neatly combed. Angry though she was, she couldn't repress her admiration. What a lean, vital man he was!

Aggravated, she tossed her head. *He's also a liar and a cheat and don't you forget it.* As he came close, she caught a whiff of spearmint toothpaste.

He smiled when he saw the passport in her hand. "Faith! I spent an hour this morning hunting for that damn thing. Where did you find it?"

Marilyn didn't trust herself to speak. As she nodded toward the coffee table, she could feel her jaw clenching and forced herself to relax.

"So that's where it disappeared to." Nonchalantly he reached for the passport.

Marilyn jerked it away. "Not until you tell me what you're up to, Dr. George McDonough, if that's really your name." She didn't try to keep the venom out of her voice.

His smile faded. He cocked one eyebrow in an expression of ironic concern. "You know that's my name. It's right there on my passport." He sat down on the sofa and patted the cushion beside him. "Why don't you sit down and tell me what's bothering you."

Marilyn didn't sit down. "I think you already know what's bothering me, *Dr.* McDonough. You lied to me. That's what's bothering me. You're no college professor, at least not one who's been in this country for two years, like you said. I'll give you exactly sixty seconds to tell me what you're up to, or I'm walking out that door."

How can he look so unconcerned when he must know I'm on to him? Doesn't he care that I've found out he's a liar? The thought hurt. She tossed his passport to him. "You know what you can do with your fancy book project."

Inexplicably, with the angry words said, the accusations made, Marilyn found herself hoping she was wrong. This man had touched her somehow, in a way that made her feel alive and vibrant. She didn't want him to be a liar. Maybe there was an explanation she hadn't thought of.

He stood and walked toward her, his face more serious than she'd seen it in the four days they'd worked together.

"You found me out sooner than I thought you would, Marilyn."

Dumbfounded, she stood rigid, as though carved in ice. "Are you saying you expected me to find out you were lying about being a university professor?"

"That I did." His expression was contrite. "I'm sorry I had to deceive you, but there was no way I could reveal my mission until I felt I could trust you." Mac studied her face and saw her porcelain skin turn dead pale. Alarmed, he leapt up and started around the coffee table toward her.

"Don't worry, I'm not going to pass out, if that's what you're afraid of." The anger in her voice stopped him midstep. "It takes more than a lying man to make me lose my senses."

She crossed her arms and stared at him as though he were a particularly obnoxious bit of trash. In her yellow shirt and billowing skirt, she reminded him of a wild canary he'd spotted once, a long time ago, in a remote part of Central Park. Instead of flying away, the little bird had chirped angrily at him when he'd got too close to her nest. This fragile woman exuded the same brave anger. Mac took a deep breath and sat back down on the sofa. If this was an act, Marilyn Wainwright was definitely a good actress.

She looked down at her watch. "You've got exactly one minute to tell me what's going on."

"It's going to take longer than a minute." He flashed her his broadest smile.

She didn't smile back. "Then you'd better get started. Five seconds have already passed."

Mac knew exactly what he was going to say. God knows, he'd rehearsed it enough in his mind. But would she take the bait? He almost hoped she wouldn't. Hadn't he told Finnegan right from the start that this woman was no spy?

"You've already guessed that I'm not really writing a book on the British army," he began.

"Get to the point, Professor." She half turned toward the door. His canary was about to take flight.

Mac smiled in a way calculated to show her how much he trusted her. "All right, Marilyn. Here's the truth of it." He paused dramatically, for effect. "I'm working for the Irish Republican Army. We need you to help—"

She didn't give him a chance to finish. "The *Irish Republican Army?* You can't be serious!" From the horrified way she said it, she might have been describing an organization devoted to devil worship. Her expression changed from steely anger to wide-eyed disbelief.

"I'm dead serious." He watched her closely. If she was a spy, she should be damned interested in what he had to say. Interested and receptive. She sure didn't look receptive, but maybe she was testing him, making sure he was for real before she bit.

"You're with the IRA," she repeated, as though she couldn't believe her ears. "Then you're a terrorist. I haven't the faintest notion why you thought I'd help you."

Before Mac could get around the coffee table to stop her, she'd rushed from the room and let herself out of the suite. The crash of the door slamming behind her echoed in his ears.

MARILYN FOUND HERSELF in the lobby without knowing exactly how she'd gotten there. The hall, the stairs, the lighted Christmas tree were blurs of line and color she never really saw. Her contact lenses played tricks on her, threatening to wash out of her eyes.

Why hadn't she believed her common sense instead of her emotions when she first saw him right here in the lobby of the Hotel del Coronado? How could she have trusted him these past few days? Why hadn't she seen through him? He was a criminal of the rankest kind, the kind that preys on innocents for political gain. Men like him deserved to rot in jail for the rest of their natural lives. Marilyn pictured Mac's lithe body confined in a cell and took no pleasure in what she saw. *The Irish Republican Army!* What on God's green earth turned a charming man like Mac McDonough into a terrorist?

She sensed a presence and smelled bourbon half a second before she crashed into a heavyset man in a short-sleeved sport shirt. His belly felt flabby against her. The whiskey in his glass splashed onto her new skirt.

"I'm sorry," she began, looking up at him. "I wasn't watching where I was going."

He leered at her with red, intoxicated eyes. "You look upset. Anything I can do to help, little lady?"

Marilyn jerked backward. "No, I'm fine."

He made a grab for her. Marilyn felt his hand tighten on her wrist. Damn. On top of everything else, this fool was going to make a scene, right here in the lobby of the Hotel del Coronado.

"Don't rush off. I've been looking for someone to…" His face twisted in pain and his hand dropped her wrist as though it were red-hot.

Mac stood beside her, his hand gripping the fat man's arm.

"Hey, let go. You're breaking my arm, guy." The fat man's voice turned into a whine.

Mac dropped his arm and, without a backward look, guided Marilyn toward the door. "You forgot your bag and your sweater." He handed them to her.

She took them without a word.

"If you won't hear me out, at least let me drive you home." He sounded exasperated, as though she were being unreasonable.

"I'll take a cab. I have no intention of ever getting into a car with you again." She refused to look at him.

"Afraid I'll tell you something you don't want to hear?" There was a challenge in his voice. "Haven't you been hiding behind your high-minded idealism long enough, Miss Librarian? The closer you get to the real world, the harder it is to be an idealist." His tone softened. "I'm fighting for a good cause, Marilyn. At least give me a chance to tell you about it. Maybe after you've heard me out, you won't think so little of me."

He paused to open the big lobby door for her. "Or maybe that's what's bothering you. You want to hang onto your prejudices."

"If you consider being against terrorism a prejudice," she snapped, "then you're right. I'm prejudiced. As far as I'm concerned, terrorists belong in jail, not roaming around free like decent people."

As soon as the words were out of Marilyn's mouth, she knew what she had to do. Terrorists *did* belong in jail. Whether she liked it or not, that's where Mac McDonough belonged. She searched her memory for something she'd heard in her security briefing, just after she'd been granted her Category five clearance. "If anybody asks you to steal classified information, if they even hint at it, report him or her immediately to the FBI." The briefer had emphasized that point. "If you get nothing else from this session, remember that," he'd said.

Is that why Mac had gotten in touch with her? Because he knew she had access to sensitive top secret material and wanted her to steal something for him? She hesitated. He seemed so sincere. Shouldn't she find out for sure before she reported him to the FBI?

A cab pulled up at the bottom of the stairs leading to the hotel's circular driveway. A couple got out. Marilyn glanced at Mac. He was staring at her with a strange cynical look. When she turned toward him, the look disappeared and he grinned.

"There's a cab available," he said, nodding at it. "Don't expect me to signal the driver. I want you to stay."

What an arrogant man he was! He'd just admitted to being a liar and a terrorist, but he still thought himself charming enough to capture her interest. She resisted the urge to spit in his face, figuratively speaking, by marching regally down the stairs to the waiting cab.

Instead, she forced herself to smile sweetly up at him. "I've decided to hear what you've got to say, Mac. After all, you did pay me in advance for a week's work, and the week's not up yet."

He grinned back at her. "I knew you'd see it my way if you gave yourself half a minute to think about it."

MAC TOOK MARILYN to the beach for his pitch about the IRA, and how it was helping the suffering Catholics of Northern Ireland cope with their British oppressors. Though the dry sand was cold, they took their shoes off and walked high on the beach, out of reach of the licking ocean waves. Mac poured his heart and soul into his words, the better to convince her he was on the level. Whether she agreed with the IRA cause was irrelevant. If she was a spy, she was doing it for the money, not for a devotion to any political ideology. What she'd be interested in was his credibility: was he really what he said he was—a soldier in the Irish Republican Army?

By the time he was finished, he was sure she believed him. No longer was he certain Finnegan was wrong. Like it or not, Marilyn Wainwright might well be a spy. If she weren't, why had she agreed to come with him tonight? Why had her horrified anger disappeared so quickly? Obviously it had been an act, designed to fool somebody trying to catch her. She'd probably left her handbag and sweater in his suite on purpose, so that he'd have a good excuse to chase after her.

Too bad, MacIntyre, he told himself. *You thought you'd finally found an honest woman. When you gonna learn they don't exist?* Still, sick as it made him to think she was a spy, at least he'd get to see her a few more times if she took the bait. They'd worked together only four days, but already he found himself looking forward to their nights together in his suite. He'd miss her when this thing was over.

Ahead of them, a bonfire flamed in a special pit constructed by the hotel. Couples were gathered around it, each giving the others plenty of space. When they reached the fire, Mac pulled Marilyn down on the sand beside him. They were close enough to the fire so that Mac felt its warmth, hot on his face. The California night pressed cold and damp against his back.

With the glow from the dancing flames reflected on her skin, Marilyn looked radiant. He put an arm around her slim shoulders. When he felt her tense, he squeezed her and then lowered his arm.

"So what's the bottom line on all this, Mac? You've spent half an hour telling me about your beloved Irish Republican Army. What does it have to do with me?"

Her high, clear voice had a bell-like quality to it. At that moment she sounded particularly innocent, like a little girl. What a perfect spy she was. Nobody who didn't know the truth would ever believe it. Hell, he hardly believed it himself, in spite of the mounting evidence.

Would she take the bait? He scooted closer so that their shoulders were touching, and was surprised at the warm feeling that coursed through him. He didn't try to resist. If his affection was genuine, instead of faked, she'd be more likely to believe him. There was a subtle trap here, but Mac chose to ignore it. He told himself he knew better than to fall for her. What he was feeling was sympathy and affection, nothing more.

Just the same, he found himself hoping she'd jump up and walk away when she found out what he wanted her to do.

Chapter Five

"You want me to steal classified information?" Marilyn was surprised at how shocked she felt. This was what she'd expected, wasn't it?

"I wouldn't put it quite that way." Mac's tone was mild, his words obviously designed to excuse any guilt she might be feeling. "All you'd be doing is letting somebody who can put the information to good use take a look at it."

Marilyn stared at his angular profile, etched in reflected firelight against the darkness. Everything about him seemed square cut, from his features to his logical way of thinking.

Stop, she rebuked herself angrily. *There's nothing square cut about him.* But that didn't stop her from feeling drawn to him.

When he turned toward her, the brightness from the fire changed his hair to molten copper. "What we need is order of battle on the British units stationed around Belfast. They've been reorganized during the past few months, and we've got to find out what's going on." His manner was low-key, as though he were asking her for something mundane, like a recipe.

Marilyn concentrated on how she was going to answer. "I think I know what you mean by order of battle, but I'm not sure." She didn't want to sound overly interested. If she agreed too quickly, he might guess she was going to report him to the FBI.

"OB refers to the organization of military units in a certain area—where they're stationed, what equipment they have, who their officers are. You should be able to get that information from one of your dedicated on-line data bases."

His glib reference to the most secret part of her job shocked her anew. "Your calling me was no coincidence, was it, Mac? You knew all along I had access to what you wanted. How'd you find out? Why pick on me instead of somebody else with the same access?"

Hurt raked through her. She'd thought he respected her and her ability to do his work. She had thought—oh, what had she thought? Foolish little dreams. She'd deal with her feelings tomorrow. Now she had to find out all she could.

Stretching his hands toward the flames he looked away from her. "The fire feels good. It sure gets chilly around here after dark, doesn't it?" His tenor voice held a challenge.

Marilyn hugged her knees, tightening her resolve. "Answer me, Mac. Why did you pick on me? There are some things you've got to tell me before I'll even consider doing what you ask."

He folded his arms in front of him and moved away from her. It was only a slight motion, but to Marilyn it was as obvious as a light switching off.

"Sorry, I can't tell you how or why we picked you. We have our secrets, too." He turned toward her and smiled in a knowing way. "It really doesn't matter why we decided you were perfect, now does it?"

Marilyn's answering smile froze on her lips. *I wonder how perfect he'll think I am when he finds out I've turned him in?* Unable to meet his gaze, she stared into the dancing flames.

He leaned toward her. Again she felt the warmth of his shoulder against hers. Somewhere inside her, a light flicked back on, ignoring the hurt she'd ruthlessly shoved aside.

He seemed to sense her heightened awareness. "Honestly, now, aren't you glad you stayed to hear what I had to say?"

"I'm not sure." The words came out slowly, carefully. Marilyn felt all mixed-up inside, as though she were being torn apart. "You realize, of course, that you're asking me to commit a crime. There's a very nasty name for it, and you go to jail for the rest of your life if you get caught."

"What I'm asking you to do wouldn't be treason," he soothed. "No harm could possibly come to the United States if you gave me the information I want about the British units." He'd put a name to the horrendous act she couldn't verbalize, even to herself.

"It'd still be... treason." She could hardly say the word. The mere thought of stealing classified material made her sick. Talking about it calmly with an admitted terrorist scared her witless. The fact that she was undeniably drawn to said terrorist scared her even more. If she hadn't considered it her patriotic duty to put this man behind bars, she would have fled right then.

"We'd pay you, of course." Mac's offer sounded like he was stating the obvious, like it was something they'd both taken for granted.

He actually thinks I'll commit treason to earn a few dollars. Marilyn put her chin on her knees and looked down at the sand so he couldn't see the disillusionment in her eyes.

Her breath caught in her throat. Hard as it was to ask, she knew she had to do it. "How—how much?"

He named a sum. A very large sum.

She didn't look up. It took her a long second to decide what to do. "Double it and I'll think about it." As soon as she'd said it, she knew it was the right response. The FBI would want to know how high he'd go.

"I'm not sure I can get that much."

"Okay. Then let's just forget the whole thing." She started to stand.

Grabbing her hand, he pulled her back down. "Hold on now. I didn't say it was impossible. I'll get hold of my organization later tonight while you're thinking about it. Tomorrow we'll reach an agreement.'' This time when she stood up, he got up with her.

"I guess we can forget about the book project, Mac," she said.

"That we can, and I can't say I'm sorry." She could hear the relief in his voice.

They started down the beach the way they'd come. The old Victorian hotel loomed beside them, its porches gaily lit with colored lights. The sound of a piano playing a Cole Porter tune drifted toward them, clear for a moment and then obliterated by the crashing waves.

"Why all the Mickey Mouse stuff about writing that book?" she asked. "Why not come right out and tell me what you were up to?"

"Because we needed to get to know each other first. I doubt you'd have been willing to listen if I'd told you who I really am the first time we talked."

Marilyn's voice quivered when she answered. "Since you didn't chance it, that's something you'll never know."

He cast a surprised look at her. "Don't tell me you would have agreed to consider my offer, right from the start?"

Keep him guessing, Marilyn. The more avaricious he thinks you are, the less likely he'll be to suspect you of going to the FBI.

She shrugged her shoulders. "For the right price, who knows?"

LATER THAT NIGHT on the way to Marilyn's apartment Mac spotted a vehicle following them again. Every night they'd been followed when he'd driven her home, each time by a different vehicle: the first night the green Olds sedan, the second a black Pontiac, the third a cream Honda. Tonight, a wine-colored Toyota trailed a block or so behind.

He hadn't said anything to Marilyn about it after the first night because he didn't want to scare her. *Scare her, hah! Don't be a fool, MacIntyre. The woman's an out-and-out spy. She's as good as admitted it. She'd be in your pocket right now if you'd agreed to pay her what she wants.*

He turned toward her. "Somebody's following us again."

She twisted to look out the back window. "How do you know? That car behind us is more than a block away."

Coming from an admitted spy, it was a naive question. "Because I know a tail when I see one." What a relief to shed the professor part of his cover. Posing as an IRA terrorist, he moved a step closer to his real self. *I may be playing a part, but at least I know who I am,* Mac thought grimly. *I wonder if Ms. Marilyn Wainwright can find her real self under that layer of innocence she affects.*

"We've been tailed every night," he went on, in a conversational tone.

"Why didn't you tell me?" Her lilting voice sounded shocked.

"I didn't want to upset you. Besides, that's not the sort of thing a college professor would notice. That's who I was pretending to be, remember?" He tried to keep the cynicism from his voice but couldn't. "The only reason I mentioned it the first night was that the fool made himself so obvious you couldn't help seeing him. Have any notion who might be wanting to keep tabs on you?" Mac doubted she knew who it was, but it didn't hurt to ask.

"You're the terrorist. Maybe it's you they're following."

Mac noticed that she hadn't answered his question. For a moment he remained silent, listening to the rhythmic thud of ocean breakers in the distance.

"The only time I'm followed is when I'm with you." He stole a quick glimpse at her face. In the glare of oncoming headlights her violet eyes were wide with alarm. In spite of himself, Mac felt a twinge of concern. Spy or not, she was still a woman, a fragile woman who could be hurt.

"Tell me this, Marilyn," he found himself asking, "are you being followed during the day? When you go to work, for instance?"

"I honestly don't know. I don't pay much attention to who's behind me." There was a breathy quality to her voice that made her sound like a frightened child.

Yesterday she would have fooled Mac, but not today. He repressed his urge to reach out and comfort her. "In the morning keep an eye on your rearview mirror when you drive to work. If you spot a tail, get the make of the car and license number. We have ways of finding out who owns them."

"You mean we've been followed by more than one car?" She leaned toward him, and he was acutely aware of a woodsy fragrance, like the smell of freshly-cut cedar boughs. It lingered in the air for a moment and then was gone.

"A different one every night. They were probably all stolen, used only one day and then abandoned." He turned onto a side road leading into an apartment complex. The car behind them drove on by.

Twisted toward the back, Marilyn breathed a relieved sigh. "They weren't following after all."

"Keep watching," Mac ordered. He made a few turns through the complex and reentered the road. A couple of minutes later the headlights appeared again, a half mile or so behind them.

"You're sure nobody's got a personal reason for following you?" He wondered if she knew and wasn't telling him. Not likely, but he couldn't rule out the possibility.

"I told you *no* the first night." Her tone was sharp. Mac wondered what was going on in her head.

"I've got a project for you, Mr. IRA Terrorist," she said suddenly. "Agree to find out who's following me and why, and I'll be a lot more receptive to your proposition."

So she doesn't know who it is. If she did, she'd never ask a terrorist to look into it. The insight gave him an unreasonable sense of relief, as though her lack of knowing removed her guilt. *Don't be an ass, MacIntyre,* he told himself, frowning. *The woman's guilty as sin.*

He turned down the street leading to her building. "Better be positive you really want to know," he warned. "Because I'm sure as hell going to find out."

He made the promise as much to himself as to her. Mac didn't like puzzles unless he was in on the game. Whoever was tailing Marilyn Wainwright better have a mighty good reason.

MARILYN KNEW SOMETHING was wrong as soon as she opened the door to her apartment. She clutched at Mac's sweater when he turned to go. "Somebody's been in here."

He peered inside. "How do you know? It looks okay to me."

"The papers are messed up on my desk, and one of the cabinet doors is ajar in the kitchen." She swallowed hard. Too much was happening all at once. First, finding out Mac was a terrorist; then, somebody was following her. Now this. The mental picture of a grubby stranger rooting through her things revolted her.

"Are you sure, Marilyn?" She heard the disbelief in Mac's voice. "Maybe you left your desk and kitchen that way."

"I know how I left them. Believe me, Mac, somebody's been here." She felt tears welling in her eyes. "I'm afraid to look in the bedroom."

She felt him pull her to him, felt the rough texture of his sweater against her cheek, the pressure of his chin against the top of her head. He rubbed the small of her back with a gentle, rhythmic motion. "We'll look through everything before I go." His soft cat's purr of an Irish brogue was oddly soothing. "If you feel uncomfortable staying here, we can get you a room at the hotel tonight and a new lock on your door tomorrow."

For a long minute Marilyn let herself savor his warmth, his special spicy scent. Then she pushed herself away. How could she let this man comfort her when she intended to betray him? He let her go slowly, as if reluctant.

"I'll be okay, Mac. For a minute or two there, I got carried away." She started toward the bedroom. He followed.

As in the living room and kitchen, nothing obvious was moved, but there were small disarrangements only an orderly person would notice. Her dresser drawer was open a fraction. The panties and bras inside weren't arranged as neatly as she'd left them. But in the drawer where she kept her jewelry, her grandmother's diamond pendant was still there, safely shut up in its velvet case.

"Any idea what they were looking for?" he asked. Marilyn noticed that he no longer questioned her certainty that someone had been inside her apartment.

She shook her head. "I have nothing of real value other than some jewelry my grandmother left me. It's all here."

Marilyn led him back to the living room. "Since they went through my desk, maybe they were looking for financial records—checkbooks, bonds, that sort of thing. If they expected to find cash, they were sadly disappointed."

"How about your checkbook and credit cards?" he asked.

She patted her cloth tote, still slung over her shoulder. "I carry them with me." Like the rest of the furniture in the room, the desk was oak. One by one, she pulled out its drawers. Nothing was missing.

"Are you absolutely certain? It's important, Marilyn. You're being followed and your home's been searched. It's pretty obvious you've got something somebody wants. What is it?"

Methodically she went through the desk drawers again. She paused at the top left-hand drawer. Her blue address book with King Tut's image in gold on the cover wasn't where she usually kept it. When had she used it last? The weekend she finished addressing her Christmas cards. She glanced at the top of the desk, where a half-full box of unused cards sat. There was no sign of the address book. An icy feeling raced up her spine.

"Something *is* missing," she told Mac, who watched her with a worried expression. "My address book."

"Now we're getting somewhere." He crossed to her sofa and sat down. Unlike the pudgy lieutenant she'd dated for the past year, Mac looked like he belonged there. Grudgingly she admired the way he made her comfortable furniture look more elegant just by sitting on it. He had a confidence, an inner sureness, that enhanced his surroundings.

"Somebody wants to find a friend of yours. Any idea which one?" His expression was knowing, as though he expected her to come up with the answer.

She folded her arms across her chest. "There are more than a hundred names in that book, Mac. There's no way I could begin to guess whose address they wanted."

He patted the seat beside him. "Then let's go at this from a different direction."

Marilyn sat down on the sofa but as far away from him as she could get. This man was a terrorist who wanted her to commit treason. She was too smart to let him get close to her again, no matter what her rebellious body demanded.

"If they wanted an address out of your book, they could have copied it," he said reasonably. "Obviously they wanted to check a number of addresses, not knowing where the person they were looking for had gone."

Marilyn eyed him suspiciously. "You sound as though you know who that person is."

He took a deep breath. "I'm only guessing, of course, but it makes sense that the person they're looking for is somebody close to you, somebody who might have gone to one of the addresses in that book of yours."

"My brother!" she gasped. "Somebody wants to find Van. That's why they've been following me."

"That's my guess," Mac agreed. "Is he on a vacation or something?"

Unconsciously she slid a little closer to Mac on the sofa. "Why didn't they just call his garage if they wanted to know where he is? I'm sure the fellows who work for him have the number."

"Then you know where he is?" Mac asked. Marilyn could see him tense. Energy pulsed through him like electricity whining through high tension wires.

Why's he so interested in Van? Marilyn wondered. "Of course, I know," she said aloud. "For the past week or so he's been visiting a friend in Palm Springs. He said he'd be back after Christmas."

Mac lifted an eyebrow. "Does he take many of these two- and three-week vacations?"

He didn't add *No wonder his business is failing,* but Marilyn could see it in his cynical expression. "Van needed this time away from the shop," she said quickly. "He's been under a lot of pressure lately and works terribly hard. Except for Sundays, this is the first time he's taken off in a couple of years. I was really glad when he called and told me he was going." She paused for a moment and then plunged on, driven by the need to defend her brother. "He's also doing some relief work for the local community. He spends most of his Sundays getting in touch with people on his list."

"People on his list? What kind of list?" Mac leaned toward her, even more alert.

"Poor…uh…families, of course. People who need help." She'd almost said "poor Vietnamese families" but caught herself just in time. She had no intention of answering questions about Van's heritage. She didn't have to justify her brother to anybody, certainly not to an IRA terrorist.

Mac was staring at her as though she'd revealed something significant. "So your brother's got a lot of contacts in the local community? Maybe one of these contacts is trying to locate him."

Marilyn leaned away from him, against the back of the sofa. "I told you, they're poor people—and the relief workers who help them out, of course. None of them would do anything crazy like this. Besides, like I said, all they have to do is call Van's shop to get the number of his friend in Palm Springs."

"Have you got the number?" Skepticism was written all over his face.

She turned her palms up and shrugged her shoulders. "Not now, I don't. It was in my address book."

"But you do know the friend's name so you can get the number from information? I think you should call your brother and tell him what's happened."

She looked at her watch. "It's almost eleven, Mac. How about tomorrow morning?"

He moved close to her and put both hands on her shoulders. "Do it now, Marilyn. Somebody's gone to the trouble to break into your apartment to find out where Van is. He needs to be warned."

The urgency in his voice scared her. "You sound like you think he's in danger. It's only a couple-hours' drive to Palm Springs. Maybe I should go there after I talk to him, make sure he's okay."

Mac stood up and gently helped her to her feet. "First the telephone call. Then if you want to drive to Palm Springs, I'll go with you. You're so loyal to this brother of yours that you've got me curious. I'd like to meet him."

No way was Marilyn going to introduce Van to an IRA terrorist. He had enough problems with his garage and his compulsion to help the Vietnamese refugees without worrying about his sister's new employer.

She didn't argue further with Mac. The phone was on her desk. She dialed information, got the number, and asked for Van Wainwright.

"Who's calling?"

Marilyn recognized the voice of Van's friend, Randy Turner, who was also half Vietnamese. "This is his sister, Randy. It's important that I talk to him."

"He's not here, Marilyn."

"Well, have him call me when he gets back."

The line went silent. Marilyn listened for the click of the receiver but didn't hear it. "Randy?"

"He hasn't been in Palm Springs since you two were here that Sunday in November. Did he tell you he'd be here?"

"You haven't heard from him since then?" Marilyn's knees felt weak. She pulled out the chair behind her desk and sat down.

"If he's somewhere in Palm Springs, he sure hasn't called me."

Then where is he? Marilyn hung up the phone with a sinking feeling that her world was on the verge of turning inside out.

BEFORE MAC WENT to his room, he stopped at his favorite pay phone on the Hotel del Coronado's lower-level arcade. Scowling, he dialed Finnegan's home number. So what if midnight in San Diego translated into three a.m. in D.C.? He had a bone to pick with his boss, and he didn't intend to wait until morning to do it.

Finnegan's "hello" was even mushier than usual.

Mac didn't waste any time with small talk. "Get these people from the local office off my back, or I'm outta here, Charley. First your Number One boy shows up in my hotel room. Now they've searched my lady's apartment. What's going on, boss?"

"What're you talking about, buddy?" Finnegan still sounded fuzzy. "I didn't authorize any search."

"You know what, Charley? I don't believe you." Mac wasn't sure whether his boss was on the level or not. A confrontation was the best way to find out.

"So somebody's gone over her place. They take anything?"

"Only an address book."

"An address book!" Finnegan's tone changed to one of wide-awake alertness. "They're looking for the brother, too. You get a line on where he's gone?"

Mac scowled into the phone. It looked like Finnegan was on the level. That meant somebody else was keeping a close eye on Marilyn, hoping she'd lead them to Van. The thought made him edgy. Who knew what kind of kook was after Van or what they'd do to get her to tell where he'd gone.

"She thought she knew, but when she called, he wasn't there. I may be wrong, boss, but I don't think she knows where he is."

Mac heard Finnegan's hoarse chuckle.

"She knows, buddy. Believe me, she knows."

Mac frowned. "Maybe you're right. I offered her the pie tonight and she bit like a pro." *Like a real pro,* Mac thought grimly. Hardened as he was, Mac had been more surprised and disappointed by Marilyn's willingness than he cared to admit.

"What'd I tell you, buddy? Now we've got her. When're you going to make the exchange?"

"Next day or two."

"Good." MacIntyre pictured a satisfied Finnegan rubbing his hands together. For some reason it aggravated him.

"Keep trying to get a line on the brother, buddy," Finnegan went on. "We need him, too."

After Mac hung up he stopped in the lounge for a Scotch. A tall blonde with a good tan sat down next to him at the bar. After a few minutes' conversation, he learned that she was a computer programmer staying at the hotel. Married, she was attending a week-long meeting in San Diego alone.

She was just the kind of woman Mac usually looked for. Attractive, available, already committed to somebody else and out for a good time. Unfortunately, tonight he couldn't work up his usual enthusiasm for her too-eager line of chatter. He finished his drink, wished her a Merry Christmas and headed upstairs to his room.

Chapter Six

Glancing nervously around her, Marilyn took in the filing cabinets, the metal furniture, the brown long-wear carpet, the receptionist's cluttered desk. It might have been any office anywhere. But it wasn't. It was the San Diego office of the Federal Bureau of Investigation.

This morning Marilyn had dressed in her plainest suit— dark blue linen with low-heeled black pumps—so she wouldn't attract attention, but she still felt conspicuous. The office's normal atmosphere made her feel a little less so, as though she were on routine business instead of turning in a terrorist who was probably wanted by half-a-dozen governments.

She focused on the receptionist. The woman was wearing a white blouse with ruffles at the neck. A nameplate on her desk identified her as Diane Rogers.

"How can we help you this beautiful morning?" Ms. Rogers asked, after she swallowed the doughnut she'd been eating and washed it down with some coffee. Plump and fortyish, she smiled benignly at Marilyn, showing identical dimples on each cheek.

"I'd like to see an agent, please, Ms. Rogers."

"What's it about, Ms.—"

"Wainwright. Marilyn Wainwright." Marilyn couldn't tell if the receptionist was being curious or if asking about her business was part of the job. "I don't mean to be uncooperative, but I'd rather talk to an agent."

Liar's Game

"Quite all right, Ms. Wainwright. A lot of our walk-ins feel that way." The receptionist broke off another piece of doughnut. Chunks of glazed frosting dropped onto the napkin on her desk.

Marilyn could feel a pulse throbbing in her temple. She hoped she didn't look as nervous as she felt. "It's pretty early. Have any agents come in yet?"

"Special Agent Dan Smith is in his office. He's tied up at the moment, but I'm sure he'll be glad to talk to you as soon as he's free." Holding the piece of doughnut in one hand, she flicked a switch on her squawk box with the other. "Agent Smith. There's a Ms. Marilyn Wainwright here to see you."

There was a moment of absolute silence. Then a baritone voice said smoothly, "Take her to the conference room, Diane. I'll be with her shortly."

The conference room adjoined the front office and boasted the same drab off-white paint and brown carpeting. It was furnished with a long table surrounded by ten chairs. A rectangular mirror hung on one wall. The receptionist told Marilyn to make herself comfortable and left the room, closing the door behind her.

Marilyn hung her leather shoulder bag over the back of one of the chairs and sat staring at the mirror. Was somebody watching her from behind it? She'd seen enough spy movies to know that was how these people operated. Well, let them look, she thought. She certainly had nothing to hide.

A moment later, a tall dark-haired man in a well-cut brown business suit entered the room through a door opposite the reception area. Movie-star handsome, except for his large nose, he had what Marilyn called a "Cassius look," lean and hungry. Above his welcoming smile were dark blue eyes as cold as glacial ice. She stirred uneasily in her seat, but met his gaze head-on.

He pulled out the chair next to hers, sat down, and held out his hand. "I'm Special Agent Dan Smith, Ms. Wainwright."

She shook his hand. It was warm. Sweaty. "Thank you for seeing me, Agent Smith." *I wonder if that's his real name,* she thought, and immediately chided herself. What difference did it make?

Agent Smith leaned back, his face expressionless. "Before we get started, do you mind if I smoke, Ms. Wainwright?" Reaching into his pocket, he pulled out a package of cigarettes and a lighter.

Marilyn's chair had rollers, and she scooted it sideways, away from him. "Sorry. I'm allergic to tobacco smoke."

Surprise flickered in his eyes and was gone almost before she recognized it. Apparently Agent Smith's walk-ins usually didn't object if he smoked. He put the cigarettes back in his pocket.

"First, let me tell you something about myself," she began. "I'm a technical librarian for the Wakefield Aircraft Corporation in La Jolla. A couple of months ago I was granted a Category five clearance. As part of my security briefing, I was told to report any suspicious contacts to the FBI."

"And you've come to report a suspicious contact?"

Was there something accusing in his tone? She examined his face and saw only alert interest. *Stop feeling guilty,* she warned herself. *You did nothing to invite Mac's overture.* It was then that she realized her guilty feelings stemmed from turning Mac in, not from what he'd asked her to do.

"Yes." Nervous but determined, she forged ahead. "Last night a man named George McDonough, who says he's working for the Irish Republican Army, asked me to steal classified information for him."

Agent Smith straightened in his chair. "McDonough's a wanted terrorist." His voice sounded tight, controlled. "Did anybody see you come in here?"

"I don't think so." Nervously she pressed her fingers together in her lap.

"With information like that, you shouldn't have come to the office, Ms. Wainwright. McDonough might have seen you." He smiled patronizingly, as if dealing with a backward child. "Any ten-year-old knows this place is watched all the time. The address is in the damn telephone book."

Marilyn's nervousness evaporated. She stood and slung her bag over her shoulder. Startled, he jumped up beside her. He was at least a foot taller, but she didn't let that stop her.

"Don't bully me, Mr. Smith." Her tone hovered somewhere around zero. From the surprised lift to his eyebrows, Marilyn could see she'd caught him off guard. "For your information, our security briefer told us to report any suspicious contacts to the FBI. Not to the police. Not to our Chief of Security. *To the FBI.* I didn't use the telephone because I knew it wasn't secure."

His patronizing look vanished. "I'm sure you did what you thought best, Ms. Wainwright." A snake oil salesman couldn't have talked more smoothly. "The important thing is that you reported it."

He led her to the door at the end of the room. "Now we need to get you out of here as unobtrusively as we can. Where did you park?"

"In a garage around the corner from your front entrance."

"Good. If we're lucky, your friend didn't see you come in our office." Agent Smith sounded exuberant, like a small boy who's just caught an exotic butterfly.

Marilyn realized it was the way she'd expected him to react, right from the beginning. After all, she was handing him a bona fide IRA terrorist on a silver platter. *Maybe he's human after all,* she thought, responding to the excitement in his voice. "Don't you want the details?" she asked.

"Later," he said. "I'll call Wakefield's Chief of Security to set up an appointment with you at your office this afternoon." He held the door open and Marilyn followed him down a long hallway. From there he led her through a maze of corridors, up several flights of stairs, across a glassed-in outside walkway, and finally to a bank of elevators.

"I'll leave you here," he said, punching the Down button. "Don't discuss this with anyone. I'll be in touch this afternoon."

On the ground floor, Marilyn found herself in a building nearly a block away from the FBI office. She walked to her car with the guilty feeling that she'd just betrayed a good friend.

WHEN SPECIAL AGENT Dan Smith, also known as Special Agent Dan Moschella, got back to his office, he went directly to the secure telephone and dialed the two-digit number for FBI headquarters in Washington.

"Mr. Finnegan, please," he said. "Special Agent Moschella calling from San Diego."

In a couple of minutes, Finnegan's raspy voice came on the line. "What's up, Dan?" He sounded grumpy, as though he'd been interrupted in the middle of a meal. But then, Finnegan always sounded grumpy.

"It's about MacIntyre's sting, Mr. Finnegan. You told me to call you if Ms. Marilyn Wainwright got in touch and not to say anything to Mac about it. Well, she just showed up. Says an IRA terrorist named George McDonough asked her to steal classified information so she reported him to the bureau."

Moschella caught the satisfaction in Finnegan's answering grunt. "That's good, Dan. We're right on schedule."

"So you expected her to turn him in?" Moschella didn't try to hide his surprise. "What the hell's going on here, Mr. Finnegan? If you don't tell me, I can't handle her right."

Finnegan sighed. Moschella heard his frustration across the three thousand miles that separated them. "We're trying to nail her brother. He's head of a syndicate controlling gangs of young Vietnamese thugs in several States. They're into drugs, prostitution, extortion and who knows what else in the Vietnamese communities. We think she's working with him, but whether she is or not, it's a sure bet she's the only one who knows where he is. They've been like two peas in a pod ever since they were kids."

"What's the secret stuff got to do with it? She said Mac wants her to steal classified information."

"It was a gimmick to get her involved, Dan. If she steals for Mac in his role as IRA terrorist, we force her to tell us where the brother is or she goes to jail." He paused. Moschella could picture the sly smile on his fleshy face.

"If she turns Mac in, we've got an alternative plan," Finnegan continued. "We get her to play along with us. As soon as she passes classified files to him, we've got her again. We refuse to corroborate her story that she's working for us, threaten her with jail, and she leads us to the brother."

Dramatically, Finnegan paused again. "Our last alternative is, if she doesn't talk, she goes to jail. Then the brother comes out of the bushes to keep his sister from being convicted as a traitor."

It was a scheme worthy of Moschella himself. He nodded approvingly. "I like it, Mr. Finnegan. So the next step is to recruit her to help us catch George McDonough, that big, bad IRA terrorist?"

Finnegan made a low growling sound that passed as a sarcastic chuckle. "You got it, Dan. Once she's hooked, get her to give him some classified info. Then we can lower the boom on her."

"MacIntyre know the whole story?" Moschella asked.

There was a moment of hesitation. Then Finnegan cleared his throat. "I thought Mac would be more convincing—would play his role better—if he was under the impression the little lady's a spy."

"He's not going to like it when he finds out the truth."

"We didn't tell you the whole story either, until you had a need to know. You're not upset about it are you?"

"Hell, no, Mr. Finnegan. But I'm not MacIntyre. You know what a bleeding-heart liberal he is—how he won't do a sting operation unless he's positive the suspect's guilty."

Awkwardly, Finnegan cleared his throat. "Mac's a good agent, Dan. After we've broken this syndicate, he'll go along. From your own experience there in Southern California, you know how bad these people are. As bad as the Mafia.''

"And as tough to crack. Unless I miss my guess, you'll be getting a promotion after this is over, Mr. Finnegan.''

Dan Moschella was grinning when he hung up the receiver.

MARILYN SAT, nervous but outwardly composed, in the plush conference room of the Wakefield Aircraft Corporation. She'd left her office half an hour before the scheduled meeting with Agent Smith to escape Edgar's curious questions.

"I'm not sure myself," she lied, when he asked her point-blank why she'd been summoned by Wakefield's Chief of Security. "I imagine it's got something to do with my clearance." The FBI agent had warned her to keep quiet. If that meant lying to her boss, so be it.

While she waited, her red leather chair pulled up to the big, round conference table, Marilyn made a chronological list of what had happened since Mac called her last Sunday night. She'd brought a legal-size yellow tablet with her and scribbled notes on the pad, trying not to forget anything.

The Chief of Security came in before she was finished. Two men were with him: Agent Smith and another man also dressed in a suit and tie. The security chief, a beefy man in his fifties named Sam Worth, introduced him as Special Agent Adam Jones. Marilyn couldn't stop her knowing smile when she heard his name. It was obviously a phony. If she hadn't been certain about Agent Smith's name this morning, she was now.

"We'll take it from here, Mr. Worth," Smith said, walking partway to the door with Wakefield's security chief. "Thanks for your help."

"Sure hope you catch the SOB." Worth paused, and Agent Smith started toward him, as though to ease him out. The security chief resumed his slow amble toward the door.

"With Ms. Wainwright's able assistance, I'm sure we will, Chief."

The agent's comment sent an apprehensive shiver down Marilyn's spine. "Able assistance" seemed to imply more than merely supplying a few details about what had happened. Would they expect her to continue meeting with Mac, an admitted IRA terrorist, in order to spring a trap of some sort? *At least I'd be able to see him again,* she thought, and was horrified at herself for even thinking such a thing.

Agent Smith returned to the table, but waited until the security chief had closed the door behind himself before he spoke. Marilyn wondered how much Worth had been told. Probably not much, if his immediate departure was any indication.

"Agent Jones will be working with us on this case, Ms. Wainwright." Smith settled himself a couple of chairs away, where he could look across the round table at Marilyn. His partner sat down beside him. Although Jones was over six feet, he was shorter than Smith. Blonde and brown-eyed, he had the same preppy good looks.

Marilyn glanced down at her list. "I've prepared a detailed summary of events leading up to the request for classified material last night. Would you like me to read it?"

"Please." Agent Smith spoke, but both men leaned toward her.

Marilyn began with the phone call from Mac in response to her ad. Mention of the ad sparked questions about why she was looking for extra work.

"Because I need the money, of course," she replied, trying not to show her aggravation. "My mother's in a nursing home," she added.

"Don't you have brothers or sisters who can help?"

Marilyn explained that Van was a half brother, struggling with a failing business. She thought that would be the end of the questions about her family, but it wasn't. They wanted to know about her father, about the circumstances of Van's birth, about how her father brought her brother to this country. Marilyn didn't hide Van's Vietnamese heritage as she usually did. After all, these men were from the

FBI. She didn't like telling the story but forced herself to be brutally honest.

After she'd finished, Agent Jones smiled sympathetically. "It must have been difficult being the second child in a situation like that. Your father went to a lot of trouble to bring your brother here."

Marilyn felt her face flush. "It wasn't difficult at all being the 'second child' as you say. My father loved both of us."

"How did you and your brother get along?" Smith asked.

Staring from one agent to the other, Marilyn took a deep breath. "Why all these questions about my family? I thought we were here to talk about a terrorist who wants me to steal classified information. What's my family got to do with it?"

"Forgive us, Ms. Wainwright." Smith flashed her a smile worthy of a toothpaste ad. "Of course we're here to investigate the IRA's request for classified material. But over and above that, Agent Jones and I are interested in you personally. You're a courageous young woman to come forward the way you did."

"We want you to feel like part of our team," Agent Jones added.

Marilyn recognized flattery when she heard it. *It'll take more than flattery to get me on your team,* she thought, frowning as another thought struck her. Maybe she had no choice.

Quickly Marilyn covered the rest of the items on her list: the way Mac had pretended to be a Notre Dame professor writing a book on the British army; the cars that followed them from the hotel to her apartment every night; the phone call she'd made to the La Jolla Institute of Geophysical Phenomena; last night's search of her apartment.

"Why do you suppose the people at the institute said he worked there?" she asked suddenly, remembering the operator's difficulty locating Mac's name on the personnel roster. "Is it possible somebody there is providing cover for an IRA terrorist?"

Special Agent Smith seemed flustered by her question. He stood up and paced around the table a couple of times before he answered. "Anything's possible, Ms. Wainwright. We'll check it out and let you know."

When Marilyn had gone through the items on her list, she eyed the two men apprehensively. What more did they want from her and where would it lead?

She wasn't long in finding out.

"We need you to help us get the goods on this guy," Agent Smith began. "If you don't, he walks away a free man, able to talk somebody else into stealing secret stuff for him—somebody who isn't as loyal a citizen as you are."

Marilyn could see where Smith was headed. She didn't like what she saw.

"I'd be willing to testify to what happened," she began, frantically searching for an alternative. The thought of facing Mac in a courtroom made her almost physically ill, but that was infinitely better than getting involved in an FBI operation to trap him.

Smith smiled benignly. "That's not exactly what we had in mind."

She waited, her heart in her throat.

"Testifying in court won't cut it," he went on. "It's your word against his. What we've got to have is an exchange of secret material for money. You hand him the classified information, he gives you the money, and we witness the transaction. That way we've got him for sure."

Marilyn didn't know how to refuse gracefully. She said the first thing that popped into her head. "I can't do that, Agent Smith. If I did, I'd be a traitor."

"You know better than that, Ms. Wainwright." His voice was patient but tinged with a fine edge of annoyance. "You'd be working for us. The FBI. The U.S. government. That makes you a patriot, not a traitor. You must realize we'd prepare the package for you to give him. You wouldn't have to steal it from your office."

"I'm not a believable actress, Mr. Smith," Marilyn went on, not acknowledging what he'd said. "I'd give the whole thing away." It was a realistic objection, not stupid like the other.

Smith didn't let her get away with that, either. "We'd train you, Ms. Wainwright, tell you exactly what to say and how to act when you're with him. Mainly, just be yourself. But instead of resisting, relax. Go along with him. Find out what he wants. You're planning to meet him tonight, right?"

Marilyn nodded. Visions of Mac raced through her head: of him working beside her at the computer, of his face in the firelight, of him comforting her last night in her defiled apartment. She took a deep breath. "I can't do this, Mr. Smith. I simply can't."

The agent's cold eyes narrowed, and his broad nose turned a pale shade of pink. "It's not that you can't do it, Ms. Wainwright. It's that you won't. Your country needs you, and you're refusing to help."

"If you're a loyal American, helping us is the patriotic thing," Agent Jones chimed in. "These terrorists are the scum of the earth."

This afternoon in the office Marilyn had done some reading about IRA atrocities. Pictures of maimed British soldiers, barely more than boys, flashed vividly in her mind. Their grotesque injuries were caused by an exploding bomb in a car driven by a hapless civilian. The poor man had been forced to steer the vehicle into the guard post or witness the brutal murders of his wife and children, held hostage by the terrorists.

She clutched her hands together in her lap. "What do you want me to do?" she asked helplessly. As she'd feared, she had no other choice.

THE SANDS INN on Mission Bay was one of the most elegant dining rooms in the San Diego area. Featuring entrées like roast pheasant in raspberry sauce, it was also one of the most expensive. That's why Marilyn suggested it when Mac offered to take her to dinner to celebrate their new agreement.

"You might as well get some good food out of it," Agent Smith had advised that afternoon, a wicked gleam in his eye. "If he's willing to pay a fortune for British Order of Battle, the least he can do is buy you a few decent meals. Besides," he added, "when you make the exchange of classified information for cash you need to be in a public place where we can witness it. Where better than a fancy restaurant? If you pick a spot fairly close to home, you won't have to worry about awkward silences during a long car ride."

Marilyn followed his advice to the letter. After some initial resistance, Mac finally agreed to the Sands Inn.

"For the money they'll charge, they ought to provide us with a king's feast," he grumbled. In his dark suit, white shirt and green silk tie, he looked elegant enough to own the place.

After her first look at him in a coat and tie, Marilyn wished she'd taken the time and money to buy new shoes to wear with her gold silk dress. Now that they'd arrived, she wished it even more. Her sensible patent leather pumps felt better suited for a walk on the beach than across the restaurant's hardwood floors.

"If I didn't know better, I'd think you were Scottish," Marilyn teased, in a feeble attempt to lighten her mood. Following Agent Smith's instructions, she was determined to relax and enjoy the evening. She tried not to think about the fact that it might be one of the last nights she shared with this man.

Mac gave her a quizzical look. "Telling an Irishman he acts like a Scot—that's equivalent to calling him a dirty name."

The haughty maître d' led them to a table near a massive aquarium. Marilyn let him help her into her chair. Mac sat opposite her.

"I'm sorry if I insulted you," she said, "but the way you try to save money for that organization of yours, they ought to give you a medal."

He grinned at her. "So that's the reason for calling me a Scot. For a minute there, you had me worried. Truth, Marilyn, I'm more inclined to be careful with their funds than with my own. Without financial support, our grand cause would fail."

"Your *grand cause* that uses car bombs to kill innocent boys?" The words spurted out automatically.

His face a mask, he crossed his arms. "Don't tell me you're thinking about backing out." He glanced at his watch. "Not forty-five minutes after you agreed to sell me what I need."

"No— No, of course not," Marilyn denied quickly. She'd have to be more careful, not let her feelings get involved. "It's just that you people do some terrible things. I can't picture myself being part of that." *Or you being part of it, either, Mac.*

Being a spy for the FBI was every bit as difficult as she'd feared. Thank goodness Mac had wanted the material as soon as he could get it—tomorrow night, if possible. That gave her only one more night of lies and pretense. Then, once this was over and done with, she could start forgetting him.

"Don't dwell on what upsets you," he advised. "Relax. Be yourself and just enjoy the evening."

Agent Smith had said essentially the same thing only this afternoon. *As though they were trained at the same school.* The thought of Agent Smith and Mac getting the same training was oddly disturbing, but she didn't dwell on it. At least the advice each gave was sound. She decided, again, to take it.

For the next hour Marilyn tried to concentrate on having a good time. She failed. Instead of enjoying herself, she became more and more miserable.

Watching her from across the table, Mac saw her unhappiness. No amount of forced gaiety could erase the pain from her violet eyes, from her lower lip that trembled with guilt, even as she smiled.

Finally, after they'd finished a flaming ice-cream dessert, he could stand it no longer. This lady might be a spy, but an unwilling one at best. The hell with Finnegan and his elaborate sting operation. Mac reached across the table and took her small hand in both of his. It was the first time he'd held her hand, and he was surprised at how well it fit into his.

"You're upset," he began, wondering if she'd admit it.

"Is it that obvious?" she said, with a sigh. "I was trying my best to be witty and entertaining." Her porcelain skin glistened in the light from the chandelier. Its glow highlighted her aristocratic cheekbones and turned her hair to dark brown velvet. For the hundredth time, Mac wondered how it would look falling loosely on her shoulders instead of piled on her head the way she always wore it.

"Let's forget the whole thing," he said. "Tomorrow night, when we meet in the hotel lobby, let's just go to dinner and forget everything else."

She jerked her hand away. Startled surprise replaced the pain on her face. "Wh—what are you saying?"

"That I'm sorry I asked you to help me. It's making you unhappy." God help him, it was the truth. He *was* sorry he'd asked. He'd rather spend ten years in jail himself than be responsible for sending her to prison.

She looked down at her coffee. He couldn't see her eyes.

"You've got it all wrong, Mac," she said. "I'm not upset because you asked me to help you. Goodness knows you're paying me enough."

"So what is bothering you then, Marilyn? I know something is." His voice sounded gruff to his ears.

She kept her eyes downcast, but he could hear a tremulous note in her voice when she answered. "It's the thought of what your organization does. I did some reading this afternoon and your—associates—do terrible things."

So that was it. He should have known from what she'd said earlier, when they'd first sat down. She didn't mind stealing top secret material for cold, hard cash. No, not at all. Being a traitor to her country didn't bother her. She was just a little squeamish about young soldiers being blown to pieces by car bombs.

"So, don't think about it," he advised roughly.

Later that night when he took her to her door, he stared down at her delicate face and yearned to feel her slim body pressed against his, the way she'd been last night. She wanted him, too. He could read it in her eyes.

For a magic moment, all sense of time and space vanished. There were just the two of them, a breath away, leaning toward each other, all else forgotten.

The moment passed. Mac forced himself to turn away without touching her. The lady was a traitor, a very clever traitor at that. Tonight she'd almost made him forget which side he was on. It mustn't happen again. Thank God he had only one more night. And then this operation would be over.

Chapter Seven

After Mac had gone, Marilyn dialed the number Agent Smith had given her to reach him during off-duty hours. "Ask for Chris Brown," Smith had told her. "The person answering the phone will contact me, and I'll call you back within an hour."

It seemed stupid to use one phony name to get a man hiding behind another, but why should she care if the FBI wanted to play silly games? Just the same, she felt a little foolish asking the crisp male voice that answered for a non-person named Chris Brown.

"Mr. Brown will return your call shortly," the voice said. "Please stay by your phone." He sounded deadly serious.

Ten minutes later the phone rang. She picked it up and heard Agent Smith's smooth baritone.

"Be careful not to mention names," he reminded her, before she had a chance to say anything but hello. "You never know who's listening."

This afternoon he'd told her that her phone, or his, might be bugged. Silly names or not, this was a dangerous business she'd gotten herself involved in.

Marilyn proceeded cautiously, weighing every word. "My friend wants the stuff." She winced at using such a nondescript word as "stuff," but couldn't think of a better one. "As soon as he can get it. Is dinnertime tomorrow night too soon? We've already made the arrangement."

"Much too soon." There was no hesitation in Smith's voice. "We'll need at least twenty-four hours to get ready. Besides, tomorrow's Saturday. Isn't your office closed?"

"No, it's open all the time." A premonition of impending disaster brought goose bumps to her skin. "I thought you said I wouldn't have to get the stuff from my office."

She heard him take a deep breath. "You won't, Ms. Wainwright. Your office is the only safe place for us to get together, for me to give you the material. But not on the weekend with a skeleton staff on board. It'd be too obvious."

"Not until Monday? We can't wrap this up until Monday?" A tremulous feeling enveloped her. She wasn't sure whether it was from anticipation, or dread at the thought of spending another night with Mac. *I can't do it,* she told herself. *He guessed something was wrong tonight. I'll give the whole thing away if I see him again before Monday.*

"That's the earliest," Smith said. "Stall him, sweetheart. My advice is to get a couple more expensive dinners out of the deal."

"Your advice stinks!"

"So eat at McDonald's."

Marilyn banged down the receiver without saying goodbye.

For the next two hours she tried reaching Mac at the hotel to break their date for Saturday night. Seeing him before Monday would be too dangerous. She dialed his room every half hour until one a.m., but he didn't answer the phone in his suite or return the messages she left for him at the desk.

All day Saturday she stayed home, waiting for him to call. When she'd heard nothing by late afternoon, she suspected he was ignoring her. Either that, or he hadn't gone back to his hotel when he'd left her the previous night.

He's probably staying with a girlfriend. Marilyn was surprised at her heated reaction to the thought. Jealousy was such a foreign emotion to her that she almost didn't recognize it. There was no way she could be jealous over an admitted terrorist, a man who manipulated innocent people like pawns in some horrible game he was playing.

By six-thirty she'd given up hope he'd call. She considered leaving another message, telling him she wouldn't be there. She decided not to. By this time she knew him well enough to realize he'd come straight to her apartment as soon as he read it. Meeting him here, alone, would be much riskier than in the hotel lobby. She had her excuse for the postponement worked out in her mind, but she was uneasy about the lies she'd have to tell. And somehow it seemed easier to lie in the crowded lobby.

Getting ready, she scrubbed herself harder than usual in the shower, trying to rub away the lies. Then, she dried her hair and dressed in a white turtleneck sweater, tucked into her freshly washed, cotton paisley skirt. It was a simple outfit for a simple meeting in a hotel lobby. No more fancy restaurants for Marilyn. Eating at the Sands Inn last night had made her feel like a gold digger, out to take advantage of an unwholesome situation. She never wanted to have a feeling like that again. Clean, and sweet smelling as laundry dried on an outside line, she headed for her rendezvous at the Hotel del Coronado.

MAC TOOK ONE LOOK at Marilyn and knew she intended to break their date. A woman didn't wear a sweater and skirt, black stockings and flat-heeled Chinese-style shoes, to a fancy restaurant, not even in laid-back San Diego. The ridiculous round glasses were perched on her nose again, as though to remind him she was still the innocent young woman he'd met five days ago.

God, was it only five days? He forced himself to ignore how vulnerable she looked in the peasant clothes. Her scrubbed-fresh scent reminded him of rain, the way it smelled on an early spring day in Central Park. She was wearing no makeup that he could see. If she'd let her hair hang down, she'd pass for a schoolgirl. For the rest of his life Mac knew he'd remember her the way she looked at that moment: clean, fresh and innocent, like a lamb being led to the slaughter.

He didn't let himself smile at her. She wasn't an innocent lamb. She was a traitor.

"Where's the package?" He kept his voice low, almost a whisper. "I've spent most of last night and today arranging for that huge amount of money you demanded." The suitcase in his hand was heavy with cash. "Don't tell me you've showed up without the information?"

Without looking around him, Mac sensed the presence of the FBI agents in the lobby. He'd guessed from her phone calls that she wanted to postpone the transaction, but he had arranged for two of Moschella's men to be there as witnesses, just in case.

"I didn't bring it." He detected no hint of apology in her tone. "I forgot today was Saturday when we made the arrangement last night. That's a bad day to take anything out of the building. The guards check packages more carefully on weekends. I tried to call you to let you know." Her voice turned sharp, accusing. "Why didn't you return my messages?"

"Because I was afraid you'd changed your mind, and decided not to go through with it. I wanted to see you tonight. I knew you'd come if you couldn't get me on the phone." It was a lie, at least the part about changing her mind. He no longer had any doubt that she'd eventually supply the information he wanted.

But the rest of what he'd said was true, Mac realized suddenly, a little surprised at himself. He *did* want to spend more time with her. That's why he hadn't returned her calls.

"Does that mean Monday's the earliest you can get it for me?" He let a fine edge of annoyance creep into his voice, not because he was annoyed, but because it suited his role.

"I may not be able to get it then, either, Mr. McDonough," she snapped. "It depends on what's happening at the office."

"Hey! What's this *Mr.* business? I'm still Mac, remember?" He smiled, not a pretend smile but one he truly felt.

She didn't smile back. "From now on, let's be as businesslike as possible," she said. "There's no need for social amenities or for you to waste your time and money taking me to expensive restaurants. Save your resources for that grand cause you were telling me about last night." She turned and started for the door. "I'll call you at the hotel Monday night at five-thirty. If you want that information you asked for, you'd better be in your suite, waiting to answer."

He swung into step beside her. "Don't do this to me, Marilyn."

As soon as the words were out, Mac couldn't believe he'd said them. They sounded so serious, so *committed,* as though she had some kind of power over him.

Marilyn stopped walking and turned to face him. "What do you mean?" Her violet eyes, peering through the thick lenses of her glasses, stared into his. Mac saw confusion there and something else—fear, guilt, hope—he wasn't sure what.

He flashed her his most charming smile. "Faith, and you can't be walking out on me, leaving me all alone on a Saturday night, a stranger in a strange land." Purposely, he used bantering words to cover his confusion. This woman was a spy, for God's sake.

She eyed his tan slacks and brown sport coat, his yellow tie and well-polished loafers. "You're much too dressed up for a date with me, Mr. McDonough."

"I can change." His tone was light, his expression confident. He yanked off his coat and tie and unbuttoned his shirt. "Now, we'll check this suitcase in the hotel safe and be on our way."

For an instant her expression lightened, and he thought he had her. Then doubt reappeared.

"I'm sorry, Mac. I've got to go. I really do. It's wrong for us to be together."

She turned and almost ran from him. The last he saw of her was the swish of her skirt, as she darted through the lobby doors. With a suitcase full of the government's cash in his hand, he couldn't go after her.

THE PHONE STARTED RINGING as soon as Marilyn entered her apartment. She turned on her answering machine and listened to Mac's entreaties—most of them humorous demands for a dinner companion—while she heated supper in her microwave oven. At eleven, he stopped calling.

His calls began again Sunday morning. Marilyn ignored them. What good could come from spending the day with a man like Mac, regardless of how attracted she was to him? Danger lurked in his charming smile and in the easy way he'd asked her to commit espionage. She dared not risk losing any more of herself to him.

After church, she headed north of the city to visit her mother in the nursing home. It was nearly five when she got back. Her answering machine showed that six calls had come in while she was gone. She flicked the switch to replay the calls, listening while she took off her cardigan and folded it. She was wearing off-white wool pants and an ice-blue sweater and matching cardigan her mother especially liked.

The first four were from Mac, begging her on bended knee to meet him that evening for dinner, a movie, whatever. She turned up the sound and listened from the bedroom while she put away her cardigan and tote bag.

When the fifth call began, Marilyn froze. It was Van's voice, speaking Vietnamese. He'd taught her the language when she was a child, and she'd never forgotten it because they spoke it often. She raced to her desk.

"I must talk to you, Little One. You are in terrible danger because you have gone to the government. Get a winning name from my picture books and call from a pay phone as soon as you can. Tell no one. Erase this message right now."

Glued to the desk, Marilyn played the tape until she had it memorized. Then she erased everything on it. Heart pounding, she sat on a tall stool at her breakfast bar with a cup of hot chocolate, and tried to figure out her brother's cryptic message. Van said she was in danger because she'd "gone to the government." How could he possibly know she'd agreed to work with the FBI? Nobody knew that except her and the bureau. Nobody. Unless . . .

A voice nagged at her. Agent Smith's voice. "Anybody might have seen you come in here," he'd said. She squirmed uneasily on her stool, remembering his annoyance. Could someone have watched her go into the FBI office Friday morning, someone who knew she was doing research for Mac? Did that someone report what he saw to Van?

It didn't make sense. Her brother had no connection to an IRA terrorist. Why would anybody report her FBI visit to Van? She dismissed the question. Van would have to explain it when she talked to him.

The "picture books" were easy. Van was a stamp collector. Marilyn had called his albums picture books when she was a child. Whoever he wanted her to call was listed somewhere in the albums. They were in his house, in a bedroom he used as an office. She had the key. It would be a simple matter to go there and get them.

The "winning name" posed more difficulty. She puzzled over it for more than half an hour, scribbling notations with a pencil on a tablet. Finally, she repeated the word "win" aloud, in both Vietnamese and English. That made more sense. The English word "win" sounded very much like the Vietnamese pronunciation of the name Nguyen. Van wanted her to search his albums for the phone number of somebody named Nguyen, the most common Vietnamese family name.

Grabbing her sweater and shoulder bag from the bedroom, Marilyn headed for her car.

IT WAS DARK when Marilyn pulled in front of her brother's modest frame house in El Cajon, but she could easily make out the yellowed lawn and withered shrubs in front. The sight made her frown. Why didn't Van arrange for a neighborhood teenager to watch the house and water the yard while he was gone? A torn screen was hanging from one of the curtained windows, adding to the dilapidation.

The place looks abandoned, she thought. Her brother would not have left it that way unless he was in a terrible hurry to leave. *Or unless he's been detained much longer than he planned.* Either possibility made her uneasy, especially since she hadn't been able to reach him in Palm Springs, where he said he'd be.

Why didn't I come right out here Thursday night when I found out he wasn't at Randy's? she chided herself. It was Mac's fault, of course. Since she'd found out he was an IRA terrorist, she'd thought of little else.

Fumbling in her shoulder bag for the key, Marilyn hurried down the walk to the front door. When she reached the small front stoop and swung the screen open, she realized she wouldn't need the key. The front door wasn't locked. It wasn't even tightly closed. She gave a tentative shove. It opened a crack. A strong odor of men's cologne hit her in the face. Her heart began pounding like a jackhammer. Something was wrong here, very wrong. She shoved harder. The door swung wider, then stopped.

The light switches were inside the door. She reached for them. Visions of touching something wet and slimy raced through her mind, but she felt only the familiar solidness of the wall beside the door. When light flooded the small porch and room inside, she stepped over the threshold. Marilyn gasped, horrified at what she saw. The place was in shambles. The walls, bashed with some kind of heavy instrument, yawned with gaping holes. Red spray paint defiled everything, from the carpet to the draperies to the battered walls.

Furniture, books and upholstery were strewn around the room as though tossed about by a giant mixer. Van's beautiful mahogany dining-room table and chairs, the only nice furniture he owned, were chopped into pieces. Blocking the door were torn sofa cushions, their covers slit and tufts of padding spilling out.

The small kitchen was littered with pans. Dishes had been swept out of cupboards and lay broken on the counters and floor. The musky smell of men's cologne was overpowering. Aghast, Marilyn picked her way through the debris to the bathroom, where she discovered the source of the smell. Whole bottles of cologne, after-shave, and toilet water had been emptied into the sink, with large amounts spilling onto the floor's shag carpet. The mirror above the sink was smashed.

Off the hall was the small bedroom her brother used as an office. The meager files he maintained for his garage business had been torn to pieces. Across the room from the desk, his desk drawers were turned upside down. The desk itself was tipped on its side.

Frantically Marilyn hunted for the stamp albums. She found three under an overturned bookcase. She flipped through them, hunting for the name Nguyen. She found it on an envelope stuck in a back pocket. It was part of the return address of a letter to Van from the Philippines. There were two other envelopes in the pocket, both from the same address in Bangkok. She slipped them into her shoulder bag.

Removing Mr. Nguyen's letter from the Philippines, Marilyn skimmed through his bold script. Since it was written in Vietnamese, she couldn't tell what it said. She'd never learned to read or write the language, only to speak it with Van. She could see nothing that looked like a telephone number. She'd have to track Mr. Nguyen down from his Manila address. She memorized it before she put the envelope in her bag.

She glanced nervously around her. What if the culprits were lurking nearby? She had a strong urge to flee, as fast as her legs would take her. But running wouldn't help her figure out what had happened. Why had someone done this? Were they looking for something? If so, why destroy the place? The mayhem committed here almost looked like an act of hate or revenge. Her brow furrowed. If Van had enemies, Marilyn didn't know about them.

A sound from the front of the house turned her legs to stone. Had she locked the door? No. She kicked herself mentally for her stupidity. Anybody could be out there, even the monster who had wreaked such destruction. Clutching the three albums to her breast, she stood motionless in the center of the room.

"Marilyn. Where are you?" It was Mac's voice.

Her petrified legs turned unexpectedly to jelly and she sagged against the side of the lopsided desk.

"In here," she called, so relieved she didn't ask herself why he'd come.

Mac found her half-sitting on an overturned desk in the ruined room. Her slim body was oddly crumpled, as though somebody had struck her in the solar plexus and knocked all the wind out of her. Extending his arms he tried to draw her to him, but she wouldn't let go of the books she was holding. Beneath her sweater, he could feel her trembling.

"My God, what happened here?" He stared down into her violet eyes—eyes that were wide with shock. What he saw there made him want to throttle whoever had done this.

"Van's beautiful little house. He was so proud of it, and now somebody's ruined it." Her eyes glistened. "Why, Mac? Why would anybody do such a thing?" She was dangerously close to tears.

Watching her, a part of him melted. "You've got no idea who's behind this?"

She straightened, seeming to get a grip on herself. "Not a clue." Then, as though to convince him, she added, "Everybody loved Van, especially the Vietnamese refugees he was helping."

Blackmailing is a better word, Mac thought grimly. This was the first time she'd said anything about her brother's connections to the Vietnamese community. Mac kept his expression blank, so she couldn't tell what he was thinking. This wasn't the time to confront her with what her brother was up to.

"It seems pretty obvious somebody didn't love him," he said innocently. "Maybe if you concentrate, you can figure out who."

Marilyn twisted away, suddenly suspicious. Mac could see the wheels spinning in her head and grinned at her.

"Just what are you doing here, Mac?" Her eyes narrowed accusingly.

"I was following you." The only reasonable explanation, it was also the truth. He folded his arms, waiting for the next question. It wasn't long in coming.

"What for? What makes you think you've got the right?" Her surprised expression gave way to outright hostility. "Just because I've agreed to do some work for you doesn't give you carte blanche to follow me around, night and day."

"I'm smitten with you, lovely lady. Can't you tell?" He kept his tone light, teasing. It was close enough to the truth that it made him uncomfortable. "I'm not going to let you out of my sight until you come with me for dinner tonight."

She smiled, a tiny little smile like a leaf unfolding. "I've also got enough sense to know that's not why you were following me. Level with me, Mac, or our deal's off."

He gestured toward the door. "All right, but let's get out of here and go somewhere for dinner. This mess is depressing."

She hesitated. "I've got to report what's happened to the police."

"Won't it wait until tomorrow? Tonight, let's just lock the door and walk away. If the police ask why you waited, tell them you wanted to sort through things first. To find out what was missing."

She nodded. By waiting, she'd have a chance to tell Agent Smith what happened before she went to the police. Maybe this was connected with the FBI's scheme to trap Mac. She couldn't imagine how. But, then, her mind didn't work like a spy's.

She followed Mac's car to a steak house on Hotel Circle, an elliptical drive paralleling Interstate eight between El

Cajon and San Diego. There, in semidarkness, seated on a red leather banquette, Marilyn sipped Beaujolais and let herself enjoy the light that seemed to shimmer around Mac's wiry frame. Something about this man made him glow, and Marilyn felt the electricity when she was with him.

Mesmerized, she responded to his lighthearted banter with a gaiety she hadn't felt since their last work night together in his suite. As usual, though he was dressed in a black sweater and blue jeans, he blended in perfectly with his plush surroundings.

Tonight he's dressed like a terrorist, she thought, aggravated with herself for having a good time. She reminded herself she'd agreed to have dinner with him for one reason only: to find out why he was following her.

"So explain yourself," she began, putting her thoughts into words. "Why have you been following me?"

Even in the semidarkness, Marilyn caught the laughter in his eyes. "Like I told you, I can't stay away from you."

She took a deep breath. "Level with me or I'll say no to your offer, Mac. I mean it."

His lighthearted expression faded. It was replaced by something serious. Threatening, even. Suddenly Marilyn felt sorry for the whole British army. With terrorists like Mac against them, they didn't stand a chance.

"Remember I told you I'd find out who was following you and why?"

She caught her breath. "You didn't—"

"Sure I did. I found out. Who, if not why. Why comes later, after I've done more checking. Shame on you, lovely lady. You have no faith in my abilities." A hint of his bantering tone returned.

Marilyn leaned toward him. "So tell me."

At that inopportune moment, the waiter arrived with their steaks. An eternity passed while he arranged the plates in front of them. When he left, Marilyn waited expectantly for Mac to go on, but he cut into his meat and took a slow bite instead.

"Let's enjoy our dinners first," he said, grinning. "Then I'll tell all."

"Right now or the deal's off." That threat had worked before; it would work again.

He put his fork down. "You win," he said, sighing. "The man following you is a hit man named Tony Benson. He's working with a couple of other guys who're keeping an eye on you. They're such klutzes, they didn't even know I was in the vicinity."

Marilyn was aghast. "A hit man! Why on earth is he after me?"

"He's not. If he were, you'd be dead by now." There was no mirth in his tone.

"If they're watching me, they know about you," she gasped. "They know you followed me to Van's house. That we're here together having dinner."

"So what?" He seemed totally unconcerned. "Eat your food. It's getting cold."

She tried to make sense of what she was hearing. "Then they don't know anything about you?"

He nodded and cut another piece of steak. "They probably think I'm your boyfriend. I've already told you. These people tailing you have nothing to do with me."

"They're after Van!" With frightening clarity she remembered her brother's voice on the tape and knew she had to warn him. Right now. Before any more time passed. She struggled to her feet. "I'm sorry, Mac. This has been too much for me. I'm feeling ill. I've got to get home."

He rose immediately. "I'll take you. We can pick up your car tomorrow." He pulled out a couple of bills and tossed them on the table.

"No, we can't do that." Her tone was sharper than she'd intended and she smiled nervously to reassure him. "I mean, I feel okay to drive. I want you to stay and finish your dinner." She slid off the banquette and started toward the door.

He came after her. "I won't stay here and let you leave alone. If you're sure you're well enough to drive, I'll follow you home."

She hesitated. "I have to stop at a pay phone and make a personal phone call, Mac. It's important." She didn't like involving him, but he seemed determined to follow her.

He gave her a strange, cynical look. "May I come along if I promise not to listen? I won't even get out of my car."

"Can I stop you?" In spite of her question, Marilyn found herself unexpectedly relieved he'd be keeping an eye on her while she phoned. There was no way anybody would get near her, not with Mac hovering in the vicinity.

He grinned. "No, you can't. Faith, Marilyn, you're getting to know me too well."

True to his word, he stayed in his car while Marilyn left hers and went to an outside phone booth on Hotel Circle. She had no trouble getting an overseas line or locating Mr. Nguyen's phone number from the address she'd memorized.

But when she tried to reach the number, nobody answered.

For a long minute after she hung up, Marilyn stood motionless. What was she going to do now? Van said she was in terrible danger. She'd just found out that her brother was in equally great danger. Did that danger somehow involve Mac McDonough, the IRA terrorist waiting for her outside the telephone booth?

Chapter Eight

"Lock your door and stay inside tonight." Mac's smooth Irish brogue quivered with terse authority. "Benson and whoever hired him are probably after your brother, not you, but there's no sense taking chances." He paused, and Marilyn saw the beginnings of a roguish smile. "As a matter of fact, it might be a good idea for me to camp out here tonight, to make sure nobody tries to break in."

Mac sounded as though he were teasing. But teasing or not, Marilyn felt sure he'd try to take a mile if she gave him an inch. The worst part of it was that she wanted him to stay. Mental pictures of him in a robe at her breakfast bar, of him shaving, bare-chested, in front of her bathroom mirror, flashed through her mind.

What am I thinking of? Her eyes cast down, she groped in her bag for her key. "I'm sure I'll be okay. Thanks for finding out who was following me." Glancing up suddenly, she saw his worried frown. It scared her. "You don't really think I'm in any danger?"

"Not as long as you stay inside with the door locked." His roguish smile was back. "Like I said, I'm available for guard duty, if you're worried." He leaned against the wall, his wiry frame coiled and ready, even in a semi-relaxed posture.

She stuck the key in the lock and opened the door. "I'm not *that* worried."

"Okay, but just do what I'm telling you."

It wasn't until Marilyn got inside and closed the door that she realized she'd left the three stamp albums on the back seat of her car.

MAC WAITED OUTSIDE until Marilyn had closed the door, and he heard the bolt slide into place. Instinctively he knew she wouldn't follow his advice. She was too concerned about her brother. Finnegan had been right all along. She knew exactly where Van was. Mac had no doubt it was Van she'd tried to call from the pay phone on Hotel Circle. She hadn't been able to reach him. That was obvious from her frustrated frown when she returned to her car.

She'd try again. He was equally sure of that. Probably tonight, and not from her apartment, either. This lady was a pro. She knew enough not to use a phone that could be bugged.

Mac drove toward his hotel. When certain he wasn't being followed, he circled back and waited. Sure enough, a few minutes later he spotted her ancient BMW heading toward town. Behind her, another vehicle, a late-model Plymouth sedan, swung onto Orange Avenue.

Mac gritted his teeth. Benson was getting on his nerves. He kept an alert eye on the Plymouth while Marilyn pulled into a nearby gas station. It had a lit pay phone booth. The Plymouth parked out of sight, half a block or so away. If somebody got out, Mac intended to tear him apart. Spy or not, Marilyn was much too fragile to be subjected to the attentions of a thug like Tony Benson.

Mac, who'd been tailing Benson the night before, recognized him when he got out of his stolen car to relieve himself. A former prize fighter, Benson's criminal connections were known to the bureau. He'd been tried three times for murder. Each time he'd been acquitted or freed on a technicality. *Not this time,* Mac promised himself. *Benson steps one inch out of line, and he's either a dead man, or in jail for the next hundred years.*

Nobody got out of the Plymouth.

When Marilyn emerged from the phone booth, Mac figured she hadn't reached her brother. Her time in the booth was too short. From her frightened glances around as she hurried to her car, he suspected she'd seen the vehicle following her.

Good. Maybe if she's scared, she'll stay put the rest of the night, and I can get some sleep. As soon as she was safely inside her apartment, he returned to the telephone booth and dialed her number.

"You're still being followed." Mac didn't identify himself.

"I know. I saw the car. Where were you while I was phoning?" Her high-pitched voice sounded breathless, like a frightened child's.

He didn't bother answering. "Whoever you're calling, it's not worth it, Marilyn. Get some sleep and don't go out again until morning."

"You couldn't pay me a million dollars to go out there again tonight."

This time he was pretty sure she meant it. Nonetheless, he returned to her apartment and waited there until dawn, watching her door and calling himself a fool. He saw no sign of the green Plymouth sedan.

MARILYN LEFT FOR WORK earlier than usual on Monday morning to give herself time to stop at a phone booth en route. This time the overseas lines were busy. Frustrated, she dialed again. Still busy.

What to do? Van had to be warned that an assassin was gunning for him. Nothing else mattered. She couldn't call the Philippines from her office phone. Neither could she spend the day running back and forth from the technical library to the pay phone in the employees' lounge on the second floor. She'd have to take time off work. Glancing at her watch, she noted that it was a little before seven-thirty. Maybe Edgar hadn't left home yet. She got his number from information.

"This is Marilyn," she said, when he came on the line. "I'm sorry, but I'm going to be late this morning."

She heard the concern in his answer. "Nothing serious, I hope, Number One?"

Marilyn squirmed nervously in the phone booth. The gray business suit she was wearing felt scratchy, right through her silk underwear. "Not terribly serious, but it *is* important. Something—uh—personal. I've got to take care of it right away."

His concern changed to alarm. "It's not your mother?"

Drat. Why hadn't she thought of an excuse before she called him?

"It *is* your mother," he assumed sympathetically. "Take all the time you need, Number One."

Marilyn felt like a rat for not correcting him, but it was a better reason than anything she could come up with on such short notice. "Thank you, Edgar. She—she had a bad night, and I want to spend some time with her." Her voice squeaked unexpectedly and she winced. Would she ever get control over her errant vocal cords?

"Understood. Call me later and let me know how she is."

Marilyn said she would and hung up. When she tried Mr. Nguyen's number, the overseas lines were still busy. Aggravated, she left the phone booth and went to her car.

What time was it in the Philippines? Last night there'd been no answer, and this morning the lines were all busy. Maybe she was calling at the wrong times. A guidebook would tell her, but the bookstores weren't open yet. Neither was the local library.

Marilyn decided to go home and wait. Until the stores opened, she'd keep trying the overseas lines from her home phone. If the lines cleared, she'd dash out and call Mr. Nguyen's number from the pay booth.

A fire engine roared by, its sirens screaming, as she turned onto Orange Avenue. A minute later, she was forced to pull to the side of the road as a second truck rumbled past. It turned down the street toward her apartment building.

Alarmed, she followed it toward her parking lot. As she approached her building, she could see the two hulking vehicles sitting end to end behind a row of covered parking spaces. Men in yellow fire-fighting gear unrolled hoses from the trucks. An instant later one of the hoses began belching water. Marilyn's eyes widened in horror when she saw where the stream of water was directed.

Into her apartment.

Her door was hanging crazily on its hinges. A jagged hole was torn in the wall beside it, as though a bomb had gone off inside.

Somebody's exploded a bomb in my apartment.

Van's words sounded crazily in her mind. "You're in terrible danger . . . terrible danger . . . terrible danger."

Sheer black fright swept through her. She wanted to speed away as fast as she could, but she was powerless to drive, frozen to her car seat. A siren sounded behind her. It was a police car. A uniformed officer got out and walked toward her. He was frowning.

"You'll have to move it, lady," he said. "You're blocking the road."

For the first time, Marilyn realized she'd stopped in the center of the street. "Wh—what's going on?" A shudder shook her body.

"A bomb went off in that apartment." He eyed her suspiciously. "You a tenant here?"

She nodded.

"Better pull over there—" he nodded toward a vacant space at the curb in front of the building "—and meet me at the manager's office. We'll need to get statements from everybody who lives here." Returning to his car, he swung around her into the parking lot.

Marilyn's heart thumped wildly, an alien organ that didn't seem a part of her. What kind of statement could she make to the police without lying her socks off? Could she tell them that she was a double agent working for both the FBI and an IRA terrorist? That her brother's house had been ravaged, probably by the same person who exploded the bomb in her apartment? That an assassin named Tony Benson had been watching her every move?

Van's words still thundered in her brain. *I must talk to you... Tell no one.*

No. She couldn't make a statement to the police until she'd talked to Van. Both she and Van were being threatened, and there was nobody she could turn to for help.

But there was. The FBI. Agent Smith could find out what this bombing was all about! Relief spread through her like a soothing balm. The agent had told her he would meet her at her office on short notice, whenever she needed to talk about their operation. Her paralyzing fear turned into an urgent compulsion to get to the Wakefield Corporation as fast as she could.

Marilyn began backing slowly toward the street that ran in front of the apartment building. When she reached it, she searched the parking area for the policeman. His car, parked opposite the two fire engines, was empty. He was nowhere in sight. Turning, she headed the BMW toward Orange Avenue.

The twelve miles on Interstate five from the Coronado Bridge to her turnoff seemed like a hundred. Marilyn kept expecting to hear the scream of a siren behind her. When she finally reached Wakefield's parking lot, she couldn't believe it was only a few minutes past nine. She went directly to the employees' lounge. From a pay phone, she called Agent Smith at the local FBI office.

"I've got to see you right away." To Marilyn, her voice sounded like a ten-year-old's, but she no longer cared. "Somebody bombed my apartment. I need to know what to tell the police."

"Have you said anything to them?" Smith sounded worried.

"Nothing so far. I left as soon as I saw what happened."

Marilyn could hear his sigh of relief. "Good. You in your office?"

"I'm calling from a pay phone in the building."

"Go to your office and wait. We're on our way." There was an odd note of excitement in his tone. "Don't say anything to anybody about this."

Feeling like a truckload of rocks had dropped off her back, Marilyn agreed.

Edgar welcomed her with a surprised smile when she walked into the library a few minutes later. He was wearing a flashy red vest. Painfully, Marilyn realized Christmas was next week. Where would she put her tree, now that her apartment had been blown up? Her lower lip trembled, and she yanked a tissue from her bag. Angrily she blew her nose. If she wanted to be around to enjoy the holiday, she'd better start concentrating on getting out of this mess alive.

"Sit down, my dear," Edgar said, apparently misinterpreting her expression. "If your mother needs you, please, take the whole day off."

His sympathy made her feel even worse. Blowing her nose again, she crossed to her desk. "My mother's better, Captain. I didn't have to see her this morning after all."

He followed her, eyeing her anxiously. "I sense that something's wrong, Number One. If you'd like to talk about it..."

Marilyn daubed at her nose. "It's this darned allergy of mine, that's all. There was something in the air on the way to work this morning." She forced herself to smile. "I'm fine, really I am. Anytime there's good news from the Good Life Nursing Home, it's a happy day for me."

It was a stupid little speech. Two weeks ago Marilyn had said things like that and meant them. Today she said it to get him off her back. The last thing she needed right now was Edgar Knowling's concerned attention. The FBI said not to talk about the bombing and, if it was in her power, she intended to follow instructions.

Still, he lingered. "Your apartment manager called." He pointed to the messages on her desk. "He called twice. Said it was urgent."

"Did he say what it was about?" Marilyn tried to look unconcerned so Edgar wouldn't see how upset she was. If the manager had said anything about the bombing to him, she'd be forced to talk about it.

He shook his head. "Negative, Number One. I told the manager you were en route to your mother's, and he could reach you there."

Relief coursed through her like a tranquilizing elixir. "You gave him the number?"

"I offered to, but he said he already had it."

"That's right. I'd forgotten." She took the little yellow sheets off her desk. After glancing through them, she wadded them up, and tossed them in the waste basket.

"Aren't you going to call him?" Her superior hovered over her like an anxious mama duck. "It sounded terribly urgent."

Marilyn smiled, trying to be reassuring. "Later. I'll call him later, after I finish this cockpit design research for Dr. Lindsey."

With a disapproving clucking sound, Edgar left her alone.

Using the library's resources, Marilyn quickly determined the time difference between Manila and San Diego—sixteen hours. At nine a.m. Pacific Standard Time it would be one a.m. the next day in the Philippines. Since it was nighttime there, perhaps she'd catch Mr. Nguyen at home, if the lines to Southeast Asia would ever clear. Waiting for Agent Smith, she couldn't leave the office, but resolved to call Manila again as soon as her meeting with the FBI agent was over.

A few minutes later Wakefield's Chief of Security phoned to let her know she had visitors in the conference room.

THE RED VELVET DRAPERIES covering the conference-room walls made Marilyn feel claustrophobic. Shrugging aside the feeling, she smiled at the two FBI agents.

Smith was wearing a dark blue striped tie that matched his business suit. "Before we left the office, we did some checking on that explosion in your apartment." His straight dark hair was combed back in a style that made him look vaguely gangsterish.

Marilyn wouldn't have minded if he were the incarnation of John Dillinger. She was so glad to see him and Agent Jones that she felt like sobbing. Here, at last, was help. Big, strong, government help.

She leaned across the table toward them. "The policeman I talked to told me it was a bomb."

"On the phone you said you didn't talk to the police." Smith's tone was sharp, accusing. Both he and Agent Jones straightened.

Marilyn caught her breath. Agent Smith was supposed to be on her side. Why did he look so hostile? "A policeman stopped me outside my apartment," she explained. "I asked him what had happened. That's when he said he wanted a statement."

The agents settled back in their chairs. "Nobody was hurt," Jones volunteered. "The manager delivered the package to your apartment as a favor, to save you a trip to his office to pick it up. It had some kind of radio-controlled device inside."

"You mean somebody was watching my apartment and set the bomb off from outside?" Marilyn clenched her hands in her lap, appalled at the thought.

"That's what we think, Ms. Wainwright." Smith's expression was grim. "Apparently they didn't mean to hurt anybody. They waited until your apartment was empty before setting it off."

Wide-eyed, she glanced from Smith to Jones and back to Smith. "Then that man who's been following me must be responsible."

"Why do you say that?" Smith leaned toward her, waiting.

"Because he and the people with him haven't tried to hurt me." Marilyn blurted the words out without thinking. Nervously she moistened her dry lips.

"Then you think they're following you to find something out, rather than to do you bodily injury?" He raised his eyebrow questioningly.

Something told Marilyn she'd already said too much. "I—I don't know." Her reply was forced through stiff lips.

Agent Jones smiled sympathetically. "It must be tough being followed all the time. Any idea who they are?"

Marilyn opened her mouth to tell them what Mac had said, that the man following her was an assassin named Tony Benson. She didn't utter a sound. The assassin was following her to get to Van. Mac was sure. So was she. Before she involved Van, she had to talk to her brother.

Smith seemed to interpret her silence as proof she was hiding something. "So you know somebody's following you but have never gotten a look at him or the car he's driving?" He frowned in exasperation. "There's absolutely no reason you can think of why somebody would be interested in your comings and goings?"

"No," she answered shortly, staring him straight in the eye. "Not a reason in the world."

"You know what I think, Ms. Wainwright?" The accusing note had returned to Smith's voice. "I think there's something you're not telling us. First you claim somebody's following you, and you have no idea who or why. Then you blame that mysterious somebody for setting off a bomb in your apartment. Why don't you tell us who it was, so we can figure out if he—or she or they—is connected to this IRA terrorist we're after."

Marilyn was almost certain the bombing had nothing to do with Mac, but she tried to act as though it might to throw them off the track. They mustn't suspect she was protecting her brother.

"You think what happened might be tied in with the IRA?" she asked, striving for sincerity.

"Anything's possible, Ms. Wainwright." Smith's eyes narrowed. "It's even possible you set that bomb off yourself."

Marilyn didn't think she'd heard him right. "I beg your pardon?" Her body stiffened with shock.

Smith's expression was grim. "A woman matching your description was seen in the vicinity a few minutes after the device went off. She left before officers could question her."

What was Smith saying? An overpowering, unreasonable fright swept over her. "I told you just a second ago that I was on my way home when that policeman stopped me. I saw what happened and left, so I wouldn't have to give him a statement."

"We're not accusing you of anything, Ms. Wainwright." Jones's tone was soothing. "Agent Smith was only suggesting a possibility."

"Why would I blow up my own apartment?" Marilyn swallowed hard.

"I can think of several reasons." Smith's oversized nose flared at the nostrils. "Maybe you wanted to throw us off track. Make us think somebody's out to get you."

Marilyn's eyes widened with alarm. "Why would I do that?" She clenched and unclenched her hands helplessly in her lap.

"Why don't you tell us, Ms. Wainwright?" He stared at her expectantly, as though he honestly thought she had a reason to blow up her own apartment.

Marilyn stared back at him. What right did he have to make such an implication? She stood up. "I don't intend to sit here and take any more abuse."

Agent Jones leapt out of his chair and hurried around the table toward her. "Please, Ms. Wainwright." Gently he eased her down. "Please excuse Agent Smith's brusque manner. The bureau's been under a lot of pressure lately. So have you, and now you're understandably upset because of what's happened to your apartment. Let's not get sidetracked from our main objective." His smile was warm.

Marilyn studied his face suspiciously. Every time Agent Smith got her angry or frightened, Agent Jones intervened. Why? *Because he's the good cop, of course.* Marilyn had read enough detective novels to recognize the good cop-bad cop interrogation method.

Marilyn stiffened. They were treating her like a suspect. But she wasn't a suspect. She was on their side, working for them. Something was going on here that she didn't understand. Hadn't Van said she was in terrible danger because she'd "gone to the government"? Could the danger have something to do with the bureau itself?

The red velvet draperies covering the walls shifted dizzily around her. The overhead spotlights shining down on the table made her feel like she was in some kind of box. A cold bead of sweat trickled down her back. Until she talked to her brother, she didn't dare continue working with these people. She rose again, with the macabre feeling that she was stepping out of a coffin lined with red velvet. "I'm sorry, gentlemen. I can't go ahead with our arrangement."

For an instant the faces across from hers reflected dismayed disbelief. Then, as though a veil had been drawn, their expressions turned predictable. Agent Smith frowned angrily. Agent Jones beamed a smile in her direction.

"Now, now, Ms. Wainwright," Jones said, "let's not be hasty. We've brought a package of secret material for you to give to the terrorist." He placed a briefcase on the table. "All you have to do is hand it to him tonight in the hotel lobby."

Would they try to stop her from walking out on them? Heart pounding, Marilyn pushed her chair away from the table. "I've told you. I've decided not to do it."

"Hold on here, Ms. Wainwright." Agent Smith stood up and glowered down at her. At least a foot taller than she, he towered over the big round table and over Marilyn who was standing beside it. He seemed as big as a mountain. "It's too late to back out." His voice was threatening.

She started for the door. "As far as I'm concerned, it's never too late, Mr. Smith."

He circled the table with amazing speed. In an instant he was beside Marilyn, his big body blocking her way.

She stepped sideways. He did likewise.

"Don't try to intimidate me," she ordered. "Get out of my way, or I'll call for help."

He didn't move. "If you back out on us, we'll charge you with espionage." The words were spoken in a hiss-like whisper.

Espionage! Was it an empty threat or was she somehow at fault simply for meeting with Mac? *Mac.* Marilyn hurt all over just thinking of him. The room began to spin again. She remembered Van's message and knew she had to reach him before she said another word. She couldn't protect her brother and work with the FBI at the same time. The agents had too many questions she couldn't answer.

She forced her lips to part in a curved, stiff smile. "Charge me with anything you like." For once her voice didn't break. "FBI or not, Agent Smith, I'd rather go to jail for ten years than work with you."

"It'll be more than ten years, sweetheart." He tensed as though to grab her. But when Marilyn stepped to one side, he didn't move. A moment later she jerked the conference-room door open. When it slammed behind her, it sounded remarkably like the lid closing on a coffin, a red velvet coffin she'd just escaped from.

MARILYN DIDN'T GO BACK to the library. Fearing that Agent Smith could somehow restrain her, she hurried out of the building to call Mr. Nguyen. Resolved to keep trying until she got an answer, she went to a pay phone at a gas station off Torrey Pines Road. Glancing at her watch, she saw that it was a few minutes past ten-thirty, two-thirty a.m. in Manila, a good time to catch him home. The first time she dialed the number, the overseas lines were busy. Sighing, she waited a few minutes and tried again.

The line was clear. Hardly breathing, she counted the rings. One, two, three, four—on the fifth ring a man, identifying himself as Toan Nguyen, answered. For an instant Marilyn was tongue-tied. She'd anticipated this moment with such a mixture of hope and anxiety that she hardly knew what to say. When she did speak, she talked so fast that Mr. Nguyen, whom she'd obviously awakened, couldn't understand her.

"This is Marilyn Wainwright, Van Wainwright's sister," she repeated slowly. "I must get a message to my brother. He is in great danger. An assassin is trying to find him and kill him."

Mr. Nguyen answered her in Vietnamese. Apparently Van had said his sister was fluent in the language, and he was testing her credibility.

"You also are in great danger, Ms. Wainwright. You must come to Manila immediately. There will be a room reserved in your name at the Philippine Village Hotel near the airport. Call me as soon as you check in. I will arrange a meeting with your brother." He paused. "Do not delay or tell anyone. Speed is of the essence. Do you understand?"

"*Ya,*" Marilyn said in Vietnamese. "Yes, I understand." To be certain, she repeated his instructions. After he'd verified them, she hung up.

Time suddenly took on new meaning. Marilyn became acutely aware of the passage of each moment. With a sense of great urgency mixed with a kind of nervous, shivery excitement, she drove to her bank in La Jolla. There, she removed her passport from her safety deposit box and withdrew most of the money in her savings account.

Next, she went to a mall in Mission Valley and charged an inexpensive overnight bag, some underwear, a couple of cotton skirts and blouses and a pair of sandals. When she left the store, she was wearing a bright yellow-and-green skirt and a matching yellow shirt. She called a cab from a pay phone inside the mall. She couldn't risk being followed and knew instinctively that the hit man would be watching the BMW, not her.

The cab picked her up at an exit at the opposite end of the mall from where she'd parked. She took it to Lindbergh Field where she boarded the first aircraft leaving San Diego, a commuter flight headed for San Francisco. Using a false name and address in case the assassin checked bus and air terminals, she barely had time to dash aboard before the craft was airborne.

In San Francisco, she had a three-hour wait for a plane going west. *God in heaven, what am I doing?* she asked herself, as she waited in the crowded airport. Never before had Marilyn so much as driven the hundred miles to Palm Springs without notifying her mother's nursing home. Now, here she was, going halfway around the earth without telling a soul. Van's life, as well as her own, might depend on her silence. She'd simply have to pray nobody got hurt by her sudden disappearance.

Tomorrow, after she talked to her brother, she could let the nursing home, her employer, and the San Diego authorities know where she was. Tomorrow, in Manila, she'd find out the truth.

Chapter Nine

When Mac's phone rang at six-thirty Monday evening, he knew who it was.

Marilyn. Nobody else in San Diego would call him in his hotel suite.

He frowned at the jangling instrument. She'd probably stayed after work to collect the secret material he'd asked her for. Now she'd want her cash ASAP. Just like all the other money-grabbing scumbags he'd nailed during the past eight years.

With a cynical smile he lifted the receiver. "Yeah."

"We've got to talk, buddy." It wasn't Marilyn. It was Charley Finnegan.

For an instant Mac was speechless. *Something's wrong,* he thought, his body tightening like a drawn bowstring.

"I'll call you back from the pay phone downstairs," he said tersely. "You at home or in your office?" He jammed his hand into his jeans pocket. Suddenly, his blue-green cotton sweater felt tight around his neck.

"At the office," Finnegan replied. "The *local* office. Don't call from a pay phone. We need a face-to-face."

Mac stiffened. What was Finnegan doing in San Diego? "Tonight's a bad time for a meeting. My deal's about to consummate."

Finnegan grunted. "Your deal's kaput, buddy. The lady's chickened out."

Astounded, Mac dropped into the chair beside the phone. "You're not serious!"

"Dead serious."

Suddenly anxious, Mac gripped the receiver so tightly his fingers turned numb. *How did Charley Finnegan find out Marilyn wouldn't go through with the deal before Mac himself knew?*

"Pick the place to meet." He spit out the words. "Anywhere but the local office."

Finnegan gave a grunt of reassurance. There was the rustle of a hand placed over the mouthpiece and the muffled sound of voices. The hand was withdrawn. "Outside Miguel's in Old Town. In, say, forty-five minutes."

"I'll be there."

THE SHORT RIDE across the Coronado Bridge to San Diego took Mac about half as long as usual, a sure sign he was driving too fast. He told himself to slow down, that he'd find out what was going on soon enough, but he still arrived at Old Town a good ten minutes before the appointed time.

A typical tourist trap, Mac thought, glancing up and down the street in front of Miguel's Restaurant. To celebrate the season, thousands of colored lights twinkled in the nighttime darkness. With a jaundiced eye, Mac took in the festive ribbons that festooned the buildings and streets. The decorations brought back painful memories of Christmases past: his father's drunken voice, always more raucous during the holidays; the frightened cries of a brother or sister who got in dad's way; hiding in the hall closet, scrunched down under mom's coat; loud alcoholic snores from the living-room couch.... Aggravated, Mac shook his head to erase the unpleasant mental images Christmas conjured up. He couldn't afford to let his mind wander.

There was a lighted tree in the window of an old building identified as the San Diego Union Museum. Mac walked toward it so that he could observe reflections of the people around him in the glass. He was certain he hadn't been followed from the hotel, but it paid to be cautious. No suspicious reflections appeared. As he'd assumed, Tony Benson and company had no interest in him. It was Marilyn and her brother they were after.

Damn! Where was Finnegan? Glancing at his watch, Mac saw that only five minutes had elapsed since he'd parked in the lot behind Miguel's. Time was passing with glacial slowness. Nervously he paced the sidewalk. The deep-fat fry smell of cheese and tortillas enfolded him, making his mouth water.

Then, across the street, he spotted Finnegan. In his brown leisure suit and beige shirt, the pudgy little man melted into the tourists. Finnegan wasn't alone. Dan Moschella was with him, his towering frame draped in dark blue trousers, a blue sport shirt and a blue cotton cardigan. In spite of his height, Moschella blended in well with the crowd.

Unobtrusively, Mac headed toward them. When he greeted them, he pretended to have run into them accidentally. In case someone was watching, they were three businessmen from out of town playing tourist.

"Too bad Lurleen's not along," Mac said to Finnegan, after they'd gotten through the initial pleasantries. "She'd love that pottery I saw down the street."

"Let's take a look." Finnegan's comment gave them a reason to move along. He swung into step beside Mac. Dan Moschella loitered a pace behind. Nobody paid them any attention.

"What's up, Charley?" Mac was burning with suspicious curiosity but kept his expression bland.

Finnegan's expression was equally congenial. "Your cookie scrammed, Mac. That's what's up."

Mac didn't let his astonishment show. "How do you know?"

"Dan's boys were tailing her. She went to—"

"Just a minute, here." Mac's eyes narrowed. He barely managed to keep his tone pleasant. "You told me we weren't tailing her."

"When you asked last week, we weren't. Dan started the tail today." Finnegan was Mr. Congeniality himself.

"Why today?" Mac's voice scratched like flint.

"Because she walked out on us today. We think she's headed for her brother."

"Walked out *on us?*" Mac felt like he'd been punched in the stomach. "You mean she's been working for the bureau all along?" How could he have been so dense? He should have known she wasn't a spy.

Finnegan cleared his throat, as though reluctant to continue. "She came to Dan's office right after you offered to pay her for stealing information."

Mac turned toward Moschella. "Why the hell didn't you tell me? As soon as she went to you, it was obvious she wasn't a spy."

Moschella grinned at him.

He's enjoying this, Mac thought, eyeing the other man's malicious expression.

Moschella's grin broadened. "From what Mr. Finnegan says, we *never* thought she was a spy."

Mac felt the heat rising inside him. His initial shock yielded quickly to anger. Mentally he began counting to ten. "You mean the joke was on both of us? On me as well as her? If you didn't think she was a spy, why did you tell me she was?"

"Now, Mac," Finnegan began hastily. "Don't get huffy. When you hear the whole story, you'll understand."

Mac felt like knocking both of them flat. "So talk, Charley."

A gaggle of teenage girls came toward them, giggling and whispering. When they'd passed, the three men started walking again, back the way they'd come. They filed into a well lighted yard containing hundreds of pottery items.

"It was the brother we wanted all along, Mac." Finnegan leaned over and fingered one of the ceramic vases. "Not that I think the woman's innocent, mind you. She's obviously in cahoots with him."

"Get to the point, Charley. Why the spy gimmick?" Mac's voice trembled with barely controlled fury.

"It was a way to get her to cooperate and tell us what her brother's up to and where he is. If she sells secrets to you, we've got her for espionage. She tells us what we want to know or she goes to jail. If she turns you in, we recruit her to work for us as a double agent. When she sells to you, ditto. Either way, she cooperates or she goes to jail."

Moschella winked at Mac. "If she says she's working for me as an excuse for selling to you, I don't even know her." He sounded gleeful at the idea.

For an instant Mac didn't trust himself to speak. He could feel a vein throbbing in his temple and ran a lean hand through his hair to hide it.

He glared at Moschella suspiciously. "You said she'd agreed to be a double agent. What happened today to make her walk out? You must have done something to scare the hell out of her."

Moschella threw him a cynical look. "Hey, don't blame me because some goon bombed her apartment."

"Bombed her apartment!" Mac felt as though someone had just punched him in the stomach again. "When did it happen? Was she hurt?"

"Relax, buddy." Finnegan put a heavy hand on Mac's shoulder. "It happened this morning after she'd left, to scare her into running to her brother. They didn't want to hurt her."

"Not a bad scheme," Moschella added, "since it looks like that's exactly what she's doing."

"Where's she going?" Mac asked tersely. He pictured Marilyn's violet eyes, wide with fright, felt her terror when she found out about her bombed apartment. She must have been scared to death.

"The Philippines," Moschella answered. "We followed her to Lindbergh Field. She caught a flight to San Francisco using a phony name. From there she headed west, to Manila."

Finnegan jabbed Mac in the ribs. "Get that, buddy? A false name. Need any more proof she's in cahoots with her brother?"

"Since somebody just blew up her apartment, maybe she was afraid of being followed." Mac's voice was dangerously quiet.

"Obviously," Moschella returned. "She never went back to her place. Left her BMW in the mall parking lot and took a cab to the airport. The bureau's old nemesis, Tony Benson, was following her."

Moschella hesitated, obviously waiting for Mac to react. Mac stared at the other man, his face expressionless. Damned if he'd let Moschella and Finnegan know he already knew about Benson.

Moschella waited another moment and went on. "He broke into her car and stole some books."

The books she took from her brother's house last night, Mac remembered, careful not to reveal his thoughts. "Where'd Benson go after he left the mall?"

"We tracked him to Little Saigon," Moschella said. "Our sources there think some Vietnamese in the community are paying Benson to knock off Van Wainwright, since he's the leader of the syndicate causing them so much trouble."

Mac knew Little Saigon was the unofficial name of the Vietnamese refugee community in Orange County, near Los Angeles. Maybe the refugees thought they could get the gangs off their backs if they got rid of the syndicate's leader. They were using Marilyn to find her brother. So was the FBI. It wasn't fair, all of them after one fragile woman, because she had a spineless worm for a brother. Mac's rage became a scalding fury.

"What we want you to do is follow her to the Philippines and cozy up to her, Mac," Finnegan said. "Find out where the brother is and get the goods on both of them."

"She booked under her own name on the flight to Manila?" Mac asked. His voice got louder in spite of his effort to keep it quiet.

Finnegan nodded. "She had to. She'll need a passport when she gets there."

Mac picked up an ugly terra cotta cupid and examined it so he wouldn't have to look at his superior. It was all he could do to keep from bashing Finnegan over the head with the thing.

"Even if I agree, I can't do it, Charley. Overseas is out of the bureau's jurisdiction. You'll have to get state and the agency in on it." Mac knew the last thing Finnegan wanted was interference from the U.S. State Department and Central Intelligence Agency on one of the bureau's cases. He wondered how his boss planned to avoid it.

Finnegan frowned. "You won't be in an official capacity, Mac. Consider it a paid vacation. Just find out where the guy is, and anything about the syndicate you can get outta the little lady. Let me worry about getting them back to the states."

"Go to hell, Charley." No words had ever rolled off Mac's tongue with a sweeter sound to his ear. Fists clenched, he stepped closer to Finnegan.

The pudgy little man moved sideways, away from Mac and closer to Dan Moschella. "Remember who you're talking to," he warned hoarsely.

Mac stared him straight in the eye. "Of all the filthy low-down tricks, the one you played on that poor woman was the worst in the book. It's hard to realize I'm working for a legitimate government agency when I hear about stunts like that."

"I told you he wouldn't like it, Mr. Finnegan." With a cynical smile, Moschella took the cupid from Mac and returned it to its place.

"Shut up, Dan." Finnegan stepped away from Moschella and planted a pudgy finger in the middle of Mac's chest. "Watch what you say, buddy. If you don't do this job for us, you're kaput with the bureau." He smiled and withdrew his finger.

Seething inside, Mac came so close to Charles Finnegan he could smell the pomade the stocky little man plastered on his thinning hair. "You touch me like that again, and I'll rip your hand off." His voice rose angrily, and he didn't try to control it. He was past caring whether anyone overheard what he was saying.

Glancing quickly around, Finnegan took a step backward. "Be reasonable, MacIntyre. The woman's guilty as hell. She knows where her brother is. He called her Sunday, you know. Our bug picked up a message from him on her answering machine. It referred to picture books and a winning name. Must have been some kind of family code."

Mac forgot the rage smoldering inside him. "What was the message?"

Finnegan told him and gave him the time the call came in.

Picture books, Mac thought. *And right after Marilyn got the message she went to her brother's house. The only things she took from the place were three books, the same books Benson stole from her car.*

"Any idea what it means?" Finnegan's shrewd smile told Mac he'd probably made the same connection.

Mac shook his head. Damned if he'd say one word that might help the bureau's case.

"I'll bet you a month's pay she's working with her brother in the syndicate." Finnegan grimaced triumphantly.

"You sound like a broken record, Charley. That's the same tune you played before, when I agreed to come out here to San Diego." Mac's determination matched the rage smoldering inside him. "I quit," he declared. "You can find somebody else to do your dirty work."

As soon as he spoke the words, he wondered why it had taken him so long.

Manila

THE CITY REMINDED Marilyn of Mexico, with its crush of brown-skinned people, its bright morning sunshine, and the disorganized clutter of its streets and buildings. The Philippine Village Hotel, where Mr. Nguyen had made reservations for her, boasted air-conditioning and all the usual amenities. She dialed his number from her room.

A woman, apparently a servant, answered. A moment later Mr. Nguyen came on the line.

"Praise God you're here," he said, after Marilyn had identified herself. "I expected you sooner. Did you have problems?"

"A twelve-hour delay in Honolulu," Marilyn explained. "Since I didn't have a reservation, I had to wait for a seat."

"I hope you're not too tired for a meeting."

"I'm not," she assured him. "I can be ready in ten minutes."

He laughed. "Patience, my dear. I'll need at least half an hour to get there in the morning traffic."

Marilyn was so relieved she could hardly speak. At last she was going to find out where Van was and, perhaps, even talk to him. "Shall I meet you in the lobby?"

He hesitated. "It will be safer if I come to your room. You will be able to identify me by the bouquet of flowers I will bring."

Her heart sank. "Then my brother won't be with you?"

"I'm sorry. No. Everything will be much clearer after we have talked."

Marilyn gave him her room number and hung up. She spent the next few minutes unpacking her few belongings, showering, and putting on clean underwear and a fresh blouse—green to match the color in her skirt. Then, nervous with anticipation, she waited for his knock on her door.

It didn't come.

When an hour had passed, she dialed his number. There was no answer. A tense panicky feeling swept over her. Something had gone wrong. The servant should be there, even if Mr. Nguyen was en route to her hotel. *Don't be an idiot,* she warned herself sternly. *He's been caught in traffic, and the servant could be anywhere.*

When two hours had gone by, and it was close to noon, Marilyn called room service and ordered a toasted cheese sandwich. When it arrived, she couldn't eat. Feeling like a caged jungle animal, she alternated between sitting on the bed and pacing back and forth across the room. Three hours after their scheduled appointment, Marilyn couldn't wait any longer. It would probably be a waste of time, but she had to go to his address. Maybe the servant was goofing off, not answering the phone. Or maybe a neighbor could tell her where Mr. Nguyen had gone. Desperate, she had to try.

The hotel doorman called her a taxi. The driver told her the address was in Makati, near the business district. In the back seat, Marilyn fidgeted while the vehicle worked its way through unbelievable downtown traffic. During the hot, frustrating drive, Marilyn stayed in a kind of nervous, round-eyed trance. She had no idea what she intended to do once she got there. All she knew was that she had to do *something*.

Finally the taxi arrived outside a high white wall with a wrought iron gate that opened on an inner courtyard. Marilyn told the driver to wait until she found out whether anybody was home. He grinned at her, showing gold-capped teeth, and parked blocking the sidewalk in front of the gate. A wizened little gardener cast him a sullen look, but didn't say anything. Several young passersby weren't so quiet. Marilyn heard their sharp comments and the driver's profane reply, but as though from a great distance. She was too anxious and upset to focus on what they were saying.

The gate wasn't locked. There was no bell so, heart thumping wildly, Marilyn unlatched it and went in. Bordered with bright flowers, the modest courtyard functioned mainly as a parking area. A Buick sedan, old but in mint condition, stood in front with its windows rolled down. Flat roofed, the house was painted the same shade of white as the surrounding concrete wall.

There was an old-fashioned knocker on the front door. Marilyn tapped it lightly, and, to her surprise, the door cracked open. Hardly daring to breathe, she tapped again, harder. The door opened wider. With frightening suddenness, she remembered Van's ruined house. His door had been open, too, just like this. Could the same people have been here? *Not possible*, she told herself bravely. *Manila's ten thousand miles from San Diego.*

She knocked again, loudly, pushing the door open wider. From the street, she heard the muffled hum of a passing car. From the house, nothing. The silence was eerie. She peeked inside. She could see a mosaic tile floor dotted with grass area rugs. Windows were open and the room was awash with light. The air moving toward her felt cooler than that outside, but not air-conditioned. Marilyn felt herself perspiring.

"Hello," she called. "Is anyone here?" Apprehension coursed through her. The house was too quiet. Where was everybody? She was struck by the silence. Was Van here, somewhere inside, where he couldn't hear her knock? Was he hiding in one of the rooms, afraid to show himself? Maybe if he saw her, or heard her voice, he'd come out. Or maybe she'd see something of his she'd recognize. Her knees shaking, she stepped inside.

"Van," she called loudly. "It's Marilyn. If you're here, come out."

Nothing. The silence was frightening. Holding her breath, she stood in what appeared to be the living room. It was attractively furnished with a bamboo-style sofa and easy chairs.

"Mr. Nguyen?" she called. "It's Marilyn Wainwright."

Motionless, she listened for the slightest sound that would mean somebody was home. Still nothing. Did she dare walk through the house?

With her breath coming in short gasps, she went through the living and dining rooms toward the back. A swinging door led to the kitchen. Almost as large as the dining room, it had a worked-in look, as though someone had been interrupted in the middle of preparing a meal. The counters were cluttered with spoons, knives and cooking utensils. Marilyn took the lid off a pan of rice on the stove. It was warm. Why had the cook left in such a hurry? Suddenly Marilyn was overcome with the strangeness of a place that should have been bustling with activity but wasn't. She couldn't wait to get out of there.

On the other side of the swinging doors, she stopped to catch her breath. Where next? On the far side of the dining room was a closed door. Marilyn knocked lightly. Then, hesitantly, she went in.

The shutters were closed and the draperies drawn, making the room seem stuffy and dark in comparison with the brightness in the rest of the lower floor. A smell, not unpleasant, like burnt matches or candle wax, wafted toward her. It mingled with another, more acrid odor that reminded her vaguely of the zoo.

Stepping inside, she peered nervously around her. As her eyes became accustomed to the dark interior, she saw that this was the house's library. On two sides of the room, bookcases extended to the high ceiling. Straight ahead of her, in front of the shuttered and curtained windows, was a desk. As she glanced toward it, Marilyn felt every nerve in her body tense. Her legs turned to leaden weights, anchoring her to the floor.

Someone sat behind the desk. A man in a dark suit. He was looking straight at her.

"Mr. Nguyen?" Her voice was a pathetic little squeak.

The figure behind the desk said nothing. His eyes stared at her with a curious unblinking stare. She moved a step closer.

"Mr. Nguyen, I'm Van Wainwright's sister, Marilyn."

Her eyes adjusted rapidly to the darkness. She observed his gaping mouth, his slack jaw. Her panic-stricken gaze dropped to his chest. Barely noticeable in the gloom was a ragged dark splotch on his jacket.

She stifled a scream.

Was he dead? She had to know. Maybe he was only wounded and needed help. She tried to move, but her feet stayed rooted to the floor.

Get a grip on yourself, she commanded. Swallowing hard, she forced herself to go around the desk. Gingerly, she reached for his left wrist to seek the pulse. His skin felt

NO RISK, NO OBLIGATION TO BUY...NOW OR EVER!

GUARANTEED

PLAY "ROLL A DOUBLE" AND GET AS MANY AS FIVE FREE GIFTS!

HERE'S HOW TO PLAY:

1. Peel off label from front cover. Place it in space provided at right. With a coin, carefully scratch off the silver dice. This makes you eligible to receive two or more free books, and possibly another gift, depending on what is revealed beneath the scratch-off area.

2. You'll receive brand-new Harlequin Intrigue® novels. When you return this card, we'll rush you the books and gift you qualify for ABSOLUTELY FREE!

3. Then, if we don't hear from you, every month we'll send you 4 additional novels to read and enjoy. You can return them and owe nothing, but if you decide to keep them, you'll pay only $2.49* per book—a saving of 40¢ each off the cover price.

4. When you subscribe to the Harlequin Reader Service®, you'll also get our subscribers'-only newsletter, as well as additional free gifts from time to time.

5. You must be completely satisfied. You may cancel at any time simply by sending us a note or a shipping statement marked "cancel" or by returning any shipment to us at our expense.

The Austrian crystal sparkles like a diamond! And it's carefully set in a romantic "Key to Your Heart" pendant on a generous 18" gold-tone chain. The entire necklace is yours free as added thanks for giving our Reader Service a try!

DETACH AND MAIL CARD TODAY!

"ROLL A DOUBLE!"

PLACE LABEL HERE

SCRATCH HERE

SEE CLAIM CHART BELOW

181 CIH AG4L
(U-H-I-01/93)

YES! I have placed my label from the front cover into the space provided above and scratched off the silver dice. Please rush me the free books and gift that I am entitled to. I understand that I am under no obligation to purchase any books, as explained on the opposite page.

NAME _____

ADDRESS _____ APT. _____

CITY _____ STATE _____ ZIP CODE _____

CLAIM CHART

 4 FREE BOOKS PLUS FREE "KEY TO YOUR HEART" NECKLACE

 3 FREE BOOKS

 2 FREE BOOKS

CLAIM NO.37-829

Offer limited to one per household and not valid to current Harlequin Intrigue® subscribers. All orders subject to approval.   ©1990 Harlequin Enterprises Limited
PRINTED IN U S A

HARLEQUIN "NO RISK" GUARANTEE

* You're not required to buy a single book—ever!
* You must be completely satisfied or you may cancel at any time simply by sending us a note or shipping statement marked "cancel" or by returning any shipment to us at our cost. Either way, you will receive no more books; you'll have no obligation to buy.
* The free books and gift you claimed on this "Roll A Double" offer remain yours to keep no matter what you decide.

If offer card is missing, please write to: Harlequin Reader Service, 3010 Walden Ave., P.O. Box 1867, Buffalo, NY 14269-1867 clammy. She jerked away. But not before she saw his hands. They were covered with blood. There were raw patches of skin where several of his fingernails should be. Below his jacket, the lower half of his body was naked.

He's been tortured. Marilyn felt as if a hand had closed around her throat. This poor man had been tortured to reveal Van's hiding place. She knew it instinctively.

The room reeled around her. She clutched the desk, fighting waves of nausea. She couldn't pass out. She couldn't get sick. Maybe the killer was still in the house. She had to get out of there! Her feet suddenly grew wings. On her furious flight she tripped once over a pair of men's trousers piled beside the desk.

The taxi was waiting outside the gate, right where she'd left it. The driver jumped out when he saw her coming.

"Everything okay?" he asked, apparently noticing something was wrong.

Marilyn took a deep breath and willed herself to speak calmly. "Everything's fine." Her voice trembled, but she managed to force the words out.

He grinned at her curiously. "Okay. You go back to hotel?"

"Yes, please." In the relative safety of the taxi, Marilyn started to shake, a series of rolling, tooth-chattering shakes that left her weak. She fought to get control of herself. By the time the cab reached the hotel, the worst was past.

MARILYN CLOSED THE DOOR to her room with the terrified feeling that she'd fallen into some kind of hellish bottomless pit. Vivid images of the horror she'd just seen played over and over in her mind. The murder should be reported, but she simply couldn't do it now. Terribly fatigued after days without sleep, she was teetering on the thin edge of uncontrollable panic. Maybe, after she'd had some rest, she could figure out how to handle it.

Rest. Her tired body demanded it. But every time she closed her eyes, all she could see was the gruesome scene at Mr. Nguyen's house—that, and the gaping hole in her apartment where the bomb had gone off. Wide awake, she stared sightlessly at the ceiling, reliving those awful moments.

Much later, a loud pounding broke through her sleep-drugged mind. The sound had an odd hollow thump to it, not at all like the comforting ring of her bedside alarm. Grabbing for her glasses, she put them on and stared at the illuminated figures beside her bed. It was two-thirty, and this wasn't her clock.

Memory flooded back. She wasn't in her own bed. She was in a hotel room in a country at the opposite end of the earth. Somebody was banging at her door. Anxiously she pushed the covers back and stepped on the carpeted floor. The air-conditioned room felt cold. She yanked the spread off the bed and wrapped it around her.

"Who is it?" She didn't open the door.

"The police, Ms. Wainwright." There was only a trace of an accent in the man's voice. "The hotel manager is with us. Open your door, or we'll unlock it with a passkey."

Marilyn froze. She felt naked, even with the spread draped around her. "Just a minute. I'm not dressed."

The key grated in the lock. The door opened. A short, slender Filipino man in a policeman's uniform stood there. Behind him were the hotel manager and two other uniformed men.

"You'll have to come with us, Ms. Wainwright." His face was impassive. "You're wanted for questioning in connection with the murders of Mr. Toan Nguyen and his cook, Mrs. Cobie Motea."

Chapter Ten

"Do you deny you were at Mr. Nguyen's house this afternoon?" The Philippine interrogator stared at Marilyn, his eyes accusing.

She peered back at him. She was sitting on a straight-backed wooden chair in a room without windows. The only other furniture was the executive chair the interrogator was using. A brilliant light hung over her head. She could feel its heat in the too-warm room. Sweat soaked her cotton shirt and dripped down the back of her neck.

"I've already told you—I won't say anything until I talk to somebody from the U.S. Embassy." She'd asked for help at least half-a-dozen times. Had they even called the embassy? She doubted it. They'd probably let her rot in jail until she talked.

But she couldn't talk, not without involving Van. Besides, who would believe an outlandish story like hers? Not the stone-faced Philippine official facing her in the cell-like room. Someone came to the door and spoke in a language she didn't know. Without a word, her interrogator left.

Alone for the first time that night, Marilyn stared down at her ink-stained fingertips. She'd been fingerprinted—booked like a common criminal—all in connection with the murders of two people she didn't even now. How could this be happening to her?

At least they'd had the decency to let her get dressed in the bathroom of her hotel room, though only with the door ajar and a woman employee summoned by the manager watching her every move. The woman had acted like Marilyn was an ax murderess. She winced, remembering the woman's frightened glances. The door to the interrogation room opened again. Marilyn shuddered, expecting to see the officer who had been questioning her.

Instead she saw Mac. She blinked. *It can't be him,* her common sense told her. But there he stood, as real as the chair she was sitting on.

He might be a terrorist, he might be guilty of horrible acts of violence in the name of his grand cause, but, at that moment, he was the air force, marines, and cavalry all rolled into one.

"Oh, Mac, I'm so glad you're here." She flew to him, and he clutched her to him. His sweaty smell, the feel of his arms around her and his rough chin rubbing against her cheek were the most comforting sensations she'd ever known. The tears she'd been fighting burst forth.

"It's been just awful," she sobbed.

He tipped her chin up and took off her glasses. "I know, darling lady, I know." His voice was thick and unsteady.

He moved his lips tenderly across her cheeks and eyes. They were feathery kisses that felt like tiny wings drying her tears.

"These people think I had something to do with two horrible murders." Another flood of tears broke through.

He handed her a handkerchief and waited, rubbing her back gently with his hand, until she stopped sobbing. "And you didn't?" His tone was mildly expectant. Did he think she'd confess, right here on the spot?

"Of course not!" Indignant, she pulled away from him. "I didn't even see the woman. The police claim her body was in a little room off the kitchen. The man was tortured. I could never do anything like that."

He whistled softly. "So the police were right. You *were* in the murdered man's house this afternoon." He led her to the executive chair the interrogator had just vacated. "Why don't you tell me exactly what happened?"

Marilyn's mind whirled. Now that her initial relief at seeing Mac was past, unanswerable questions assailed her. What was an IRA terrorist doing in a Philippine police station? Why did the authorities leave her alone with him?

Mac yanked the wooden chair closer to hers and straddled it, facing her. "Start with why you were at the murdered man's house."

She drew back, suddenly wary. "You sound just like that detective, Mac. Before I say anything, I want to know why these people are letting an IRA terrorist question me."

He took her hand, cradling it tenderly in his. "I'm not an IRA terrorist, Marilyn. I am—or was—an FBI special agent."

For a moment she was shocked into silence. Then the pent-up emotion of the past twenty-four hours exploded.

"An FBI special agent?" She yanked her hand away in stunned disbelief. "Quit lying, Mac. How much are these people paying an IRA terrorist to squeeze the truth out of me? Ten thousand for the grand cause?" She glared at him. "A hundred thousand? Just how much is my story worth to them?" She swallowed hard to kill the sob in her throat.

He swung his chair around and, facing her, hunched forward, the picture of dejection. "I don't blame you for not believing me." He sighed heavily, his voice filled with anguish. "After we get you out of here, I'll tell you the whole story."

"What do you mean 'after we get you out of here'?" Marilyn eyed him suspiciously. "Are you telling me all I have to do is talk to you, and they'll let me go? How stupid do you think I am? These people believe I murdered somebody. They're never going to let me go that easily. It's just a trick, another one of your nasty little lies."

"It's not a trick. As soon as your hotel manager told me you'd been arrested, I came down here." Leaning toward her, he rubbed the stubble on his chin. "I want to help, Marilyn. Why else would I follow you all this way?"

"Heaven only knows." Marilyn stared at his face. His usual roguish look was gone, replaced with an earnestness that seemed sincere.

What if he's telling the truth? She remembered her odd awareness that Mac and Agent Smith had been trained at the same school. An urgent sense of relief washed over her. Mac wasn't a criminal. He was an upstanding citizen, like herself.

But her relief was short-lived. If he was an FBI agent, everything he'd told her was a lie. She gave him another hostile glare. And it meant something even worse—he'd been trying to trap her—send her to jail for treason.

"I'm going to get you out of here, but you have to tell me what happened." There was a pleading tone to his voice. He took her hand again. "Hate me if you want to. God knows I deserve it. Just let me do this one thing for you, and you can walk away from me forever, if that's what you want."

His words somehow sounded different than they had in California. With a start, she realized why. There wasn't a trace of an accent. She withdrew her hand, but not as quickly as before. "You've lost your accent, Mr. IRA Terrorist."

He stared levelly into her eyes. "Because I'm no longer playing that role."

The door opened and a heavyset black man wearing a beautifully embroidered, hip-length white shirt over dark trousers came in. Partially bald, his high forehead glistened with a fine sheen of perspiration.

"Neil Warner from the U.S. Embassy," he said, extending his hand to Marilyn.

Gratefully she clasped it. "Marilyn Wainwright, Mr. Warner. Thank God you're here."

Mac stood up and nodded.

Putting his briefcase on the floor, Warner shook hands with Mac. "What the hell you doing here, MacIntyre? You're about ten thousand miles out of the bureau's jurisdiction."

Marilyn's eyes widened. Mr. Warner, an official from the U.S. Department of State, had just verified Mac's story. Could it be true? Or was somebody playing another horrid trick on her?

"I've got a personal interest in Ms. Wainwright," Mac said. "As soon as I found out she was in jail, I came to help. The people out front were happy to cooperate with a fellow officer."

Squatting on the floor, Warner opened his briefcase and took out her passport. He handed it to Marilyn, along with his card. "The police want your story. Then you'll be free to go."

"Just like that?" Mac seemed surprised. He stared at Neil Warner.

The official smiled. "In spite of what you read in the papers, we've got pretty good relations with the people here, MacIntyre. She'll have to keep the embassy informed as to where she is so the police can get in touch if they need her. Other than that, she'll be free as a bird as soon as she tells me what happened."

"Then they don't think I—uh—murdered poor Mr. Nguyen?" Marilyn had to force the words out.

Warner sat down, facing her. The chair creaked under his weight. "From what I understand, they never thought you did, Ms. Wainwright. But they do have eyewitnesses, a cab driver and a gardener, who saw you go into the building and then leave in a shaken condition. Unless you were wearing gloves, the police probably found your fingerprints inside the house."

He smiled at her encouragingly.

Marilyn took a deep breath, wondering how much she could say without involving Van. She glanced toward Mac and saw him nod slowly.

Warner followed her gaze. "If MacIntyre's bothering you, he can wait outside while you tell me what happened."

An odd panic grabbed at her insides. "No—please—let him stay."

How can you want him here after what he's done to you?
Annoyed with herself, she glanced at Mac's face again. Despite his reassuring smile, he looked tired. His eyelids were puffy, and there was dark stubble on his chin. His wrinkled turquoise sweater drooped over jeans that looked slept in. *Why did he follow me all this way?* An unaccountably elated feeling gave way to a horrible new suspicion. *Because he wants me to lead him to Van. Maybe the assassin isn't the only one after my brother.* Sweat rolled down her forehead. She dabbed at it with the handkerchief Mac had given her.

Warner leaned over and took a tape recorder from his briefcase. "Mind if I record this, Ms. Wainwright? The police will type it up, and you'll have to sign it."

"No, of course not." What *was* she going to say?

In the end she repeated exactly what had happened from the time she got out of the taxi, until she returned to it. Warner wanted to know why she'd gone to see Mr. Nguyen in the first place. Marilyn said he was a friend of her brother's. She'd sought him out because his was the only familiar name in a strange city, where she hoped to enjoy a short vacation.

Warner seemed to accept her explanation. On the way out, he said a few words to the Philippine officials. They returned her tote bag with the curt order not to leave Manila for a few days.

The embassy staff car was parked outside, a driver inside. "Let me drop you at your hotel, Ms. Wainwright," Warner offered.

Tenderly, Mac took Marilyn's arm. "If it's all right with her, I'll escort her."

She didn't pull away. For her brother's sake, she had to know what Mac's game was. This scholarly Notre Dame professor turned roguish IRA terrorist turned considerate FBI special agent had said he was ready to tell her his story. She needed desperately to hear what he had to say. *And not only for Van's sake,* she admitted to herself.

"Thanks for coming down here so early in the morning," she told Neil Warner. "Mr. McDon—uh—Mac can take me to the hotel.'' She stumbled over the name but caught herself. What had Warner called him?

I don't even know his name. Indignation swept over her, and she moved a step away from him. In that instant, she very nearly accepted Neil Warner's offer. But the danger to Van, along with her mounting curiosity, made her swallow her aggravation. She couldn't afford to postpone hearing Mac's explanation.

Warner didn't notice her confusion. ''The Fils weren't kidding when they told you not to leave Manila, Ms. Wainwright. If you try to leave, they'll stop you.'' He got in the car's back seat and rolled down the window. ''Let me know if you move to another hotel. My number's on the card I gave you.''

Beside her, Mac squeezed Marilyn's arm. In the humid, early-morning air she caught his scent again. A distinctive male odor with no hint of cologne, it made her head spin and was oddly reassuring. Wary but determined, she watched the embassy vehicle pull away from the curb.

''SHALL WE GO BACK to your hotel?'' Mac helped Marilyn into the cab.

She winced, remembering the woman employee who had watched her dress. ''After what happened to me in that hotel last night, I don't want to go near the place until I've had breakfast.''

''What I've got to say might ruin your appetite.'' He wasn't smiling. ''It's pretty bad—bad enough to make me sick to my stomach when I found out how you were being framed.'' He told the driver to take them to a restaurant.

Marilyn let her breath out in a tired sigh. ''You mean you were the agent in charge, and you didn't know I was being framed? C'mon now, Mac. I find that very hard to believe.''

''If it's hard for you, imagine how I felt.'' He clenched his jaw. His lips turned to a thin hard line. ''When I found out about the lousy scam my boss pulled on you, I quit.''

"You quit the FBI? Because of me?" *This can't be true,* she thought wearily. *It's some new kind of trick, like his professor trick and his IRA terrorist trick.*

Mac's eyes narrowed. "They didn't let me in on the whole scheme, Marilyn. My boss knew I'd never frame an innocent person, so he convinced me you were a spy."

Memories of Agent Smith's angry face flooded Marilyn's mind. "The agent in San Diego said I was guilty of espionage, Mac. Even after I'd turned you in and agreed to do what he wanted."

Unspoken sympathy glowed in Mac's eyes. In his expression, Marilyn recognized understanding of what she'd been through.

"I know." He took her hand and kissed it. "They played hardball with you."

The stubble on his chin felt rough against her hand. It made her feel guilty about insisting they talk, but not guilty enough to suggest returning to the hotel so they could both clean up.

The cab stopped in front of a hotel with a commanding view of Manila Bay. The driver, a young man barely out of his teens, glanced down the driveway. "Your friends not turn off Roxas when we did." He eyed Mac with a sly smile.

Marilyn saw the startled look on Mac's face.

"Did you see them in the rearview mirror?" He handed the driver a couple of bills.

The young man glanced at the money, grinned, and shoved it in his pocket. "Yes. Thank you very much. They follow you from police station."

When the cab had left, Marilyn stared at Mac with frightened eyes. "Somebody's still following me."

"Us," he corrected. "I'm with you now, for as long as you want me." Ignoring a couple of street vendors who had set up stands outside the hotel, he guided her inside the impressive marble lobby. The restaurant was on the far side. He slowed his stride so that she could keep up with him.

"Could that hit man—that Benson character—have followed me all the way from San Diego?" she asked.

Marilyn sounded scared, more frightened than Mac had ever heard her. Small wonder. During the past forty-eight hours she'd seen sights no one should have to see, been accused of crimes she could hardly comprehend, let alone commit. Tenderly, he put his arm around her waist.

"It's possible, but I doubt it," he said to reassure her. "According to the FBI agents who followed you from your office, Benson lost you at the mall." He smoothed his hair back with his fingers. "Maybe the Manila police are keeping an eye on you. It might even be someone from the U.S. government. The bureau wants your brother, Marilyn. They say he's the head of a crime syndicate."

"That's stupid!" She tossed her head. A lock of hair came undone and fell to her shoulders.

Mac had a sudden urge to loosen the whole velvet brown mass and run his fingers through it.

"Either somebody's crazy," she said hotly, "or they're framing him, the same way the FBI tried to frame me."

Mac chose his words carefully. "I'm only repeating what I was told. Apparently gangs of young Vietnamese have been organized into a syndicate operating over the three coastal western states. They're terrorizing Vietnamese communities."

"And the bureau thinks Van is the leader?" She spat out the words contemptuously.

He waited until they were seated in the coffee shop before he answered. An airy room filled with plants, the place overlooked Manila Bay. To the west, at the entrance to the bay, stood Corregidor, barely visible in the hazy morning light.

"The bureau also believes you're helping him run it, or at least that you know what he's doing." He watched her closely, but saw no reaction other than outraged astonishment.

"That's crazy, Mac. Why would they think such a thing?" She was starting to look frightened again.

Mac thought she seemed shaky and told the waitress to hurry with their coffee. He yearned to see her smile again, to watch the color return to her pale cheeks.

"The bureau gets information from many different sources," he explained carefully. "Fact is, an operation like the one against you isn't undertaken unless there's a lot of firm evidence."

"There wasn't any evidence against me. None at all. You said so yourself."

"Not against you, Marilyn. Against your brother." He spoke quietly, trying not to upset her.

The waitress brought their coffee. Marilyn took a swallow. "Somebody in your office is crazy, Mac. Van isn't the head of any syndicate. If he were, I'd know it." There was no doubt in her voice.

Mac admired her loyalty, even if he didn't understand it. "People change," he suggested gently. "Maybe you've lost touch with him the past few years."

She shook her head. "It's simply not possible." Her eyes widened. "Mac, that assassin from San Diego must have been the one who killed poor Mr. Nguyen, trying to get him to tell where Van is."

Mac frowned. The idea had already occurred to him, and he didn't like it. "If Benson did it, that means he figured out the connection between the dead man and your brother. Since Nguyen was dead when you got there, Benson couldn't have followed you." He eyed her curiously. "Just what *is* the connection, Marilyn? Why did you go straight to that address?"

She hesitated long enough for Mac to see she didn't want to tell him. "Forget I asked," he said. "For now, it's enough to know Nguyen was a friend of your brother's. You obviously thought he knew where Van was. Is Nguyen the one you called from the pay phone Sunday night?"

"Yes." There was another moment of silence. It lengthened, became unbearable.

He searched her face. She didn't look away. In her firm gaze he caught sight of a hidden strength he hadn't suspected. This lady wasn't fragile. Her courage and determination were like a rock inside her.

"I don't trust you, Mac." There was no hint of an apology in her tone. "I'm telling you up-front, so you won't ask any more questions about how I got Mr. Nguyen's name."

Her words left him empty. He leaned across the table toward her. "You don't have to trust me, Marilyn. For now, just let me stick around until everything's cleared up."

"Why are you doing this, Mac?" Her voice was tinged with suspicion. "First you follow me all this way and now you're offering to help me out of a bad jam. Why?"

Why, indeed? He'd asked himself the same question a hundred times on the long flight from Los Angeles. After talking to Finnegan, he hadn't even been sure she was completely innocent. Maybe she *was* working with her brother. The one thing Mac was certain of was that she wasn't a spy. And that's what he'd been trying to frame her for. He wanted to make it up to her.

But there was more to it than that. Something about her intrigued him. Whether it was the spunky way she defended her brother, or the musical sound of her voice, or her proud bearing, or any one of a hundred other things, she evoked tender feelings he'd rarely felt before, feelings he reserved for children and animals. He couldn't let her disappear from his life without finding out more about her. That's why he'd come after her, he realized suddenly.

Now, sitting across the table, she looked so defiant—in spite of her tired, disheveled appearance—that he yearned to reach out to her, to smooth away the lines above her eyebrows and make her smile again. He cleared his throat. "When I found out you were innocent of those espionage charges, I suppose I felt guilty. I wanted to make it up to you somehow."

To his surprise, she pushed her coffee cup away and stood up, glaring at him. "Now that you've assuaged your guilt, you can be on your way, Mr.—what is it you're calling yourself these days?"

She was going to walk out on him! He leapt to his feet. "You haven't heard the whole story, Marilyn. Please stay. It's important that you do." He leaned toward her and touched her lightly on the arm.

Pushing her chair aside, she backed away. "I've heard enough, thanks." What kind of fool did he take her for? Nobody chased a woman halfway around the world because he felt guilty. There had to be another reason, and Marilyn was pretty sure she knew what it was. *He's still working for the bureau. This is another elaborate hoax to trap me into leading them to Van.*

"You know who hired Tony Benson?" Mac's quiet voice followed her as she turned to go. "The Vietnamese community. They thought they'd break up the syndicate if they killed your brother."

Marilyn sagged into her chair. "How do you know?"

"An agent from the San Diego office followed Benson after he left the mall. He went to Little Saigon. A bureau source said he was working for the Vietnamese."

Looking down, Marilyn stirred her coffee so Mac wouldn't see the pain in her eyes. "Is that the same source who said Van was the syndicate's leader?"

"Probably," he admitted.

"Well, he's wrong." Marilyn was silent for a long while. "Van would never take advantage of refugees he's tried so hard to help."

Mac hesitated. "The bureau's source sure wasn't wrong about somebody wanting to kill your brother. Mr. Nguyen's death proves that. It couldn't be a coincidence that he was tortured and killed only hours before you got there looking for Van. Somebody else wants to find him, Marilyn."

"I know." She shivered, remembering the hellish scene.

The waitress brought dishes of freshly peeled mangos, along with their French toast and ham.

"I'm not sure I can keep anything down," she said.

His forehead wrinkled with concern. "Try a small bite of fruit. After all you've been through, you need to build up your strength."

Squeamishly, she cut off a small section and bit into it. It had a rich sweet taste unlike anything she'd ever eaten. After she'd had a few more bites, she tried the toast. Made of thick French bread, it dripped with butter and syrup.

Mac smiled across the table at her. "You're looking steadier already."

She smiled back at him. From the way he beamed, she realized how downcast she must have looked for most of this morning. After she tried the ham and enjoyed a few more bites of French toast, she took another swallow of coffee.

"Do you have brothers or sisters, Mac?" When he didn't answer right away, she added, "My brother's been my best friend and added so much to my life. I always feel sorry for people who don't have brothers and sisters."

"Then you won't feel sorry for me," he said shortly. "I had nine."

"Nine! How wonderful." Her voice rose with delight. "Your whole childhood must have been like a picnic. Tell me about it."

Mac took a deep breath. "It wasn't exactly a picnic. Good old dad was an alcoholic who was sick most of the time. *Sick*—that's another word for drunk."

"Oh, I'm so sorry, Mac." Her face fell. "Where did you grow up?"

"New York City's lower east side." He felt the old hostility rising up inside him, in spite of his efforts to put it down. "Two of my brothers are in jail right now. A third died of a drug overdose. My youngest sister had an illegitimate baby. Should I go on? Like I said, it wasn't exactly a picnic."

She put her fork down and leaned toward him. "It's no wonder you don't understand my feelings for Van when you grew up in an atmosphere like that. Do you keep in touch with any of them?"

"Not since my oldest sister died. She was the only one I was close to."

Mac felt her sympathy. But he was unprepared when she reached across the table and took his hand in her two small ones. A strange tenderness swept over him, as he gazed at her sweat-stained shirt and disheveled hair. With all the pain she'd suffered recently, *ever since I came into her life,* he thought, she was still trying to comfort him.

She withdrew her hands quickly, as though embarrassed by her show of affection. "I'm sorry, Mac. I didn't mean to get personal. I know you're helping me out of a sense of duty." A pensive look crossed her face. "At least that's what you're telling me."

He drew his breath in and held it, not trusting himself to speak. "What do you mean?"

She hesitated. "Only that I'm not sure what to believe. It's hard for me to picture a worldly man like you growing up in such a deprived atmosphere. Your other story fit you better—the one about going to school in England and traveling on the continent during your college years."

He groaned. "But the other story was a fabrication, made up to go along with my cover. What I've just told you is the complete, unvarnished truth."

She didn't believe him. He could see the doubt in her eyes.

Chapter Eleven

"You don't believe me, do you?" Mac's expression was tight with strain. His voice sounded tired. "You know, it's ironic. The first time I open up to a woman, she thinks I'm lying."

Marilyn tried to ignore the pain in his eyes. "Do you blame me? After all the lies you've told me? I'm sorry, Mac. I want to believe you, but I just can't, at least not everything."

He studied her intently. "Why would I lie? I've told you my whole story, why the bureau wanted to frame you. Everything."

Marilyn swallowed another bite of French toast. What harm would it do to tell him what she suspected? At least then, he'd realize she wasn't a gullible fool.

"The most logical reason in the world," she replied firmly. "You just told me the bureau wants to find my brother and thinks I know where he is." She flashed him an accusing look. "Maybe you're still working for them. Maybe you think I'll lead you right to him if you play your cards right."

He flinched, as though she'd struck him in the face. A muscle clenched along his jaw. Feeling sorry, she started to tell him to forget what she'd said, that she didn't mean it, but the words stuck in her throat. He'd looked hurt before, when he was playing college professor. That had been a sham. Maybe this was, too.

"Whether you trust me or not is irrelevant." He sighed heavily, a bleak smile on his lips. "What you've got to do is go home and put yourself under the FBI's protection. I really mean that, Marilyn. It's the only way you'll be safe."

"I'll be safe all right. Safe in jail." A suffocating sensation tightened her throat.

He drew a sharp breath. "Don't worry about going to jail. Don't even worry about them giving you a hard time. After what I've told you—about the sting and how they were planning to frame you—you can make life miserable for Finnegan and company. There's a nationally syndicated columnist on the *Washington Post* who gets his jollies from exposing government—uh—shall we say, *irregularities.*"

What he said sounded so *right* that Marilyn almost believed it. Why would he suggest she go home unless he were truly concerned about her safety? For an idyllic moment she let herself picture the two of them flying off into the sunset, the harsh events of the past few days behind them.

Then reality struck, and she hurtled back to earth. This was probably another trick to get her to trust him. By now he knew her well enough to realize she'd never give up her hunt for Van, not with an assassin and the FBI and God knew who else after him. All Mac had to do was stick around and, when Marilyn found her brother, Special Agent MacIntyre could arrange for him to be returned to the United States. Well, she was too smart for that. She'd continue her search alone.

Marilyn had a good idea where to start: Bangkok. At the return address on the other two envelopes she'd found in the back of her brother's stamp album. Unfortunately, the trip to Thailand would have to wait a few days, until the police were ready to let her leave the country. *So that's Mac's game,* she thought, with new insight. *He knows I can't leave Manila so he advises me to go home. That's a great way to get me to trust him.*

He was staring at her with a quizzical expression. His eyes searched her face as though trying to read her thoughts. "So how about it?'' he asked. ''Let's head for the hotel to pick up your things and then to the airport and home.''

Suspiciously, she stared back across the table at him. ''What about the police statement? I haven't signed it yet.''

His roguish grin reminded Marilyn of the old Mac. How much of this new Mac was part of the old one, the one she'd half fallen in love with?

''If we call Warner at the embassy and tell him you want to leave Manila,'' he said, ''I'll bet the police or someone from the embassy will bring that statement right to the airport for you to sign.''

''Why would they go to that trouble? Do you know something I don't?''

Obviously in no hurry to answer, Mac finished his last piece of ham. ''Since you've asked and since I've decided to be completely honest with you from now on—'' His words were measured. ''It's only a gut feeling, but it seemed to me the police let you go too easily.''

Her eyes widened in agreement. ''Do you think the embassy put pressure on them?''

He nodded. ''The embassy's probably doing the bureau a favor. They'll make it possible for you to leave the country.'' His curious gaze searched her face. ''The bureau wants you to run to your brother. But you can't do that stuck in Manila. Unless, of course, this is where he is.''

He still thinks I know. Marilyn looked down at her empty plate so he couldn't tell what she was thinking. ''I have no idea where Van is, Mac. For all I know, he *is* here.'' She took a swallow of coffee. It tasted cold and bitter, the way she felt. ''As long as there's a remote possibility, I'll keep looking.''

His brows drew forward in a worried frown. ''You've got to let me help you, Marilyn. It's too dangerous for you in Manila on your own.''

His compelling hazel eyes, the firm line of his mouth and the confident set of his shoulders impressed her with his take charge assurance. Why did he have to look so darned sincere? She wondered who he really was, this man sitting opposite her.

"I don't feel like I know you, Mac." To Marilyn, her voice sounded a long way off. "You seem so different from the professor I worked with at the hotel." *The man I fell in love with.*

He reached for her hand. Before she could pull away, his fingers, warm and strong, grasped hers. "I *am* different. I'm not a make-believe IRA terrorist out to involve you in espionage. I'm a real man who wants to help."

His earnest gaze held hers. "It's only been a few hours since you found out the truth about me. Give yourself another day or two to get to know me." His voice broke with huskiness. "You don't have to trust me first crack off the bat. Just let me hang around to keep an eye on things."

Intensely aware of the warmth of his hand around hers, Marilyn felt herself relenting. This proud man, with his air of confident authority, almost seemed to be pleading with her. What harm could come from letting him do as he asked, especially since she had to remain in the city anyway? While she was here, she'd advertise in the English-language newspaper for Van on the chance her brother was in Manila and might see it. Mac didn't have to know what she was doing.

A smile found its way through her mask of uncertainty. "You've got to promise not to snoop if I want to go somewhere alone."

With a satisfied nod, he held up two fingers on his free hand. "Boy Scout's honor. I'll respect your privacy."

Somehow, this time, she believed him.

ON THE WAY BACK to the hotel, Mac suggested they stop downtown to buy more clothes. Like Marilyn, he'd brought only a few essentials.

The cab driver brought them to a shop on a crowded narrow street. Mac eyed the place dubiously from the car window. It didn't appear to be the kind of store frequented by foreigners. Its front was open and piles of clothing and shoes were displayed on tables on the sidewalk. A small crowd of women dressed mostly in brightly-colored cotton shirts and baggy dark pants had gathered around one of the tables. They were grabbing at the merchandise as though it might vanish momentarily.

"This isn't what we want," he told the driver. "Take us to a nice place."

"This is nice place," the man insisted. "Many bargains."

Mac felt Marilyn lean against him, as she peered around his shoulder. The touch of her body against his did strange things to his pulse. Annoyed, he reminded himself that he was here to right a wrong, not seduce this woman.

"It's probably got everything I need," she said. "The way we look, we'd probably get thrown out of a decent store."

"I doubt that," he grumbled. "Not as long as we've got U.S. green in our pockets." Despite his misgivings, he opened the taxi door and helped her out. "Wait for us," he told the driver, after paying him.

Eyes narrowing, Mac watched the bright yellow vehicle disappear in the heavy morning traffic. Either the taxi driver hadn't heard Mac, or he chose to park out of sight. The car's hasty departure bothered Mac. So did the milling crowd. The shoppers were pressing against them. He was jostled a couple of times as he followed Marilyn inside.

"Stay close," he said tersely. "We don't want to get separated."

She flashed him an elfin smile. "If we do, we can meet back at the hotel."

Mac was thankful she didn't seem to notice his apprehension. She'd faced enough trouble the past few hours, without worrying about every step she took.

Inside, two big fans whirring at top speed provided relief from the humid heat. Fluorescent lights shone down on tables like those outside, also piled high with merchandise.

Mac stuck to Marilyn like molasses, while she selected a couple of flimsy cotton nightgowns and some underwear. Eyeing the transparent nightgowns, he visualized the gauzy cloth clinging to her slender body. The image brought unwanted warmth to his loins. Even more annoyed than in the cab, he spoke to the salesgirl who'd latched onto them as soon as they entered. "Where are dresses for sight-seeing?"

"I'll bring some, sir." The clerk turned to Marilyn. "We have many in your size. You're small, like us Filipinas." She went to the rear of the store. In a moment she returned with the promised garments.

Frowning, Marilyn examined them. "Don't you think they're a little...ah...colorful and ruffly for me?" she asked Mac.

"Try one on. See how it looks." He'd noticed changing booths along a side wall. Privacy was provided by a shower-curtain-like arrangement. There was no way to enter the booths except through the curtain so Marilyn would be safe, even out of his sight.

"The pink is beautiful with your skin, ma'am." Young, probably in her early twenties, the clerk spoke flawless English.

While Marilyn was behind the curtain, Mac plopped down in a nearby chair. *It's probably provided for the husbands,* he thought wryly. Reflecting on the picture of domesticity he and Marilyn made, he found, somewhat to his surprise, that it didn't bother him. What the hell was wrong with him these days? First he chased halfway around the world after a woman who rated him somewhere between Judas and Saddam Hussein for trustworthiness. Now, here he sat, waiting patiently while she picked out a new wardrobe.

When she appeared in the pink dress, he couldn't repress a whistle of admiration. Fitted at the waist, with big sleeves and a full skirt, the dress accented her slim, vibrant beauty. Why had he thought Marilyn was plain? She was the most lovely thing he'd ever seen.

"Buy it," he said, his tenor voice gruffer than usual. "Get the others, too, if they look half as good."

She ended up buying the pink dress and two others.

Back on the sidewalk, Mac picked out socks, underwear and washable shirts from an outdoor display table. He stuffed them into a sack provided by the store. For now, the jeans he had on would have to do. There were no pants to fit him. Filipino men were shorter and their hips slimmer than his.

After he'd paid for his purchases, he glanced up and down the traffic-snarled street, hunting for the cab. Buses, jeepneys loaded with passengers, and private automobiles crawled by leaving noxious clouds of exhaust fumes in their wakes. Across the street, in the middle of the next block, a dilapidated old building was being torn down. The sharp rattle of a jackhammer competed with the roar of unmuffled automobile engines in the dust-filled air. There was no sign of the taxi.

"Since we're in town, let's stop at a drug store," Marilyn said. "I don't even have toothpaste."

Glancing down at her, Mac took in her animated look, the flush of excitement on her cheeks. Amazingly, in spite of all she'd been through, her tiredness seemed to be gone. Apparently she'd developed a stamina at odds with the seeming fragility of her slender body.

Taking her shopping bag from her, he pulled her hand through his arm. "The hotel will have everything we need. We should probably go back and clean up before we do anything else." He tried to sound reassuring, but a measure of his concern must have slipped into his voice.

Her expression changed to one of alarm. "We're not in danger are we, Mac?"

Eyes sharp, he studied the people on the street around them. From his six-foot-tall vantage point, it was like looking down on a waving stream of black-haired heads, a few wearing frayed bandannas. He saw nothing suspicious but remained on guard. The stream was flowing too close to them for Mac's peace of mind.

"Crowds make me nervous," he said evasively. "And this doesn't look like the best part of town. Keep a good grip on your purse."

He felt Marilyn tense as she tightened her hold on her bag, pulling it closer to her body.

As though to reinforce his warning, a flock of ten or twelve ragged young boys clustered around them, their hands outstretched. "Five P and we'll carry your things," shouted the largest. He jerked at one of the three shopping bags over Mac's arm.

Mac took three bills out of his pocket. "Here's three pesos." The spokesman grabbed for the money. Mac let him have it. "Now go away." The group vanished as quickly as it had appeared, melting into the passing crowd.

Suddenly the cab turned onto the street. The driver had apparently been watching for them from a hidden vantage point. When it reached them, Mac helped Marilyn inside with the relieved feeling that, for the moment at least, they were safe.

Outside the hotel, the usual hawkers jabbered at them in pidgin English as they got out of the taxi. Obsequiously, one of the men thrust a reed basket toward Marilyn.

"Souvenir of Nayong Pilipino," he said, referring to the model Philippine village located next to the hotel. "Made by Bontoc tribe. Special price for you, missus."

He edged toward them and then lunged. Mac glimpsed a flash of steel. He managed to jerk Marilyn back and sideways before the blade fell. The thrust probably meant for her heart stabbed into her upper arm instead.

Restricted by the three shopping bags over his arm, Mac was unable to grab her assailant. Dropping the reed basket at their feet, the man darted across the drive, heading for the street. Nobody tried to stop him.

FOR THE FIRST few minutes, Marilyn didn't know what had happened. She felt a blow to her arm, as though someone had struck her hard, then a strange numbness.

Around her, she saw the curious looks of the hawkers and a Japanese couple who were coming out of the lobby. The uniformed doorman elbowed his way toward them.

"What happened here, sir?" he asked Mac.

"My wife's had an accident," Mac said. "She needs a doctor."

"We have one on staff." The doorman cleared the way and hurried toward the registration desk to get help.

Mac put his arm around Marilyn's back and half carried her inside. Only then did she look down and see the spreading red stain on the sleeve of her green shirt.

My God, I've been stabbed! Why hadn't Mac told the doorman?

Panic like she'd never known before constricted her throat. Unable to speak, she clutched at Mac's arm with her other hand, until her fingernails left tiny red marks on his skin. She felt herself being lowered to a chair, felt his hand gently removing her bag from her shoulder.

He examined the wound. "The bastard only got the fleshy part of your arm, thank God, but it's deep." He pulled a white T-shirt from one of the shopping bags and wrapped it around the cut.

Even as Marilyn watched, a spot of pink appeared. It turned moistly crimson and oozed outward, into a widening circle of red. Mac muttered an oath and wrapped more layers of the cotton around her arm, applying pressure as he did so.

A clerk who had been summoned by the doorman ran up to them. "Can she walk?" he asked. "The doctor's office is down the hall, off the lobby."

The pain began, an insistent sharp throbbing that left Marilyn drained. She gritted her teeth. "I'll be okay, Mac. Let's go."

She felt his arm around her, helping her to her feet. Ignoring the curious glances of people in the lobby, she forced herself to start moving. "We've got to report this to the police." She could hardly lift her voice above a whisper.

"Let's get your arm fixed up first. Then we'll talk about what we should do next."

It was an equivocal reply, but Marilyn was hurting too badly to argue. When she glanced down at her arm she saw that the blood had soaked through again. She put her head down, fighting the dizziness that swept over her.

Mac's strong arms lifted her off her feet. Pressed against his warm body, she was enfolded in his familiar masculine scent. It gave her a protected feeling, as though she were safely wrapped in an invincible cocoon.

The doctor was a buxom Caucasian woman who took immediate charge. As though it were happening to somebody else, Marilyn watched the doctor's hands removing the bloodied T-shirt from around her arm. Gently she was eased onto an examining table and her wound was cleaned. From a great distance, she heard Mac explaining his wife's accident.

His wife. An odd picture formed in her mind. Dressed in a flowing white gown, she was standing in front of a deep crimson pool. There were two men with her, one on each side. She couldn't make out the men's faces. She knew only that the picture was wrong. There should be one man beside her, not two.

A woman's voice—the doctor's—broke through her reverie. "I'm going to close that up for you, Mrs. Wainwright. Then you should rest in your room overnight. The stitches can come out in two or three days."

The doctor turned away. "Be sure she stays put tonight, Mr. Wainwright."

Mr. Wainwright? Marilyn's eyes widened. What kind of weird game was Mac playing now?

MARILYN WAITED until the nurse had tucked her in bed, and she and Mac were alone in her room before she asked him what he was up to.

His answering smile held a hint of apology. "I pretended to be your husband because I wanted to stay close, without having to answer fool questions about our relationship. Since you were registered under Wainwright, that made me Mr. Wainwright."

Lie or not, what he said made sense. It also made her feel warm, safe. Until she remembered he'd lied about the way she'd gotten hurt.

"Why did you tell the doctor it was an accident?" She tried to keep the fear out of her voice. "Somebody tried to kill me, Mac. Shouldn't it be reported to the police?"

"We can't trust the police. Hell, Marilyn. We can't trust anybody." He dragged a chair between the bed and the door and sat. His tense expression gave him a fierce, wrathful look.

"We can't even trust Mr. Warner from the embassy?" A cold knot formed in her stomach.

"Especially not anybody from the embassy. Finnegan's probably got them keeping an eye on you right now, hoping you'll lead them to your brother."

Aghast, Marilyn could feel her heart thumping madly. "You can't think somebody from the embassy tried to kill me?" She struggled to sit up. The room began whirling.

"Whoa, take it easy." He jumped up and put an arm behind her back, easing her down on the bed. His brow creased with concern. "After you've had some rest, there'll be plenty of time to talk."

"Now, Mac. Tell me now. It's only a flesh wound. The doctor said so herself."

Marilyn lifted herself on one elbow. The room stayed in place. She watched him grab a couple of pillows from the closet. He thrust them behind her head and shoulders. Gratefully she sank against them.

Pulling his chair closer to the bed, he sat down again, facing her. "Probably nobody at the embassy was behind this attack, but we can't take chances. Maybe somebody there sold out. The stabbing's added another dimension to this nasty game we've been playing." He rubbed the stubble on his chin thoughtfully. "Up until now, people have been after you to get to your brother. Nobody's tried to harm you."

"How about that bomb in my apartment?" She shivered, remembering how scared she'd been and how she'd run to Agent Smith for help. What a big mistake *that* had been.

"The bureau says the bomb was set off purposely, when you weren't there."

She shivered again. "That's what Agent Smith said. He even suggested I might have done it myself."

Mac's mouth curved down with disgust. "Sounds like the kind of stupid comment Dan Moschella would make." His voice lowered in annoyance. "Was Agent Smith tall, with a big nose?"

"That sounds like him." She paused. "So what's your theory? Why the sudden attack?"

"Think about our situation for a minute." He folded his arms and stood facing her, his mind searching rapid-fire for answers. "We've got two groups who want to find your brother—Vietnamese refugees who've hired an assassin to kill him and the U.S. government who wants to put him in jail. These people don't want to hurt you. They want you to lead them to him."

"So why the sudden attack on me?" she repeated.

His eyes narrowed. "Whoever's behind the stabbing has a different motivation from the others. They want to keep you from finding your brother and will go to extreme lengths—even kill you—to stop you."

"Who could it be?" Her violet eyes opened wide.

He shrugged. "Who knows? Since the attacker was waiting outside the hotel, he probably wasn't the one who followed us from the police station."

"That was someone from the embassy, right? Hoping I'd lead them to Van." There was a tremulous quiver to her voice.

They were going around in circles. "You need some sleep," he said softly. "We'll talk more later." He leaned over and kissed her gently on the forehead. "Take this pain pill the doctor left for you. It'll help you sleep." He brought a glass of water from the bathroom and watched while she swallowed the pill.

"I'm scared, Mac." Fear, stark and vivid, glittered in her eyes. "It seems like everybody's against me. Whoever did this could be waiting outside the hotel for me right now."

"Shush," he said, running his fingers lightly over her cheek. "I'm going to be right here, remember? Like I said before, it's not you alone anymore. From now on, it's us."

Much later, Mac sat dozing in a chair beside the door. He didn't dare stretch out on the room's empty bed. Tired as he was, he knew he'd never be able to stay awake. At least he'd been able to shave. A nurse, sent by the doctor to check on Marilyn, had provided a disposable razor. Later, the same nurse brought him the chicken adobo dinner he'd just eaten. Yawning, he folded his arms across his chest.

He didn't stir when a uniformed woman using a passkey slipped by him into the room an hour later. In her hand she carried a small square case. The case contained a single hypodermic syringe.

Chapter Twelve

Through a curtain of codeine-induced sleep, Marilyn heard rustling sounds and sensed a presence nearby.

Somebody's standing beside my bed.

Every muscle in her body seemed to contract. Then she remembered. Mac was with her. Eyes closed, she breathed deeply, searching for his scent. Instead, she smelled a faint, sickly sweet gardenia odor.

She forced her eyes open, blinking in the semidarkness. The only light came from a dim lamp on the dresser. Without her glasses, everything looked blurry. She made out the fuzzy outline of a woman in a nurse's uniform standing beside the bed. The woman leaned down and pulled back the sheet. Marilyn got a close up glimpse of her face. She looked more Vietnamese than Filipino.

Then Marilyn saw the hypodermic needle.

"No!" She lifted her arm and twisted away. She didn't want an injection that might make her woozy for the next twenty-four hours.

"*Seen ba.*" The woman's words sounded so familiar that Marilyn didn't realize they were Vietnamese. All her attention was focused on the hypodermic needle.

"Please, *madame,*" the woman repeated in English. "Your doctor ordered morphine for pain." Her voice was low and oddly toneless.

Wide awake now, Marilyn gazed frantically around the room, hunting for Mac. Sprawled in a chair by the door, he looked as though he'd been asleep for hours.

"Mac!" Marilyn called as loudly as she could. "Wake up!" Her cry came out a hoarse screech.

The nurse seized her arm.

Marilyn heard a shuffling sound and a low grunt. Mac grabbed the woman by the shoulders. "She's . . . ah . . . not supposed to have shots." He stumbled over the words, and his voice sounded thick.

The nurse put the hypodermic syringe in a small white case on the nightstand. She snapped it closed.

"Sorry, *monsieur.* I was told to give morphine. I will check with *madame's* doctor."

"Do that." He followed her toward the door, his steps uneven.

Suddenly remembering that the nurse had spoken in Vietnamese and that she looked more Vietnamese than Filipino, Marilyn stiffened. Fear spurted through her. Was that woman really a nurse on the hotel staff?

"Stop her," she cried to Mac. "Don't let her get away."

The woman sprinted the last few steps to the door, yanked it open and slammed it shut behind her.

"Go after her." Marilyn's voice rang with alarm.

Mac jerked the door open and lurched into the hallway.

From the bed, Marilyn watched him stand motionless outside the door. In a moment he returned to the room.

"Why didn't you go after her?" she fumed.

"I'm sorry," he mumbled, his words thick. "She got away before I could catch her."

Why did he sound so strange? Marilyn's fear for herself turned into a desperate concern for Mac. Something was terribly wrong with him. Had somebody poisoned him? But if he'd been poisoned, would he have awakened when she called?

Hiding her alarm, she patted the bed. "Come and sit beside me." When he plopped down, she rubbed his hands briskly between hers—first one hand, then the other, letting her energy flow into him.

"Wake up," she said sharply. *Please, please wake up,* she prayed silently. "Wake up, Mac."

"Damn it all," he said thickly, after several agonizing minutes had crept by. "Something in that dinner I ate must have been drugged. The oldest trick in the book and I fell for it."

"Go in the bathroom and splash water on your face," she urged. "Maybe that'll help."

He shuffled across the floor. She heard the water running. When he returned, he dropped into his chair and put his head in his hands. He looked so dejected Marilyn started to climb out of the bed to go to him. Her flimsy nightgown reminded her of her near-naked condition. She sat on the edge of the bed, the sheet pulled up to cover herself.

"That woman wasn't a hotel nurse, Mac." She shivered and lay down again, pulling both the blanket and sheet over her.

He straightened. "Why do you say that?" The drug-induced fuzziness was rapidly leaving his voice.

"For one thing, she was Vietnamese, not Filipino." Marilyn tried to control her anxiety but could feel herself gasping for air. She concentrated on taking slow, even breaths.

"Are you sure?" Tensing, he leaned toward her.

"She *looked* Vietnamese, Mac. And she spoke a couple of words in Vietnamese, probably without knowing she did it. Plus, she addressed me as *madame* and you as *monsieur.* Those are French terms the Vietnamese use but not the Filipinos."

"You've convinced me." His expression was grim. "Let's find out if there are any Vietnamese nurses on the staff here."

He picked up the phone and dialed the lobby.

From his short conversation, Marilyn knew she'd guessed right. The woman didn't work for the hotel. Still shivering, she pulled the sheet and blanket tighter around her neck.

"Mac, that woman was going to kill me with whatever was in the hypodermic." She felt trapped, like a rabbit with a pack of hounds after it.

He sat down beside her on the bed. Pain glowed in his eyes. "And I almost let her get away with it. Damn! How could I be so stupid? I should have known better than to eat something I didn't order."

That he was angry with himself touched Marilyn deeply. She slid her hand from under the covers and gently patted his arm. "It wasn't your fault. Besides, you woke up in time. That's what's important."

Mac's mouth tightened into a firm, hard line. "One good thing has come out of this. Now I realize what we're up against." His eyes burned with wrathful fire.

Marilyn tensed, waiting for him to go on.

"In less than twenty-four hours, two people have tried to kill you, my food's been drugged by a phony nurse, and a second woman masquerading as a nurse has somehow gotten hold of a hotel passkey. What does that sound like to you?"

She shrugged, wondering what he was getting at. "Not like Tony Benson. He didn't even have an extra man available to follow me into the mall."

"Exactly." He leaned toward her, his eyes gleaming. "We've become the target of an organization with significant resources."

"Not the FBI?" She gasped the question, the memory of Agent Smith's accusations still fresh in her mind.

He shook his head decisively. "No way. The bureau doesn't run around assassinating innocent people. In any case, Finnegan wants to find your brother, not get rid of you. No, this is somebody else."

She took a quick sharp breath. "The ones who killed Mr. Nguyen? To keep me from finding Van?"

Mac stood and paced along the side of the bed. "It's possible, but I don't think so. You said Nguyen had been tortured. The only reason would be to make him talk. The people after you might want him dead, so he couldn't help you reach your brother. But they'd have no reason to take the risk involved in torturing him.''

"Then Benson did it." There was no doubt in Marilyn's voice.

Mac stopped pacing. He nodded his head in agreement. "That's a damned good guess. It looks like we've got two different outfits involved in this mess. Three, if we count the U.S. government. The FBI wants to find your brother and arrest him. The American Vietnamese want to find him to assassinate him. So they've hired Benson."

He paused, his hand stroking his chin. "It's the third organization that poses the real threat to us. For some reason, they want to keep us from finding Van."

Suddenly Marilyn felt overwhelmed by what he was saying. "I feel like some horrible monster is out there, waiting to pounce on us." A shudder racked her body. This couldn't be happening to her. Weird monsters didn't attack run-of-the-mill people who lived mundane lives and minded their own business.

Mac smiled at her description. "That's not a bad way to put it. One thing's for sure—the monster can't find us if we're invisible."

"What do you mean invisible? We can't just disappear."

His smile split into a roguish grin. "Yes we can, Marilyn, my lovely Miss Librarian. Tomorrow morning, that's exactly what we're going to do."

THEY LEFT THE HOTEL at nine o'clock the next morning. Mac brought the three shopping bags containing yesterday's purchases. He insisted Marilyn wear the same skirt she'd worn the past two days. With it she put on a fresh shirt, a bright yellow-and-green print, the last clean one she had.

"We want the staff to recognize us when we leave for a day of sight-seeing," he said.

Marilyn didn't argue with him. She felt more comfortable in the clothes she'd brought from San Diego than in the ruffly new dresses. It wasn't until they were settled in the back seat of the cab that she realized they wouldn't be returning to the hotel.

He grinned at her. "Anything in the room you can't live without?"

She clutched at his arm. "I can't just walk away without paying my bill."

"Didn't you use a credit card?"

"Yes, but I didn't—"

"Yes, but nothing. You can pay the bill after we get this mess straightened out."

Marilyn's stomach clenched into a tight little knot. "What about the police? Won't they arrest me if I don't come back?"

"Not if they can't find you."

"I can't do this, Mac." Marilyn fought to keep her voice from cracking. "There's got to be a more responsible way to handle this."

His mouth twisted into a cynical smile. "Not unless you want to get us both killed."

The taxi let them off in front of a small curio shop in Manila's Chinatown. Watching the cab pull away, Marilyn breathed heavily. The throbbing pain in her arm was getting worse. She hadn't wanted to take another sleep-inducing pain pill before they left the hotel. It had not been a wise decision.

Mac touched her face gently, seeming to feel her discomfort. "Your arm hurts, doesn't it?" There was compassion in his eyes.

Marilyn's heart thudded. "Like somebody's cutting it off." She managed an apologetic smile. "If I don't sit pretty soon, I'm apt to fall down."

No sooner were the words out than Marilyn felt his arm around her waist. For a brief moment she leaned against him. It felt good.

"Can you walk to that restaurant?" He nodded toward a tiny hole-in-the-wall place next to the curio shop.

Sighing, she straightened. "I think so."

Once inside, he led her to a back table where they couldn't be observed from outside. Sitting next to her, Mac faced the door. There were only ten or twelve tables. They'd see anyone who came in. Doors and windows were open. An oscillating fan moved the air, but it was still warm inside.

"Maybe you should take one of your pain pills," he said sympathetically.

"They make me sleepy." She didn't want to make things more difficult by feeling woozy and sluggish.

He handed her a pain pill. "Take it. Being sleepy's better than hurting." He ordered tea and pastries.

With a sigh, Marilyn swallowed the pill, washing it down with some water supplied by their teenage Chinese waitress.

"Now, we'll have a cup of tea while the codeine kicks in. When we're done, whoever's following us will have a chance to earn his pay."

She appreciated his confidence. "You think you can escape with a helpless woman in tow?" Her mouth curved into a smile.

"You bet. Just watch me." He smiled back at her. There wasn't a hint of anxiety in his tone.

Marilyn could hear muffled voices in the kitchen. Several sounded like children's. Apparently the entire family helped out in the restaurant.

Mac motioned to the waitress. "Do you have a little brother?" He'd heard the voices, too.

Giggling, the waitress held up three fingers.

"Three little brothers? Could you send out the oldest? I want to hire him."

She hurried away, still giggling. Mac turned to Marilyn. "How're you feeling?"

"Much better," she said truthfully.

"Good enough to follow a small boy through some back alleys? I'm betting a kid who lives here can help us lose whoever's after us."

Marilyn nodded, feeling stronger by the minute. "The tea and the codeine seem to have done their work."

A woman entered the restaurant and sat at a table near the door. Dressed in a red shirt over black slacks, she was indistinguishable from a thousand other women.

"Does she look Vietnamese?" Mac asked.

Marilyn studied her face. "She might be. She's definitely not Chinese. Everybody else in here is."

Mac's brows drew together in a frown. "Anyone out of the ordinary is suspect. We've got to assume she's keeping an eye on us."

The waitress returned with a boy about ten years old. "He is Chiang," she said.

The boy frowned. "Not Chiang. Joe. After Joe Louis."

"You gonna be a heavyweight champion, too?" Mac asked.

The boy nodded seriously. "Joe practice every day."

Eyeing his skinny frame, Marilyn admired the child's optimism.

Mac took a five- and a ten-dollar bill out of his wallet and laid them on the table. "We've got to get away from some people who are following us, Joe. This is yours if we lose them."

The boy's almond eyes widened. He reached for the cash. Mac covered the ten-dollar bill with his hand. "Five now and ten afterward."

Grinning, the boy pocketed the five. Mac returned the other bill to his wallet. He glanced toward the kitchen. "Is the back door through there?"

Joe nodded, grinning.

The woman in the red shirt was clearly watching them. When Mac turned toward the kitchen, she stood.

Mac pushed his chair back. "We've got to go. Right now. She's guessed what we're up to."

The youngster took a quick look at the woman. "Follow Joe," he ordered, darting through the rear door.

The kitchen's heat struck Marilyn in the face like a steamy wall filled with cooking smells: onion, rice and the enticing odor of meat broiling over charcoal. Iron pots bubbled on an ancient black stove. Two adults dressed in baggy dark

cotton clothes supervised five or six children, the oldest in
her late teens.

As the boy hurried by, he said something to the man, then
grinned at Mac. "He stop woman if come through kitchen."

"With Joe's family here, she probably won't try," Mac
said to Marilyn, his hand anchoring her firmly to him. "All
these places have a back way out. She and her friends will
just barge through the one next door."

Joe led them into an unpaved muddy alley behind the
restaurant. Though the rainy season was over, puddles remained from a recent shower. Dented, dirt-streaked vehicles were parked haphazardly along the perimeter. Trash
barrels overflowed with garbage. Flies buzzed everywhere.
Two gaunt children pawed hungrily through the trash,
strewing rotting food on the ground.

Marilyn turned away, sickened by the sight. The air stank
with the fetid odor of garbage.

"Get us out of here fast," Mac ordered.

Suddenly two men with guns burst through a door directly ahead of them. They were both Vietnamese.

Marilyn wheeled and began running in the opposite direction. She heard a popping sound. Mac caught her hand
again and jerked her to the side.

"Get behind that car," he said. They darted around an
ancient Chevrolet sedan on the opposite side of the alley.

Their young guide was no longer grinning. "You no tell
Joe these guys shoot at us, mistah. Worth many more dollars."

For a panic-stricken minute, Marilyn thought the boy was
going to stop right there to negotiate for more money, but
he headed toward an open door.

"Ten dollars extra," Mac said.

"Twenty," Joe yelled over his shoulder.

"Okay, twenty. Just get going."

They followed the boy into a shop filled with Chinese girls
hunched over sewing machines. Even with the doors open,
the heat was oppressive. The young women bent over the
whirring machines, their thin fingers guiding the cloth. Joe

made an excited comment in Chinese to one of them who clucked at him disapprovingly.

They emerged on a street clogged with horse-drawn carriages. Joe ran to an adjacent market, its front open to the sidewalk. A stairway at the rear led upward. Panting, they raced up it. On the roof, laundry was stretched out on racks, drying in the sun.

The boy grinned at them. "How Joe doing?" He motioned them to stay low, so they couldn't be seen from the ground.

Mac handed him twenty dollars. "Get us off this roof and into a cab, and there's another twenty where that came from."

Silently Joe pocketed the money, a satisfied grin on his face. He might be only ten, but he was as money-wise as any Shylock. He took them to a spot shaded by a taller building next to it. "You stay here. Joe see if they gone."

The boy took off for a walk around the perimeter. Marilyn sagged against the wall, lowering herself to the roof's granulated surface. She could feel sweat pouring down her back. In the hot open air, she felt exposed, vulnerable.

"Are you all right?" Mac sat down beside her, his brow creased with concern.

"Won't somebody tell those men we're up here?" Marilyn cast frightened glances around her.

"The Vietnamese and the Chinese have no love for one another, Marilyn. Nobody's going to tell them about us. If they start up here, someone will warn Joe." He smiled reassuringly. "We're probably as safe here as we'd be anywhere in Manila."

Safe. The word sounded strange, foreign somehow. "Oh, Mac, do you think we're ever going to make it home?" Her voice wavered. She'd been stabbed, threatened with a hypodermic needle, then shot at. Would she ever again live a normal life in a normal house, doing normal things? Like watching TV? Strangely, when she pictured herself in that other, normal life, Mac was sitting beside her, the way he was now, with his legs thrust out next to hers.

He seized her hand and held it. "It's not too late to make a run for the airport. Like I said, once we're back in San Diego, we can put ourselves under the bureau's protection. We'd be perfectly safe there. It would be obvious to whoever's after us that we'd stopped looking for your brother."

Mixed feelings surged through her. She knew she was risking their lives, but couldn't just leave and let her brother be killed. Resolutely, she straightened. "Something terrible will happen to Van if I don't find him." Her hands balled into fists.

Mac examined her face. Her momentary confusion had been replaced with a determined, confident look. She wasn't going to take his advice. How she could have such faith in her worthless brother was beyond Mac's comprehension. None of Mac's own siblings was worth an ounce of loyalty, let alone the life-and-death commitment Marilyn seemed willing to make.

He had to try again, harder, to get her to realize how dangerous her search was. He had to get her home, where he'd have half a chance to protect her. There was no gentle way to tell her what he suspected. "Has it occurred to you that these people after us may be connected to your brother's syndicate?"

Her eyes widened with alarm, but she didn't pull away. "If the syndicate's after us, that's all the more reason he's got to be warned. They're probably after him, too."

Mac groaned under his breath. She refused to believe the obvious—that her brother was the syndicate leader. "Maybe Van doesn't want you to find him, Marilyn. Maybe that's why his people are after us."

She jerked her hand away. "How can you say that, Mac? From what I've told you about Van, you should know he'd never try to hurt me, or anybody close to me, including you."

He pressed the length of his body against her side, being careful not to jar her bandaged arm. "I'm glad you feel close to me." He didn't let on how surprised he was that she'd said so. "The last thing I want is for your faith in your brother to come between us. But you've got to consider the possibility that he doesn't want you to find him, and that's why his syndicate's trying to stop us."

She shook her head defiantly. "Van's not the head of that syndicate, Mac. If he didn't want me to find him, he wouldn't have told me to come here."

Mac recalled the message, intercepted by the bureau, that Van had left for Marilyn on her answering machine. In it, he'd said nothing about her coming to Manila.

"Don't tell me you've been in touch with Van since he left San Diego?" Mac's astonishment was genuine.

"He left a message on my answering machine for me to call Mr. Nguyen. When I finally reached Mr. Nguyen on Monday morning, he told me to get to Manila as fast as I could. I'm sure he was following Van's instructions."

"So that's why you left in such a hurry." Slowly the pieces were falling into place.

She nodded. "He said I was in great danger."

Mac wanted to find out more, but, at that moment, their young guide returned from his walk around the roof. He squatted on his haunches, facing them. "Strangers still look for you."

"Can you see them in the street?" Mac asked.

"No. They inside shop."

"How do you know they haven't gone?"

The boy inclined his head toward a woman gathering sheets into a basket. "She tell Joe."

They stayed on the roof for more than an hour. Occasionally Joe would take off for another ten-minute patrol of the roof's perimeter, studying the street on one side and the alley on the other. While they waited, Chinese women came and went, taking dried sheets off the racks, hanging wet ones in their places. Joe spoke to each woman to learn where the Vietnamese strangers were. Finally, he announced that they had gone.

NOT UNTIL MAC WAS convinced their taxi wasn't being followed did he take Marilyn to the Mabuhay Hotel, a middle-class establishment catering to American tour groups. He registered them as a married couple from Atlanta and paid the bill with cash.

"Get some rest," he said, when they reached their room. "I'll be gone awhile arranging for some fake ID. I hope it won't take too long."

Marilyn's heart sank. She, who had always been so independent, was suddenly afraid to be alone. "Can't I come along?"

He took her in his arms and held her close, pressing her face against his chest. "You need to rest." His voice was husky with concern. "I'll go later, if that would make you feel better."

She pulled away, embarrassed by her momentary weakness. "I'm sorry, Mac. Go ahead. I'll be fine."

"You're sure?" He examined her face.

She managed a smile more confident than she felt. "I'm positive."

After a few minutes he left.

Alone, Marilyn showered and awkwardly washed and towel dried her hair with her good arm. Then, leaving her hair loose, she put on one of her new nightgowns and crawled into bed. Sighing, she sank down on the pillow. Ever since they'd left the rooftop in Chinatown, she'd had the uneasy feeling that something dreadful about her brother was being unveiled before her eyes.

Was it possible that Mac's suggestion was true? Van wouldn't try to kill her. But what about somebody else in the syndicate? Maybe somebody else wanted to keep her from talking to her brother. Could Van truly be involved in a sinister organization like that?

No. It's not possible. Then why was the FBI so certain? Why were the American Vietnamese so certain? Why was Mac so certain? *Mac.* Where was he?

Marilyn glanced at her watch. He'd been gone over an hour. This room wasn't as luxurious as the one she'd had at the Philippine Village Hotel, but it was clean and air-conditioned. It was also terribly empty. Her arm began throbbing, and she took another pain pill. Still, she couldn't fall asleep.

When three hours had passed, she gave up on sleep. Wrapping a sheet around herself, she went out onto the tiny balcony. Even five stories up, the humid air smelled of exhaust smoke. The modern skyscrapers of downtown Manila stretched out on one side. On the other, the wide Pasig River snaked its way through a maze of lower buildings, bisecting the city.

Shivering in spite of the humid heat, she went back inside the room and climbed into bed. Propping pillows behind her, she stared at the wall.

What if something had happened to Mac? Even worse, what if he'd decided to abandon her here in the Mabuhay Hotel? She couldn't blame him if he did. Because of her he'd been drugged and shot at. And when he'd offered to take her home where they'd both be safe, she'd turned him down.

What would I do without him?

She heard footsteps outside. Moving the pillows to one side, she turned toward the door, a relieved smile on her lips.

A key grated in the lock. The door swung open.

The man standing on the threshold wasn't Mac.

Marilyn's smile vanished. Panic swept over her, and she jerked the sheet up around her chin. Coming through the door toward her was a bald stranger she'd never seen before.

Chapter Thirteen

The man entering the room didn't look especially threatening, but that did nothing to relieve Marilyn's panic-stricken paralysis. His dark trousers were wrinkled and a little too short. The embroidered white cotton shirt he was wearing needed pressing. His wire rim glasses were lopsided, giving his face an odd, unbalanced look.

But the most interesting thing about him was his hair, or rather, his lack of it. Except for a fringe around his ears, he was almost totally bald. His bushy eyebrows and dark, muttonchop sideburns gave Marilyn the feeling that what should have been on top of his head had somehow been misplaced.

The apparition approached the bed. Instinctively she scooted to the other side, as far from him as she could get. The sheet slipped, leaving her shoulders bare.

"You look like you've just seen a ghost," he said.

It was Mac's voice. Marilyn felt such enormous relief that her muscles seemed to collapse. She fell back against the pillows. "Mac, is it you?" Her voice squeaked like a child's.

"Of course it's me. Who else has the key to our room?" He tossed a couple of packages on the bed. "Maybe I overdid it with the fake sideburns."

Her vast sense of relief made her slightly hysterical. She burst out laughing. "Who're you supposed to be?"

He bowed deeply, from the waist. "Doctor Henri La-Fitte of Paris. You aren't supposed to break out in peals of laughter every time you look at me."

She quivered, trying to hold back her mirth. "Who am I?"

"You, *madame,* are my half Vietnamese, half American wife. Since I speak French and you, fluent Vietnamese, it seemed like a good cover."

Her laughter died in her throat. "How did you know I speak Vietnamese, Mac?"

Pushing his wire rim glasses to the top of his shaved head, he sat down on the foot of the bed. "I'm one of those people who knows everything about you and likes you anyway." His smile was almost apologetic.

"You've seen my security file, haven't you?" She should have known. But somehow that hadn't occurred to her. Strangely, it didn't bother her. It made her feel closer to him, if anything.

He nodded. "You know what my first reaction was, after I'd gone through your file?"

She shook her head, half-afraid of what he was going to say.

"That you couldn't possibly be a spy. Your record was too clean." Frowning, he pressed his lips together. "Damn it all. I should have trusted my intuition and made Finnegan eat his dirty little operation."

"I'm glad you didn't. If you'd trusted your intuition, I never would have met you." Amazed at her boldness, Marilyn pulled the sheet over her bare shoulders.

What was she saying? Here she was in bed in her nightgown, alone in a hotel room with this man, registered as his wife, and she'd as good as told him she was overjoyed about it. Warmth surged through her at the thought. She felt herself blushing and hated herself for not having better control.

He raised a bushy eyebrow and smiled at her, a tender look in his eyes. "Much as I like what you're saying, if you hadn't gotten involved with me and the FBI, you probably wouldn't be in this mess.''

He was right, she realized suddenly. What had Van said in his message? That she was in danger because she'd *gone to the government*. She never would have done that except for the FBI's plot.

You are in terrible danger because you have gone to the government. Her skin prickled. How could Van have known that? He couldn't. Not unless he was connected to the syndicate and knew somebody in the organization was after her. Marilyn felt as though someone had kicked her in the stomach. Maybe the syndicate was watching the FBI office in San Diego and saw her go in. Maybe somebody thought she was informing on the syndicate and was after her now to shut her up.

That meant the FBI was right, that Van was part of a vile organization that preyed on its fellow Vietnamese. Even worse, it meant he might have something to do with these attempts on her life. Her suspicion made her feel sick. *It can't be true,* she thought, ashamed for even thinking such a thing. *There has to be some other explanation.*

Watching her from the foot of the bed, Mac saw her frown. Was it because of what he'd said about getting her into this mess? She seemed so helpless, peering at him through those scholarly glasses, her long hair trailing over the sheet. It was the first time Mac had seen her with her hair down. He wanted to feel it beneath his hands while he held her pressed tightly against him....

Aggravated with his errant thoughts, he bent his head toward her. ''I'm glad we met, too, Marilyn. I just wish I hadn't been the one to get you involved in that stupid sting operation.'' His voice sounded raspy to him, and lower than usual. He inched closer to her on the bed.

She gazed at him reflectively. ''If it hadn't been you, it would probably have been another agent, Mac. Your Mr. Finnegan was out to trap me, one way or another.'' She shivered. ''Think what a mess I'd be in if somebody like

Agent Smith had been playing the IRA terrorist. I'd be here in Manila all by myself. I might even be dead."

He couldn't bear the thought. "Don't say that, Marilyn." He moved nearer to her, so near he could smell the floral scent of the shampoo she'd used.

He reached for her, wanting to comfort her, to feel her slender body pressed against him, to let her know he would never let anybody hurt her. She leaned toward him, and the sheet she'd been holding slid down. His gaze dropped from her eyes, to her bare shoulders, to her small, well-formed breasts, the hardened nipples pressing tautly against her thin cotton nightgown. The sight turned his urge to comfort her into something more primitive. Heat rippled through his loins, and he felt the beginnings of an unwanted arousal.

God help him, he wanted her. Hair, eyes, mind, heart, body and soul, he wanted her. An awareness he'd been suppressing for the past two weeks surged through him.

But there was a danger here. Marilyn Wainwright wasn't someone he could enjoy for a night or two and then forget. He had feelings for her that he wasn't yet ready to acknowledge. Instinctively he knew that intimacy with her meant commitment. Mac had spent a lifetime resisting commitment. He wanted no relationships like those he'd seen in his own family, with the fighting, the unwanted children, the deliberate hurting. How had this waif of a woman—who wasn't his type at all—managed to get past all his barriers?

He didn't know. What he did know was that his wanting was a kind he'd never felt before, a kind that couldn't be denied. He leaned toward her. In one motion, she came into his arms. Gently he rocked her back and forth, his cheek against hers, his hands stroking her hair. He was struck by the clean, fresh scent of her. Then he covered her mouth with his. Her lips, moist and warm, welcomed him. He traced their inner fullness with his tongue, savoring their sweetness.

Without releasing her, he slid his hand along her neck, to her bare shoulder, then to her breast. Shuddering, he rubbed the palm of his hand over the hard nub of her nipple. He felt her tense, move backward. Reluctantly he let her go. "Are you okay?" he whispered, his voice thick. He cradled her face in his hands and stared into her eyes. Her vulnerable, open look made him want to shield her from harm.

"No. Yes. I'm all mixed-up, Mac." Her face showed her confusion. She pulled the sheet up, covering herself again.

"What's wrong, darling lady?" He didn't try to hide his desire. "Is it this disguise I've got on? Underneath, I'm the same old Mac."

"That's just it." Her voice was almost a whisper. "I'm still not sure who that is. Your personality seems to change with each new role you play. When I think I'm getting to know you, somebody else shows up I don't even recognize."

He forced himself to back away from her. For a moment he felt pain, even though his logical mind understood how it must seem to her. Sighing, he said, "The changes are only skin-deep, but I guess you don't know me well enough yet to appreciate that."

Her violet eyes regarded him with unmistakable anguish. "I'm not sure I ever will. As long as I don't trust you, I—"

"You still don't trust me?" he interrupted. "After all we've been through in the past two days? What more can I do to show you I'm on your side?" There was a roughness in his voice.

"Oh, I know you're on my side." She tilted her head quizzically. "What I'm not sure of is why."

"Then I'll tell you." His voice was tender, almost a murmur. "Because I care about you, Marilyn Wainwright. I don't want anything to happen to you. After this is all over, I want us to be together. Really get to know each other." He reached for her hands, gripping them tightly.

Doubt crossed her face. "How can we do that, when you're in Washington, and I'm in San Diego?"

Mac took a deep breath and let go of his inhibitions. "I don't work for the bureau anymore, remember? When this is all over, I'll move to San Diego."

Her doubt was replaced with wide-eyed amazement.

"You really mean it?" Marilyn felt her face flush. He sounded so serious. Would he actually do it?

"Why not?" He grinned the roguish grin she knew so well. Somehow it didn't look out of place on the bald Dr. Henri LaFitte.

"I like to swim and the beaches are great," he continued. "So's the climate."

"San Diego sounds like just the place for you, Dr. LaFitte," she teased, to give them both time to think. She sensed that, with his talk of a move, he'd made a commitment of sorts, and it bothered him. She'd already guessed that he didn't make commitments easily.

"Maybe Dr. LaFitte can set up a medical practice near the beach," she went on, still in a teasing tone. "Combine business with pleasure, as it were."

His expression turned serious again, but a corner of his mouth was tugged upward in a slight smile. "Since you're Dr. LaFitte's wife, I'd counted on you to—er—provide for us both until I found a suitable position."

He'd switched to a French accent that was almost as soothing as his Irish brogue had been. She rewarded him with a winning smile. "Get us home all in one piece, my dear doctor, and I'll gladly support you. If I still have a job, that is."

His grin flashed briefly, lighting his features. "Hey, you're playing the doctor's wife like a pro. It's easy to be somebody else. All you have to do is make up a story about Mrs. LaFitte and then act the way she'd act. That's what we've got to do now."

"So tell me about Dr. LaFitte's Vietnamese-American wife." Marilyn dropped her teasing tone.

He was silent for a moment. When he spoke, his eyes narrowed speculatively. "Let's say you were raised in Vietnam and met this French doctor—me—when you were a teenager. The French have strong ties to Indochina from their colonial days. I was helping set up a hospital in your province."

"What's my name?" There was a decided lilt to her voice. She was enjoying this.

"You tell me. This is your story."

Her brow furrowed with concentration. "It's Li. I've always thought that was a pretty Vietnamese name."

"Good. How many children do we have?" Mac stared at her, brows lifted.

"Two boys. They're in school in France." She paused, then went on, amazed at how easy it was. "After we married, my dear husband persuaded me to go to school while he was working for a hospital in San Francisco. That's why I speak English with an American accent."

"You've got the idea," he said, sharing her enthusiasm. "If anybody says anything to you in French, don't try to answer. I'll make excuses for you."

He handed her a package. "You're going to have to wear high heels. Here are some shoes that ought to fit. I checked your sizes while you were asleep."

Frowning, she examined them. "I'm not used to high heels, Mac. They don't suit me."

He nodded patiently. "That's why you've got to wear them. When we leave this room, Marilyn Wainwright stays behind."

Mac passed her another package. Opening it, she discovered cosmetics designed to make her skin color look more Oriental, along with some black hair dye.

Marilyn held up the box containing the dye. "Is this absolutely necessary?"

He grinned mischievously. "You're more familiar with Oriental appearances than I am."

She groaned. "I hate to do it. The color won't grow out for years."

"We don't have to go through with this," he reminded her gently. "Say the word and I'll get the embassy on the phone. I'm betting we can be on our way to San Diego within twenty-four hours."

How wonderful it would be to go home.

Marilyn glanced from the small box in her hand to Mac's face. His hazel eyes burned with sincerity. He wanted to take her home. She was convinced of it. In that moment she almost trusted him.

Almost. A shred of doubt remained. Was he playing another game with her that might somehow hurt Van? She didn't doubt her brother was in danger. She had to talk to him, to learn the truth. She shook the box in her hand. "I'm going to find Van, Mac. If it takes dyeing my hair, so be it." Her face was resolute.

Mac leaned back with a sigh of resignation. "One more thing. Let's take a look at your dark glasses. I seem to recall they're the same shape as your everyday ones."

Her purse was on the table beside the bed. She took out her sunglasses and handed them to him.

"These won't do," he said, examining them. "They look too much like Marilyn Wainwright. Here. Try these." He handed her a pair with the frame slanted at the upper corners.

She put them on and gasped with alarm. "I can't see a thing, Mac. They've got no correction. Without glasses, I'm so nearsighted I might run into the side of a bus."

"We'll get you some brown-tinted contacts to wear under them. We can't have you running into the side of a bus, now can we?" He examined her face. "How are you feeling? Strong enough to get started with all this?" He waved his hand in a vague gesture that took in the packages scattered on the bed.

"After the hours I've spent in this room? You bet I'm strong enough."

"Good. I'd like to get out of this hotel as soon as it's dark."

Wrapping the sheet around her, Marilyn went into the bathroom. After she'd left the room, Mac switched on the TV and positioned himself in a chair facing it. The set was tuned to an English language channel featuring an American talk show. He kept his eyes on the screen, but his mind kept wandering to Marilyn.

She was probably still in her flimsy little nightgown, its material clinging loosely to her slender form. He pictured her with her hair flowing over her bare shoulders, her breasts clearly visible through the transparent fabric. A ribbon of a belt cinched her tiny waist. Below, her hips flared, and beneath them, perfectly formed legs. God, how he wanted her.

He heard the bathroom door open. Then, the air stirred behind him and he smelled the strong, not unpleasant, earthy scent of the hair dye.

"Don't turn around," she said. "This gunk takes twenty-five minutes to work. I might as well watch TV with you as sit in the bathroom all by myself."

"After all we've been through, a little hair dye isn't going to bother me." He was itching to see her and had to resist an almost overpowering compulsion to glance behind him.

"I'm still in my nightgown, Mac. If you insist on turning around, I'll have to sit in the bathroom while this dye works."

"Fine." He kept his eyes resolutely trained on the TV set.

He heard the bed squeak when she sat on it, heard an enticing rustle when she pulled the sheet up to cover her legs. He pictured her delicate face fringed in black from the dye, her glasses perched on her nose, her lathered hair piled up on her head. She probably had a towel wrapped around her shoulders to keep the dye off her neck.

Lucky towel, he thought irrationally.

Those twenty-five minutes were the longest Mac had ever lived through. Striving to earn her trust, he didn't turn around.

MARILYN FROWNED at the strange reflection looking back at her from the full-length mirror in their hotel room. Straight black hair hung below her shoulders. Her skin had a darker, rosier tone to it. The embroidered pink dress she was wearing, with its big sleeves and cinched middle, made her shoulders look broader than they were, her waist narrower. Her legs were bare, her feet shod in sandals with heels at least three inches high. Raspberry-red toenails peeked through the straps across her arches. At Mac's insistence, she'd painted her fingernails the same garish color.

"I thought the idea was for us to disappear," she said. "In this outfit I stand out like a peacock in with a bunch of barnyard chickens."

"The idea is for Marilyn Wainwright and George Mac-Intyre to disappear. You've got to admit you look like a different person from the one who checked in to this hotel."

She frowned again. "Maybe so, but nobody will ever believe I'm Vietnamese. Not with my eyes." She examined them in the mirror. The makeup she'd applied, to make them look more slanted and the lids heavier, made a little difference but not much.

"You're half American, remember?" Mac said. "Wait till we get you the brown contact lenses." He paced around her, eyeing her slender form. "You're a mighty good-looking woman, Li LaFitte."

"Don't tell me you like me better in this outlandish costume?" Marilyn kept her tone light to mask her disappointment. She'd seen the stunned approval in his eyes when he got his first glimpse of her.

His expression turned instantly serious. "I'd be lying if I said you weren't gorgeous in that outfit. But no. I don't like you better dressed this way. The woman I chased halfway around the world was wearing low-heeled shoes, glasses and no makeup."

Mollified, Marilyn smiled at her reflection in the glass. Maybe the disguise wasn't as outlandish as she'd thought.

Leaving the key on the dresser, they slipped out of the hotel through a rear exit so they wouldn't have to go through the lobby. A short time later they checked in at still another hotel, registering as Dr. and Mrs. Henri LaFitte of Paris.

During the next couple of hours, Marilyn learned something about doing business in Asia. Apparently one could buy almost anything at any hour if he or she had enough cash. Marilyn was surprised at how adept Mac was at greasing palms.

Their first stop was at the optician's. In less time than she believed possible, she was walking out of the shop wearing well-fitting brown contact lenses. Their next stop was at a small photo shop in Quiapo District. Passport Pictures Our Specialty read the sign. The young proprietor made up the nameboard and seated Marilyn in front of his camera. Brusquely, he told her to take off her dark glasses.

She glanced at Mac and he nodded. Hesitantly she pulled them off, squinting in the bright light. *It's never going to work,* she thought dismally.

The photographer fiddled with his camera. Surprisingly he paid no special attention to her. "Look this way please, ma'am." Marilyn didn't smile. A bulb flashed once, then again.

"These will be ready in two minutes," the clerk said, disappearing behind a curtain.

"Don't forget your glasses, darling," Mac said, in his French accent. Quickly she put them back on.

A moment later the photographer handed five copies of each print to Marilyn. The woman in the picture didn't look Oriental, exactly, but neither did she look like Marilyn Wainwright.

"How about you, sir?" the clerk asked.

Mac shook his head. "*Non.* She is the one who lost her passport." He smiled fondly at Marilyn, looking for all the world like an indulgent husband.

The photographer grinned. "How about a portrait of the two of you together?"

"No, we're in a hurry." Mac handed the man some cash.

"Why not, Ma—Henri?" Marilyn said, biting her tongue. "The picture would be a nice souvenir, something to show the boys when we get back to Paris."

Mac turned to the photographer. "Can it be done right now, *s'i vous plaît?* We don't want to come back for it."

The little man beamed. "Yes. Right now. A beautiful eight-by-ten color photograph."

"And we'd like to buy the negative, too."

"That can be arranged, sir." The photographer replaced the chair Marilyn had used with a bench. "Sit down, please."

Taking off her dark glasses, she sat next to Mac, enjoying the secure feel of his arm around her waist. His body heat, emitting a faint musky smell, penetrated the thin cotton of his embroidered shirt. He'd showered that afternoon in their room, before leaving on his shopping expedition, but the water hadn't washed away all his scent. Marilyn was glad. She snuggled closer to him.

"Good," the photographer said. "Look at the camera."

Marilyn didn't. With her head half-turned, she looked at Mac instead. The instant the bulb flashed, he glanced toward her. The photo that resulted was of a devoted couple basking in their devotion to one another. *Of course, the picture's a lie,* Marilyn thought. It looked nothing like either one of them. Nonetheless, there was something about it that made her feel wistful.

Washington, D.C.

CHARLES FINNEGAN PICKED up the secure phone and punched in the code for the U.S. Embassy in Manila. When someone answered, he asked for Neil Warner. Warner had been assisting with the bureau's operation against the syndicate ever since Marilyn Wainwright got herself involved in a murder investigation.

While he waited, Finnegan eyed the note in his hand. "We have a problem. Call ASAP," the note read. Finnegan grunted sourly. So Warner had run into a problem, had he? So what else was new?

The embassy official came on the line almost immediately. "I'm sorry to have to tell you this," he said, after Finnegan had identified himself. "The agency boys lost MacIntyre and Wainwright."

For an instant Finnegan didn't trust himself to answer. Then he exploded. "Damn it all, man, how could they lose two round eyes in a city full of Orientals?"

"The woman got stabbed, and MacIntyre—"

"Stabbed!" Finnegan jumped out of his chair. "Who did it?"

Silence. Then Warner cleared his throat. "You didn't ask, but she wasn't badly hurt, Mr. Finnegan. The wound was in the fleshy part of her left arm."

Another longer silence. Finnegan plopped back down in his chair. "So who did it, Warner?"

"The agency says somebody in Vietnam's behind it. They think MacIntyre got scared and took her undercover to hide. He probably can't get her out of the Philippines, though, Mr. Finnegan. You remember that murder she was involved in? The local cops are watching the airports."

Finnegan grunted again. "When MacIntyre wants to leave, he'll get her out of there. Cops or no cops. What's this about somebody in Vietnam being behind the attack? Are you talking about the Government of Vietnam or somebody else in the country?"

"Our source couldn't tell us."

Typical State Department answer, Finnegan thought cynically. "If there's a connection between Hanoi and the syndicate, we've got more trouble than we thought."

"The agency station chief here in Manila's pretty excited about the possible connection," Warner returned. "His boys are doing their damnedest to find both Van Wainwright and his sister."

"Watch the classifieds, Warner."

"I beg your pardon?"

Finnegan sighed. Why were these foreign service people so dense? "The little lady likes to advertise in the classifieds. That's how she drummed up research business in San Diego. I'm betting Van Wainwright's in Manila. Since somebody killed their contact, Wainwright's sister might try to reach him through an ad in one of the English language newspapers."

Warner promised he'd assign somebody to read the classifieds.

"Look for anybody trying to get together with someone else," Finnegan added, implying that Warner couldn't figure it out for himself.

After he'd hung up, Finnegan returned to his desk and dialed the bureau's San Diego office on his open line.

"Any reason you can't take off for a week or two?" he asked Dan Moschella, after he heard the big man's voice.

"I'm always ready to go, you know that, Mr. Finnegan," Moschella said smoothly.

"Get a flight to D.C. as soon as you can. I've got a special job for you. Brief you on the hush-hush stuff when you get here."

What Finnegan planned was highly unusual, too unusual to be talked about on the phone or sent over insecure fax lines. Dan Moschella, with his down-to-earth, somewhat amoral approach to his work, was exactly the right man for the unorthodox operation Finnegan had in mind.

Chapter Fourteen

A rock band played loud, brassy music in a room filled with smoke and the scent of expensive perfume. Marilyn and Mac sipped white wine at a tiny table across from the big, square, dance floor, where a mass of young bodies writhed to rhythms punctuated by heavy drumbeats. Shiny balls and Christmas tinsel hung overhead, a glittery reminder that the Philippines was a Christian nation, the only one in Southeast Asia.

Marilyn had suggested stopping for a glass of wine after dinner because, secretly, she wasn't ready to face the challenge of their small hotel room with its one double bed. Mac had asked for a larger room, but there hadn't been one available. It had been too late to find another hotel catering to French visitors.

How were they going to manage in that little room? Mac had had very little rest for days. She couldn't expect him to sleep on the floor. Neither could she imagine the two of them lying chastely side by side in bed. The mere thought set her pulse to hammering and made her cheeks flush pink. After what had happened this afternoon, the attraction between them was obvious. She wouldn't be able to resist him again.

What *was* she going to do? *Stop worrying and enjoy the moment,* she told herself sternly, glancing at the throbbing life around her. Who would have thought she'd ever find herself in a place like this, the kind of place she avoided like the plague in her real life? Not only was she here, but she was surprised to find herself liking it. The air seemed charged with an electric tension that heightened her senses. Was it because she'd been attacked and almost killed? Was this why people took risks? To savor the sweetness of life after they'd faced their challenges and survived? Or was it because Mac was smiling at her across the table? She glanced at him.

"Do you like it?" He inclined his head around the room. "I understand this is a favorite hangout for the younger members of the diplomatic corps."

She broke into a wide smile. "What I like most is not having somebody take potshots at me."

Mac surveyed the room again, his bald head turning in a slow arc. "We'll have to keep our eyes open, of course, but for now we seem to have lost whoever was using us for target practice."

Their table was against a wall near the entrance. The couple next to them, a dark-skinned girl in a very short skirt and a fair-haired young man wearing a hip-length embroidered shirt like Mac's, were leaning very close to one another. While Marilyn watched, the man took the girl's face in his hands and kissed her. From the reverent way he touched her, Marilyn guessed this was a love affair, not a casual encounter.

She sighed. What was happening to her? Two weeks ago that scene would have annoyed her. Tonight she felt only a bittersweet sense of empathy with the young lovers.

"I'm starting to like being Li LaFitte," Marilyn said. "She enjoys life more than I ever did."

"Don't like her too much," Mac advised. "One of these days you'll have to leave her behind."

Marilyn studied his face, with its high forehead, dark eyebrows and sideburns. It was a face totally different from that of the college professor she'd worked with at the Hotel del Coronado, and from the FBI special agent who had rescued her from the Manila police. Yet, underneath a shallow layer of camouflage, weren't they all the same man?

"Why, Mac?" she asked. "Why do I have to leave her behind? Isn't part of you in all these characters you play? And part of them in you, when the playing's done?"

Mac chose his next words carefully. "I'm in them, of course. And I suppose, over the years, I've adopted some of the characteristics of the personalities I've played. But I've never let them change my perception of myself, or who I really am."

"And just who is that?" Eyes sober, she probed his face.

He reached across the table and caught her hands in his. "I'm the man who loves you and wants to spend the rest of his life getting to know you better." Mac was surprised at how easily the words came. God help him, it was the truth. "Darling lady, I want to grow old with you."

He saw her eyes widen, heard her quick gasp of amazement. Did she believe him? He sensed that she still didn't trust him, not completely. Would that ruin his chances with her?

"You're still pretending, aren't you Mac? Because we're playing a married couple?" Her hopeful expression reassured him. He knew she *wanted* to believe what he was saying.

He raised her hands to his lips, kissed them and felt them tremble. "There's nothing phony about the way I feel for you, Marilyn. Look behind this disguise. See a man who wants you more than life, who will do anything to keep you safe."

The pounding music increased in volume. Dumbfounded by what Mac had said, Marilyn didn't try to make herself heard over the brassy noise. Could it be true that he loved her?

Her heart sang with delight at the thought. Then logic took over. No matter how he felt about her, he might still be working for the bureau. As long as there was the slightest chance of that, she couldn't trust him with Van's life. With her own, yes. Hadn't Mac already saved her not once, but three times in the past two days?

She studied the planes of his face in the semidarkness. What an attractive man he was, even with his hair shaved off and the bushy sideburns. She caught her breath. Something about the intent way he was staring at her reminded her of the roguish IRA terrorist, ready to risk everything for his grand cause. The slight tilt of his head recalled the serious college professor gazing across the table at her over a bowl of yellow roses. His hopeful smile was the same one she'd seen on his lips outside the police station, when he'd asked to take her back to the hotel.

They were all the same man. Peering at him through the smoky haze, Marilyn wondered why she'd thought there was such a big difference. Underneath the cover personalities, he was Mac. The same yesterday, today and forever. The man who loved her. *The man she loved.* Finally Marilyn admitted it to herself. Whether he called himself McDonough, MacIntyre, or LaFitte—she loved him. Whether he had red hair, or black or no hair at all—she loved him. And would as long as she lived.

The deafening noise abated, and she leaned toward him, her eyes warm with emotion. "I feel the same way you do, Mac."

An eager, hopeful look replaced the uncertainty his face had held. His hands tightened around hers.

"I love you, too, Mac." To Marilyn's own ears, her voice rang like a paean. Gone was the squeaky shrillness she hated. "Before, I was confused about your cover personalities. I thought I was in love with an IRA terrorist and it terrified me. I was still terrified when I found out who you really are, because I thought I'd lost you."

He gripped her hands until they tingled. "You didn't lose me, darling. All you did was uncover the authentic version."

Marilyn felt a warm glow flow through her. "I finally figured that out. A couple of minutes ago I didn't even see that disguise you're wearing. You were the same old Mac you've always been."

He beckoned the waitress. "Let's get out of here."

Outside, the night air was humid, the street almost as crowded as during the day. Laughing, they joined hands and ran through a brightly lit arcade smelling of popcorn and french fries, to the next avenue where Mac flagged a horse-drawn calesa.

In the rig, listening to the clop-clopping of the pony, he hugged her, being careful not to jostle her sore arm. "I feel like I've just won the lottery. I finally realized how I felt about you, but didn't dare hope you felt the same." He nuzzled her face.

"I wasn't sure," she confessed, loving the feel of his skin against hers. "I guess I was pretty mixed up until everything came together in my mind. Believe it or not, when I became Li LaFitte..."

Tightening his grip on her arm, he put his finger over his lips and pointed at the back of the driver, seated on a pedestal box in front of them. He saw the alarm in her eyes and cursed himself for reminding her of their danger. On this, of all nights, he wanted her to feel safe, protected.

"Anyway, when I changed into this outfit—" she glanced down at her dress's pink skirt, at her bare legs, at her high-heeled sandals "—I understood how you could act and look differently, but still be the same person underneath."

He slid his arm around her shoulders. "Actors do it all the time." There was a faint glint of humor in his eyes.

She snuggled closer. A thoughtful smile brightened her expression. "But there's never any doubt what an actor's up to. He's entertaining an audience. With you, if your victim guesses you're acting, it ruins your whole show."

He turned toward her, so that his mouth was very close to her ear. "What you're saying is that you didn't like being fooled, but you're going to forgive me because I'm such a nice guy." His voice was a low murmur. "And because I love you."

Her answering smile lit up her whole face.

IN THEIR LITTLE ROOM, with the door bolted, Mac took Marilyn in his arms. The warmth of his body was so male, so protective, that she was overcome with yearning for him. Her whole being throbbed with wanting.

"After what happened this afternoon, I don't trust myself in the same bed with you." He nuzzled the hair on top of her head. "If you don't mind giving up a couple blankets, I'll sack out on the floor."

"You don't have to trust yourself," she whispered.

Mac caught her face between his hands. The skin on her cheeks and throat came alive where he touched her. His gaze was so intense she felt transparent, like he could see what she was feeling.

"Are you sure, darling?" he asked, after a breathless moment. "God knows I want you, but we don't have to rush things."

His willingness to wait made Marilyn even more convinced. "I'm sure," she whispered. She felt her knees weaken as he bent toward her.

Crushing her to him, he brought his lips close to hers, brushing them with nibbling kisses.

Waves of desire coursed through her. She put her arms around him, let her hands feel his sinewy muscles through his thin Philippine shirt. He pulled her closer. His lips left hers to caress her neck.

Hot lava flowed through her at the warmth of his breath on her skin. She delighted in the pressure of his hard chest against her tender flesh. "Yes, I'm sure," she said again, her voice breathless.

Mac moved his mouth over her cheeks and eyelids, as though touching would burn her image into his memory. His lips recaptured hers, more demanding this time.

Standing on tiptoe, she melted into him, her mouth a willing harbor for the gentle probing of his tongue. An incredible need overtook her. Sensing it, Mac scooped her into his arms and carried her to the bed.

Marilyn wasn't sure exactly how it happened, but moments later their flimsy tropical clothes were piled on the room's one chair. The light was off. Mac was lying on the bed with her, his body half covering hers. She could feel the heat of him course down the entire length of her.

"You do believe I love you?" he asked, his voice a thick whisper.

"I believe you." Her voice trembled with yearning. Her fingers moved over his face, over the false sideburns he'd applied so he could better protect her.

"Now—slowly, easily—you're going to see how much." He lowered his mouth to hers while his hands began an arousing exploration of her soft flesh. Then his mouth followed the same sensuous trail.

When Marilyn's desire was so intense that she thought she'd go mad, he took her to a place she'd never been before, a velvet-lined garden lit with exploding stars. Love flowed in her like warm honey, and she knew the flooding of uncontrollable joy. In her limited experience, no other man had come close to releasing the thrilling sensations she'd just felt. Had it been the same for him?

"No, don't move," she said, when he started to turn over.

Obediently, Mac lay still, his hand stroking her long hair. "I feel like I just got shot out of a cannon." There was an awed huskiness to his voice.

"I know." She trailed little kisses down his face.

Minutes later, their bodies still naked and moist from their lovemaking, they lay facing each other in the darkness.

Mac slid his arm around her slender shoulders. He winced when he touched the bandage on her arm. "Damn. I didn't hurt you, did I?"

In the heat of passion, he'd completely forgotten about her wound. Her ardor had astounded him. It had wiped everything out of his consciousness except his desire for her.

She sighed in pleasant exhaustion. "My arm's the farthest thing from my mind right now—and no, you didn't hurt it. It feels just fine."

"I'll take a close look when I change the bandage tomorrow." He pulled her close. "But, tonight, Mrs. LaFitte, your husband wants you to know how much he appreciates you." Surprisingly, thinking of himself as Marilyn's husband didn't dredge up the usual painful memories of his early family life.

Marilyn giggled. "I knew I was going to enjoy being Li LaFitte, but I didn't realize how much."

There was a long silence, then she added—somewhat pensively Mac thought—"I wonder what it would be like to really be someone like Madame LaFitte, to feel safe and secure with a man you loved and trusted."

Mac didn't miss her meaning, though he doubted she was aware she'd given herself away. *She might love me, but she still doesn't trust me,* he thought, fighting a wave of discouragement. It was going to take time to overcome her mistrust. He'd simply have to be patient.

He squeezed her arm with his hand. "In time you'll know exactly how it feels to trust me."

A disturbing thought surged into his mind, a thought that would haunt him during the rest of their days in Manila.

If she refuses to trust me, how in God's name can I protect her?

MARILYN SLEPT THAT NIGHT snuggled against Mac's long wiry body. In the morning, after he came back from the bathroom, she smiled up at him and patted the empty space beside her. "Please don't get up yet." She needed to reassure herself that he was real, that what had happened between them last night wasn't just another move in some cat-and-mouse game they were playing.

He slid beneath the covers and kissed her deeply, until their need for each other was as great as it had been last night. Trembling, she felt an overpowering joy along with her shuddering ecstasy.

"It was better than last night," she murmured.

He smoothed her tousled hair. "It's going to keep getting better and better."

Suddenly, they were gazing at each other, realizing they shared an extraordinary gift.

"I'm never going to let you get away, Mrs. LaFitte," Mac declared, his voice a husky whisper.

Marilyn offered him a slow, shy smile. "Whatever makes you think I'd want to go, Doctor LaFitte?" *It's going to work out,* she thought, her heart singing. *I won't have to go to Bangkok alone after all.*

FOR BREAKFAST that morning they ate steak and eggs and thick slices of toast at a hotel restaurant a few blocks from their own modest establishment. When they were finished eating, Marilyn stared at Mac over her coffee. Instead of his dressy Philippine shirt, called a barong Tagalog, he wore a plain white cotton shirt, perfect for his morning task.

Leaving her pink dress for the hotel maid to launder, Marilyn had put on the yellow one she'd bought. Lord, had it been only yesterday? She leaned across the table toward him. "Do you really think you'll be able to get us French passports, just like that?" She snapped her fingers.

"Trust me." Mac smiled cynically. "There's a big black market for them. As long as I've got U.S. passports to trade and good old American green for added incentive, I'll be able to buy us French ones with no trouble."

Marilyn sighed. "It's all so illegal. I can't believe we're doing these things. We've got the police in two countries after us, and now we're trafficking in stolen passports. Where's it going to end?"

He took a long swallow of coffee. "Wherever we find your brother."

Marilyn heard the determination in his voice. She tried to read his expression. "You still think Van's the head of that syndicate, don't you Mac?"

"Everything that's happened so far seems to point that way. I hope you're not going to be too disappointed when you find out the truth." His eyes softened with compassion. "We're going to find out, you know."

"Yes, I..." Marilyn almost told him about the address in Bangkok, the address she'd found along with Mr. Toan Nguyen's, but something held her back. She swallowed her words.

Mac stared at her intently. She shrugged to hide her confusion. "I'm sure we'll find him. And I'm not going to be disappointed when we do. He'll be able to explain everything."

"I hope you're right." He didn't sound convinced.

Mac seemed so sure of Van's guilt. Later, alone in their room while she waited for him to come back with the French passports, Marilyn wondered if that's why she hadn't told him about the address. No, she decided, she hadn't told him because there was no need to, not yet anyway. They were stuck in Manila for a day or two, until her arm completely healed. She'd tell him when she had to.

Meantime, there was a reasonable chance Van was right here. If so, he knew about the events surrounding Mr. Nguyen's death. He must be aware that she was here, too. But he'd never be able to find her in her new identity as Li LaFitte.

She sat on the bed with her arms around her knees, thinking. Van knew she'd used the classified ads to get research jobs. Might he not guess she'd use them to find him? In any case, what would be the harm of running an ad? If the Manila newspapers carried such ads...

Their room was on the fifth floor. Marilyn took the elevator down to the cubbyhole of a lobby and bought a copy of an English language newspaper called the *Manila Monitor*. Leafing through it, she spotted a slim section devoted to small ads. Most of them listed phone numbers to call or addresses to visit. That was going to be a problem, she realized. She couldn't reveal her new name or the name of this hotel in a newspaper ad. Listing a box number for a reply seemed risky because she'd have to make daily visits to the box to check for a response. Finally, she decided to meet him somewhere.

She returned to the room and scribbled some notes. After a couple of false starts, she came up with:

Collector with winning picture game—Meet me at Rizal Monument Two p.m. Thursday

The ad would run for three mornings, if she got it in right away. Van would understand it, she was certain. He'd used the same words in the message he'd left on her answering machine. And the message was obtuse enough so that nobody else could identify either her or Van from it.

A statement in the newspaper said payment for ads was required in advance. She'd have to deliver it in person. Mac had given her strict instructions not to leave their hotel room, but this was a necessity. Besides, with any luck she'd be back before he returned. After a quick check of her makeup in the bathroom mirror, she headed downstairs to call a taxi.

MARILYN WAS GONE. Mac sensed it as soon as he pushed the door to their room open. His first panicky thought was that she'd left him to set out on her own search. Then he saw her cosmetics on the top of the dresser. Relief flooded him. The picture of the two of them together, as Dr. and Mrs. La-Fitte, was propped up against the mirror. A large wooden locker stood against one wall. He jerked its doors open. There was her freshly laundered pink dress, already returned by the hotel staff, plus a pale green one she'd also bought yesterday.

What was she up to? he wondered anxiously. Why had she left? Didn't she realize how dangerous it was for her to be prowling the streets alone, especially in broad daylight when her makeup was more obvious? Perhaps he hadn't been forceful enough when he told her to stay in the room. Well, as soon as she got back, he'd remedy that.

He turned on the tiny black-and-white TV set and moved the room's one chair close to it, but he barely heard the voices. His mind kept remembering the sensations, the tantalizing sounds and the musky fragrances of last night.

It wasn't that she was an experienced lover. Far from it. He doubted she'd known more than a few men intimately. But there was something about the way he felt when he was with her and the way she responded to him, that turned on every cell in his body.

The fifteen minutes he sat there felt like hours. When he heard a key in the lock, he swung around, facing the door. His breath escaped in a great sigh of relief. Marilyn seemed to float across the threshold, adding a special brightness to the room's drab interior. With her long black hair swirling carelessly around her shoulders, she appeared ethereal, somehow, yet radiantly alive at the same time. Just looking at her, Mac felt his loins quicken. He groaned, his intention to admonish her fading rapidly.

"You got back sooner than I expected," she said. A flicker of apprehension crossed her face.

Watching her, Mac felt his stomach muscles tighten. She was hiding something from him.

"I couldn't wait in this room by myself a second longer," she went on. "When the walls closed in, I decided to do some shopping."

"Is that all you did?" He was surprised at how severe his voice sounded.

Her eyes narrowed. "You promised to give me time to myself. I'm going to hold you to it, Mac."

"But it's dangerous, darling. You can't run around in Manila on your own. Don't you want me with you when you go out? Didn't last night change anything between us?" He didn't try to hide his distress.

A smile trembled on her lips. "Of course it did. But it didn't change my need for time alone, outside this room. You can't expect me to stay locked up in here every time you have an errand to run."

Reluctantly, Mac gave in. "You've got to promise you'll be very careful when you get these urges to wander on your own."

"I'm always careful." There was a note of finality in her tone. With a pang of regret, Mac realized she wasn't going to say anything more.

Much later, after they'd explored each other's bodies and taken satisfaction in the way of lovers, Mac unwrapped the bandage from her arm. The cut was healing nicely.

"It's been itching," she said. "While the dressing's off, I'm going to take a shower."

"Don't scrub it," he warned. "I'll clean it with antiseptic and put some ointment on it when you're finished."

Mac waited until he heard her turn on the water. For her own safety, he had to know what she planned to do. There would never be a better time to look through her handbag for clues.

It was on the dresser. Repressing his guilt, he opened it. The first things he spotted were three envelopes addressed to Marilyn's brother. One contained the return address of the man who had been murdered. The other two were from Bangkok. The letters inside were written in Vietnamese.

So this was how she'd gotten the murdered man's address. Her brother's message on her answering machine must have told her where to find these envelopes. Quickly Mac memorized the Bangkok address. Sooner or later she would go to these people, just as she'd gone to Toan Nguyen. When she did, Mac intended to be nearby, whether she wanted him there or not.

Chapter Fifteen

In spite of the nagging fear that was her constant companion, the next two days were the happiest Marilyn had ever spent. The hours passed in an idyllic haze of closeness, laughter and intense pleasure. In some strange way she felt transformed into Li LaFitte, beloved wife of an adoring husband. She acted the part, refusing to let her concern for Van and the ever present threat of danger steal her sense of completeness with Mac.

During the day they did the things every newcomer to Manila does. They visited Corregidor, the aquarium, St. Augustine Cathedral, Fort Santiago, Malacanang Palace. They ate breakfast overlooking Manila Bay and lunch along the Pasig River. Their nights were fantasies in black velvet.

At least half-a-dozen times Marilyn came close to telling Mac about Van's stamp albums, the Bangkok address, and the ad she'd placed in the *Manila Monitor*. Each time something held her back. She loved Mac. She knew he loved her. But she didn't completely trust him. Was he still working for the bureau? She was ninety-five percent sure he wasn't, but as long as a smidgen of doubt remained, she dared not jeopardize Van's freedom. She had to talk to her brother before she told Mac what she was doing and what she planned.

Each of the two days after the ad appeared, Marilyn spent an hour or so alone, in a shopping area near the hotel. She used this time to determine whether Mac was following her.

By the afternoon of the second day, she was fairly well convinced that he wasn't. But not completely. She was a rank amateur. He was a skilled professional. It was possible she'd missed seeing him, or that he'd somehow managed to get to their room ahead of her when she doubled back there unexpectedly. She burst in to find him sitting on the bed, reading the newspaper she'd bought that morning.

"Why didn't you get one with more international news?" he asked, glancing at her with a quizzical expression. "This covers mostly what's going on in the local area."

A wave of alarm stopped her in her tracks. *Has he guessed about the ad?* Awkwardly she cleared her throat. "I'm interested in the local news, Mac. We might as well learn something about the Philippines while we're here." She studied his face. A watchful, almost predatory, alert glinted briefly in his eyes, vanishing almost as soon as it had appeared.

"I missed you, darling. I'm glad you're back earlier than yesterday." There was a faint tremor in his voice, as though some emotion had touched him.

He knows I'm lying to him about why I bought the paper, Marilyn thought, hating herself. She felt her cheeks flush pink. *But he can't possibly have guessed about the ad, not the way I worded it.*

She sat down beside him on the bed. "I'm glad too, Mac." She closed her eyes, waiting for his kiss.

THURSDAY MORNING, Mac took the stitches out of her arm.

"You missed your calling," she said, after he'd applied a new bandage.

"What do you mean, *madame?*" he purred in his lovely French accent. "Have you forgotten you are married to the renowned Dr. LaFitte?"

She giggled mischievously. "When you talk like that, I think I'm married to Charles Boyer. Seriously, Mac, where did you get your medical training?"

He shrugged. "When you're in my line of business, or rather, the line of business I used to be in, you learn how to treat everything from knife to bullet wounds."

Marilyn caught his slip. Maybe it meant something and maybe it didn't. Was he really still involved with the FBI?

Lunch was a disaster. They went to a French place where the waiters responded with snail-like slowness. Fifteen minutes passed before their orders were taken, another fifteen before the soup arrived. It was nearly one when Mac's sweetbreads and Marilyn's stuffed sole were served.

"Bon appetit," the waiter said, with a pert little bow. "Enjoy your lunch, *madame, monsieur.*"

Marilyn knew she had to leave by one-thirty to make it to Rizal Park by two. She tried to eat slowly, but finished her sole before Mac was half-through.

He chewed with infuriating thoroughness. "You were really hungry," he said, eyeing her empty plate. "We'll have some flan for dessert." Flan, a burnt sugar pudding, was her favorite.

"I don't want dessert." She fidgeted on her chair. The walls around them featured oil paintings of the Moulin Rouge. She forced herself to concentrate on the pictures so she wouldn't stare at the formidable cluster of sweetbreads that remained on Mac's plate.

He put his fork down. "Is something wrong?" His concern was evident in his voice. "You seem a little nervous."

Marilyn glanced at her watch. If she didn't leave in five minutes, she wasn't going to make it. "I've got to go, Mac." He looked worried. How wonderful it would be when she could tell him everything.

She stood up. So did he. "Please finish your dinner," she urged.

He seemed to sense she was headed for more than a shopping expedition. "I wish you wouldn't do this, darling." He sighed heavily. "Can't you trust me enough to let me come along? I promise I won't interfere."

She was convinced his concern was genuine. But there was still a chance he was after Van. "I can't, Mac. Not this time. Maybe when I get back to the hotel, I'll explain...."

"Explain, nothing!" Jumping up, he stepped around the table toward her, his face filled with worry. "You can't do this, Marilyn. Whatever you're up to, it's bound to be dangerous. You've got to trust me. Believe me, I won't interfere." His voice rang with determination.

"You can't," she gasped. "You promised. Remember?" Time was slipping by. How could she prevent him if he insisted? "If you come, I'll just go back to the hotel, and take care of my business another time."

There would never be another time, but Mac couldn't know that. For a tense moment, he frowned at her. Then his worried look changed to one of anxious resignation. He kissed her lightly on the mouth. "Promise you'll be very careful. Don't go in crowds or let anybody come close. Watch what's going on around you."

She smiled at his concern. "You sound like a proud papa with a teenage daughter. Don't worry. I'm as interested in preserving my own skin as you are."

"Good." He returned to his place, but didn't sit down until she'd started toward the door. Looking back at their table, Marilyn saw him watching her, his face grim.

Outside, even wearing her dark glasses, she felt blinded by the afternoon's humid brightness after the air-conditioned semidarkness of the restaurant's interior.

She waited for her eyes to adjust and then searched up and down the jammed street for one of the ubiquitous yellow taxis. There was none in sight.

A group of young urchins crowded around her. "You want taxi, miss?" one asked. "We get one for you. Only five P."

It was an outrageous price, but Marilyn was behind schedule. The minute she paid them, almost as though in collusion with the youngsters, a cab appeared.

"Rizal Park," she told the driver as she climbed in.

While he threaded his way through the omnipresent crush of traffic, she kept an eye out the rear window. If Mac tried to follow her in another cab, she'd be sure to see him.

Nobody followed her. Rizal Park, a vast area comparable to San Francisco's Golden Gate Park, fronted on the sea. Instead of going directly to the monument specified in her ad, Marilyn instructed the driver to patrol along the streets ringing the central area of the park where the monument was located. Eagerly she searched for Van, along with any indication of danger.

Nothing. No Van. No milling crowds. Only people strolling and children playing the Philippine version of tag on the grass and in the gardens. She swallowed her discouragement. It wasn't quite two o'clock. He might be on his way, looking the area over first, just as she was.

The cab pulled into a crowded parking lot about a block from the monument. There were no parking spaces, so Marilyn told the driver to come back for her in about half an hour.

It's a long shot, she warned herself, praying she wouldn't be too disappointed if Van didn't show up. Trying not to hurry, she started down one of the paths leading to the monument. A huge statue of Jose Rizal, The Pride of the Malays, dominated the area. Casually she circled it, pausing to read the plaques, admire the obelisk, and gaze at a uniformed sentry. There was no sign of Van.

Marilyn headed for a vacant stone bench near some shrubbery. Although it was a distance away from the monument, she could easily spot Van from there, as well as anybody who looked suspicious.

Seated on the bench, she studied the people in the vicinity. A tall Caucasian man about a quarter of a mile away caught her attention. Like her, he seemed to be looking for someone. He was dressed in white Bermuda shorts and a dark blue T-shirt. Even at this distance, there was something eerily familiar about the erect, almost military, way he was standing. When he turned toward her, Marilyn swung around so that her back was to him. She forced herself not to glance in his direction until a full minute had passed.

When she finally did look, a wave of apprehension swept over her. He was coming down the path toward her. In that short time, he'd bridged about a third of the distance between them. She gasped, recognizing him. It was Agent Smith! Marilyn couldn't believe her eyes. Had he come all the way from California to arrest her for espionage?

She had to get away from here. Slowly, concentrating on every move, she stood and began walking away from him. Her heart thumped crazily, pounding in her ears. Would he recognize her?

Don't be an idiot, she told herself, remembering what Mac had said about the dirty trick the bureau had played on her—about the heyday the U.S. newspapers would have if they found out about it. *He's not going to arrest me. He's after Van. Somehow he's found out about my ad, and thinks Van will come.*

Peering through the foliage of a large bush, she watched Agent Smith stroll along the path toward the bench she'd just left. He didn't glance in her direction. All his attention was focused on the monument.

How had the bureau found out about the ad? Marilyn felt the blood drain from her head. Mac had told them. There was no other answer. Some way, she couldn't imagine how, Mac must have figured out her message.

He's still working for the bureau, she thought, feeling an aching sense of loss. Were the past three days just another ruse designed to get her to trust him? She refused to believe it. Yet, he was a cunning, clever man. Nobody knew that better than Marilyn herself. How far would he go to get Van in custody? A sob caught in her throat. She tossed her head angrily. If there was ever a time when she needed her wits, this was it. Sobbing like a schoolgirl wasn't going to help.

She cast another quick glance at Agent Smith. He'd sat down on the bench, in almost the same place she'd been. *He's watching someone, probably another agent, near the monument,* she realized, her heart sinking. *They've got a*

*trap set to catch Van if he shows up and they intend to fol-
low me.*

Smith leaned back and lit a cigarette. Marilyn forced
herself to stay where she was for another full minute. Then,
slowly, she turned and began strolling away, keeping the
bushes between them. She didn't dare go near the monument. Mac had probably told Smith about her disguise. She
couldn't let him see her.

Twice, from the cover of the bushes, she stopped for a
close look at the people clustered around the monument.
From that distance she couldn't be positive, but she was
fairly certain Van wasn't among them. She'd take another
look from the cab. Still hidden, she glanced toward the
parking area where the cab had let her off. It hadn't yet returned. While she watched, another taxi pulled into the
crowded lot. A man got out. Bald, he was wearing a white
shirt and dark trousers. The vehicle pulled away as soon as
he paid the fare.

Marilyn's body stiffened in shock. It was Mac. If she'd
needed further proof that he was working for the bureau,
this had to be it. First Agent Smith appeared, then Mac. A
gamut of confusing emotions made her feel like screaming.
If he truly loved her, how could he betray her to the bureau? She realized suddenly that she'd never really believed
he was still lying to her about working for the bureau. How
wrong she'd been.

She stayed hidden until a taxi pulled into the lot and
parked there, obviously waiting for someone. Agent Smith
was no longer on the bench, she noticed anxiously. He was
probably on his way to meet Mac. She walked as fast as she
could without breaking into a run. She reached the taxi. It
was hers. The driver got out and helped her inside. "Take
me around the monument again," she said.

From the relative anonymity of the cab, she peered out the
window but saw no one familiar. Not Van. Not Mac. Not
Agent Smith. Did she risk going back to the hotel to get her
things? No, she decided quickly. She could buy herself some

time if Mac didn't realize she'd gone. "Take me to the air-port," she told the driver.

A clerk at the Thai Airways ticket counter told her there was space on a flight leaving for Bangkok in less than an hour. Not until she was in the air, high over the South China Sea, did Marilyn yield to the compulsive sobs she'd been fighting since she left Rizal Park.

MARILYN WAS NOWHERE in the park. Mac prowled its path-ways and gardens for almost an hour and a half searching. Maybe the boys he'd quizzed in front of the restaurant had been wrong when they heard Marilyn tell the taxi driver to take her here. Or maybe her appointment was somewhere in the vicinity, at the Rizal Library or the post office, per-haps, instead of at the park itself.

Damn! He should have gone right after her instead of waiting. When the youths gave him her destination, he'd hesitated just long enough for her to get away. He'd figured to keep an eye on her without her knowing about it, just as he'd done the past couple of days. Who would have guessed she'd get away from him on this, the most critical day of all, the day she was obviously planning for?

In any case, the park was calm, with no excessive crowds or other signs of recent disaster. If she'd been here and he'd missed her, he doubted anything had happened to her. *She's probably back at the hotel,* he told himself hopefully, wav-ing for a taxi.

But she wasn't. Their room was empty, with no indica-tion she'd been here in his absence. Where was she? Had something happened to her? Again and again he cursed himself for losing her outside the restaurant. How could a trained special agent have allowed such a damn-fool thing to happen? He told himself to be calm, that she'd be walk-ing through the door any minute. It didn't help. Restlessly he paced back and forth between the dresser and the foot of the bed, consumed with impatience and a growing fear that she was in some kind of trouble.

Mac had been waiting more than two hours when there was a light knock at the door. *Thank God.* He felt like he'd just won the lottery. *She's lost her key somewhere. She's probably late because she's been hunting for it.* He rushed to the door and opened it.

Dan Moschella stood there smiling, his white teeth dazzling against his olive skin. "Aren't you going to invite me in, MacIntyre?"

Mac had rarely been as astounded as he was at that moment. Of all the people in the world he expected to see, Dan Moschella was among the last. Keeping his face impassive, he stood aside to let the agent enter.

Moschella strode past Mac to the chair and dropped into it. He cast a knowing eye at the cosmetics on the dresser. "Looks like you and the lovely Ms. Marilyn have set up housekeeping." His baritone voice held a vaguely envious note. "Where is she, by the way? I waited downstairs for a couple of hours, hoping to spot her. When I didn't, I figured she must have come up the back stairs."

Mac resisted the urge to knock Moschella's front teeth out. "What makes you think Marilyn Wainwright's here? Manila's full of charming women. These things—" he waved toward the dresser top "—belong to someone else."

"My dear Doctor LaFitte," Moschella began. "That picture of the two of you on the dresser looks too much like her to be anyone else, in spite of the long, black hair."

Mac took a deep breath. Their cover and their disguises had been penetrated. His alarm mounted. If the bureau knew who they were, did the people gunning for them know also? He imagined Marilyn, terrified, running from some cruel-faced little man, her long hair streaming out behind her....

"Besides, I doubt you'd have been searching Rizal Park for anyone but Ms. Wainwright," Moschella continued. "What happened? She give you the slip?"

So that's where the agent had stumbled onto him—Rizal Park. Moschella had probably followed him back here to the hotel afterward, and asked the desk clerk what name he was

Liar's Game

registered under. Mac cursed himself for not being more careful.

Ignoring Moschella's flippant questions, Mac stood in front of the dresser and studied the other man. Why had Moschella turned up at the park at the same time Mac did? Mac didn't believe in coincidences, not where the bureau was involved.

"What the hell were you doing in the park, Moschella?" he asked bluntly.

The agent gave him a sly smile. "The same thing you were. Trying to find your girlfriend."

Mac's eyes narrowed. "Why did you think she'd be there?"

"Because of the ad, of—" Moschella broke off abruptly. "You didn't know about the ad, did you MacIntyre? Well, shame on you. You let the little lady put one over on you."

Mac remembered Marilyn's guilty look yesterday when he'd asked her about the newspaper. Damn! He should have known she was embarrassed about something printed in it. He'd been so worried about her afternoon excursions, he'd overlooked something obvious.

He sat down on the bed. "What kind of ad did she place?"

"Classified. Finnegan thought she might arrange a meeting with her brother that way. He told the embassy to be on the lookout for anybody advertising in the English language papers to get in touch with someone else." Moschella pulled out a pack of cigarettes and lit one. "I thought we'd struck out until I spotted you rushing around like some kind of lovestruck fool."

Mac glared at him, and he added, "Never would have recognized you if I hadn't seen you bald on the O'Brien case a few years back."

"So what did the ad say?"

"Read it yourself." Moschella handed him a slip of paper. "We knew right away it was her. She used almost the same words her brother did when he left that message on her answering machine.''

Mac remembered that the bureau had a tap on Marilyn's telephone. His heart sank when he saw her pathetic appeal to her lost brother. Didn't she know there were people who made a business of reading ads like this to track people down? Of course she didn't know. She was an innocent, unfamiliar with the dirty tricks of the cloak-and-dagger trade.

"She coming back here?" Moschella watched Mac with an odd, humorless smile.

"Damned if I know." Mac's careless words hid a wrenching pain in his gut. What was she going to do out there all alone? She was an innocent among assassins, Little Red Riding Hood searching for the big bad wolf in a forest filled with ravenous vultures. Again Mac visualized her running from an assassin, only this time her face was tight with panic. He had to find her.

Dan Moschella seemed to read his mind. "Let's see if she's still in town." He went to the phone on the table beside the bed. "U.S. Embassy, please," he said to the operator. A moment later he had Neil Warner on the line. "Like I said when I talked to you yesterday, I'm only here on vacation, Neil, so my authority is limited. I wonder if you could do me a big favor? Have your people check the trains, planes, buses, rental car agencies to see if Ms. Wainwright's left town?"

Mac heard the buzz of Warner's voice.

"Then try LaFitte. She's registered under that name at this hotel. Call me back as soon as you know anything."

The phone rang not ten minutes later. It was for Moschella. He listened for a few moments, then turned to Mac with a triumphant look. "She took off for Bangkok a couple of hours ago. You must have gotten her a fake passport. If you want to catch up to her before she gets herself killed, I suggest we start moving."

Bangkok

THE TAXI STOOD motionless, its horn blaring, in the worst traffic jam Marilyn had ever seen. If Manila's traffic was bad, Bangkok's was horrendous. Exhaust fumes choked the air, but she couldn't close the windows. The taxi wasn't air-conditioned. Though early evening, it was still hot and humid.

She stared out her open window at the shining dome of an ancient temple. Next to it was a modern, multicolored office building. A flock of saffron-robed monks, their heads shaved, held out begging bowls to everyone who passed on the crowded sidewalks.

Will Van be here? she wondered tiredly. *Will his friends know where he is?*

Or would this be a fool's errand, leading nowhere? And if she couldn't find him, what in God's name was she going to do? She felt momentary panic. Her money wouldn't last much longer. She didn't dare reveal her true identity, not with a killer on her trail. The Philippine police were after her, too. So was the U.S. government. On this entire planet there wasn't a soul she could turn to.

Certainly not to Mac. She felt like crying every time she thought of him. Mac with his gentle surgeon's hands. Mac the considerate lover. Mac who had betrayed her at every turn.

Marilyn's eyes filled with tears, and she shook her head angrily. She couldn't let herself get distracted this way. For now, at least, she couldn't afford the luxury of hating Mac for what he'd done to her. She forced herself to focus on the married couple she'd be meeting soon. From their name, she knew they were Vietnamese, like Mr. Nguyen. It was important that she be clearheaded and convincing when she talked to them. She had to make them understand how important it was that she see her brother.

Incredibly, the traffic straightened itself out. Her taxi began inching along the jammed street. The driver flashed her a toothy smile. "Only two blocks more to Tri Petch Road."

"But we're not in a residential ... in a place where people live." Somehow she'd expected Van's friends to live in a house in a nice neighborhood, like Mr. Nguyen.

"People live everywhere in city," the driver said.

He turned off the main street onto another that was less crowded. A moment later he stopped in front of a small shop featuring Vietnamese handicrafts. The sign read Treasures from Vietnam.

The door was open.

Marilyn took a deep breath and stepped inside.

Chapter Sixteen

The shop had a musty smell, as though everything displayed were centuries old. Wood carvings, bronze statuary, colorful scarves, and pillows were arranged on shelves in jumbled disarray. Standing on the floor were painted glass elephants, temple dogs and vases.

Nervously Marilyn glanced around her for a clerk. The silence was unnerving. *Just the way it was at Mr. Nguyen's.* She swallowed hard, remembering the terrifying scene in the murdered man's library. *Please God, don't let it happen again.*

"Chao?" she called out in Vietnamese. "Hello? Is anybody here?"

The curtains at the back parted. Out came a tiny Vietnamese woman. Marilyn breathed more easily. In spite of the heat, the woman was dressed in the traditional *ao dai,* a garment with a stiff high collar and long skirt split up both sides to reveal white silk trousers underneth.

"Ba Dinh Thuy Phoung?" Marilyn asked. "Are you Mrs. Phoung?"

"I am Madame Dinh Thui Phoung," the woman replied, her face a mask that revealed nothing. "How may I be of service?"

Marilyn took a deep breath. It was now or never. She felt her dress sticking to her back from nervous perspiration.

"I am Marilyn Wainwright, Van Wainwright's sister. It's urgent that I find him."

The woman's bland expression did not change. "The name is not a familiar one."

Marilyn yanked off her dark glasses.

Mrs. Phoung's eyes narrowed. "You are not Vietnamese."

"I'm an American," Marilyn said in English. "I truly am Van's sister. I must find him. It's a matter of life and death." She opened her bag and pulled out one of the envelopes she'd taken from Van's stamp album. She handed it to Mrs. Phoung.

"Here's a letter you sent him. I found it at his house."

The woman glanced at it and gave it back to Marilyn. "Why do you think I know where he is?" Her English was excellent. "This letter concerns a stamp transaction. Nothing more."

"He left a message telling me to contact him through you." It was stretching the truth, but Marilyn was desperate.

"How do I know you are his sister?"

Marilyn reached for her passport and remembered she was masquerading as Li LaFitte. If this woman saw the passport, she'd never believe it was a false identity.

What would Mac do if this happened to him? Marilyn pictured his face, heard his voice. "Don't get too attached to Li LaFitte," he said. "You'll have to leave her behind...."

Inspired, Marilyn yanked out her wallet instead of her passport. "Here's my driver's license, Mrs. Phoung. And my library card. And a credit card."

The woman examined them carefully and then handed them back. "You look very much like your brother, Ms. Wainwright."

Marilyn expelled her breath. Angry and disappointed though she was with Mac, just the thought of him had been enough to pull her through this crisis. *Mac.* How could he betray her?

At last, the woman smiled. "I do not know where your brother is, but there is someone who may."

Hope gushed through Marilyn like a spring flood. "His life, and mine, may depend on my finding him."

"Where are you staying? Perhaps a message can be left for you if this person wants to see you."

"I—uh—nowhere." Embarrassed, Marilyn felt her cheeks flushing. "I told the immigration authorities at the airport I was registered at the Siam Intercontinental, but I can't go there. Somebody may be following me, and that's the first place they'd look."

Mrs. Phoung eyed her with disbelief. "Where did you leave your luggage?"

Wearily Marilyn sagged against the wall. "I have no luggage. A killer's after Van and me. That's why I have to find him." She raised her dress's floppy sleeve, revealing the bandage Mac had applied that morning. "This is the result of one of his attempts. I had to leave my things behind in Manila." Her voice was tight in her throat. This woman must believe her.

The suspicious look disappeared from Mrs. Phoung's face. It was replaced by startled alarm. "Ask your taxi to take you to the Chitr Pochana, a restaurant on Sukhumvit Road. Order dinner. Someone will contact you."

Marilyn wheeled and was starting for the door when Mrs. Phoung's voice stopped her. "Don't come back here. It isn't safe. Tell no one about me." The woman's voice was low, frightened.

Marilyn had the panicky feeling that she was being cut off. She couldn't lose contact with this woman. Mrs. Phoung was her last hope of finding Van.

Marilyn turned and faced her again. "Please let my brother know I'm here in Bangkok." She didn't try to keep the pleading tone from her voice.

Fear flashed in the woman's eyes. "Someone will come to the restaurant. Now, go. Quickly."

Outside, night had fallen with the swiftness of a blind dropping over a window. In the darkness, the neon lights flashed on, advertising the good life in a dozen different languages.

As Marilyn's taxi inched its way along the glittering streets, she noticed the entrance to a bar gaily draped in red and green. With a shock, she remembered this was Christmas Eve. What was Mac doing tonight? Had he followed her to this Buddhist city a million miles from home? *Probably,* she thought, her nostalgia giving way to anger. Since she'd used her French passport, he and Agent Smith would have no trouble tracking her to Bangkok. But once here they'd never find her, since she hadn't checked in at a hotel.

At last she arrived at the restaurant. After looking around to see if she was being followed, Marilyn chose a table in an outside garden. "I'm expecting someone," she told the waiter, who spoke passable English. When her order arrived, Marilyn forced down a few bites. But she spent the next twenty minutes pushing rice and curried prawns around on her plate. Her stomach was clenched so tight that nothing tasted good.

Nobody's coming, she told herself. Mrs. Phoung was too frightened, too unnerved, to send anyone. Marilyn stalled another half hour sipping tea. Finally, she signaled for her check. Beside it on the tray was a folded piece of paper.

The waiter inclined his head toward the doorway. A child stood there, a girl not more than ten or twelve. Marilyn strained to see through her dark glasses. The child looked Vietnamese, not Thai.

"She want to be sure *madame* get message," the waiter said.

Marilyn took a twenty-baht bill out of her wallet. "Please give this to her."

With trembling fingers, she opened the note.

Emerald Buddha. Ten p.m. by front entrance, it said. That was three hours from now. Relief washed over Marilyn, along with a shadow of fear. Would Van be there, or someone to guide her to him? What would this night bring?

She beckoned to the waiter.

"Where's the Emerald Buddha?" she asked.

"Wat Phrakaeo closed after dark," the waiter replied.

Marilyn bit her lip to stop the impatient remark that trembled on her tongue. "What is Wat Phrakaeo? What does it have to do with the Emerald Buddha?"

Obviously used to dealing with tourists, the waiter smiled and bowed slightly. "Sorry, *madame*. I not know you are new in city. Wat Phrakaeo is temple where Emerald Buddha sits."

From the doorway, the child watched her intently. Marilyn caught her eye, and nodded to show she understood.

AS SOON AS MAC FLASHED his fake French passport, the Thai immigration authorities at Bangkok's Don Muang Airport were happy to tell him where his wife was staying. He and Dan Moschella went straight to the Siam Intercontinental as soon as they'd picked up their luggage. They were both dressed in the clothes they'd worn in Manila, Moschella in white Bermuda shorts and a blue shirt and Mac in brown pants and a white shirt.

The desk clerk checked the hotel guest list, but found no Li LaFitte registered.

"My wife didn't have baggage," Mac said, a tight feeling in the pit of his stomach. "Has anybody checked in this afternoon without suitcases?"

The clerk cast him a disparaging glance. "Nobody checks into this hotel without luggage, *monsieur*."

Frowning, Moschella turned away from the counter. "Any idea where she might have gotten to, Mac?"

"If I knew, I sure as hell wouldn't tell you." Mac clenched his fist. Nothing would please him more than flattening Moschella. He had to figure out a way to get rid of Moschella, the sooner the better. The last thing he wanted was an FBI agent tagging along when he went to the address he'd found in Marilyn's handbag. His fear for her was growing. Where was she?

"Hey, I'm on your side, remember?" Moschella sounded hurt. Mac wasn't fooled. The agent was almost as good an actor as Mac himself.

"So I'm out to nail the brother," Moschella said. "Okay, I'll admit it." He turned back toward the desk clerk. "Where's the bar?" To Mac he said, "Let's have a couple of beers and talk this over."

Reluctantly Mac agreed. Moschella could have him detained by Thai authorities if he refused to cooperate. He was in Thailand on a fake passport. He'd provided a fake passport for a woman wanted in the Philippines in connection with a murder. The police could pick him up on either charge. He'd be of no help to Marilyn stuck in an interrogation room in some Thai police station. She needed his help, he knew. Right now. Dear God, if anything had happened to her... He couldn't bear the thought.

The bar throbbed with music and the singsong voice of a Thai announcer on the TV set. Moschella took a long swallow of his beer. "We both want the same thing, Mac. The sister safe in your capable hands. The brother in custody in mine. Let's work together on this. If we don't, we may not find her soon enough."

He didn't continue. He didn't have to. Mac tried to relax and failed. He hoped his tension wasn't obvious in the bar's semidarkness. For a long minute he remained silent, torn by conflicting emotions. Finally he made his decision. He'd pretend to cooperate.

"All right, Dan," he said slowly. "I've got to find her."

Moschella studied Mac's face. "Now you're talking sense, MacIntyre. So what's your best bet about where she's gone?"

Mac shrugged. "Damned if I know. My suggestion would be to wait for her right here at the hotel. Since she told Immigration this is where she'd be, she'll probably show up sooner or later."

"You wait here for her," Moschella said. "I've got an old buddy assigned to the embassy who owes me a favor. I'll run him down. Maybe he can help us find her. I'll meet you in the lobby in a couple of hours."

It was almost too easy. One minute Mac was sure he'd never get away from Dan Moschella. The next, Moschella was gone and Mac was in a taxi, heading for the address he'd found in Marilyn's handbag.

Was he being followed? Mac didn't think so, but to be safe he told the driver to let him out at a pharmacy several blocks away. He went inside and bought toothpaste and shaving cream. A few minutes later, he left through a rear entrance. Not until he was absolutely certain no one was tailing him, did he go to the address he'd memorized.

DAN MOSCHELLA WAITED in a corridor off the hotel's spacious lobby until he saw MacIntyre leave the bar. He smiled. Good old Mac was doing just what Moschella had expected him to, heading out of the lobby. He'd undoubtedly call a taxi.

Moschella was almost one-hundred percent sure where MacIntyre was going, but planned to have him followed anyway. He nodded to a slim Vietnamese man waiting for his signal across the lobby. The little man nodded back and glided after MacIntyre. Moschella had worked with him before. Ruthlessly efficient, he rarely botched a job.

If MacIntyre spotted the agent—not very likely, since the little man had been instructed to disappear as soon as Mac arrived in the vicinity of his destination—Moschella knew he'd connect his follower to the Vietnamese thugs trying to kill him and Marilyn. There was no way he'd link Moschella or the bureau with the tail.

When the agent's car had pulled away from the entrance under the hotel's massive curved roof, Moschella went to a phone in the lobby and dialed an outside number.

A woman answered.

"Where is she now?" he asked, letting his voice identify him.

"She waits for someone by the Temple of the Emerald Buddha."

"Good." Moschella smiled, pleased. "Maybe we're finally going to locate the elusive Madame Vinh."

"Our people will maintain surveillance from a discreet distance. When will you join them?"

For a moment, Moschella was silent. "Soon. I'll have someone with me. He must not talk to Madame Vinh or the brother."

"I understand, *monsieur.* Is that all?"

"When Sami calls, tell him I've left for Tri Petch Road. If the man he was following is not there, I'll return to the hotel. Sami can contact me here."

"Very good, *monsieur.*"

Moschella hung up without saying goodbye.

MAC HAD BEEN EXPECTING to see a house or apartment, not a store. He double-checked the address. It was the right one. Had Marilyn been here? Would he find some trace of her inside? The place looked closed. Its door was shut, its front lights off. In back, a single fluorescent tube was burning.

Crossing the street, Mac mingled with passersby so he could observe the entry. The shops on either side were also closed, with iron gratings pulled down over their display windows. The grating in front of the Vietnamese shop had not been pulled. Maybe somebody was still inside. Mac crossed to the door and tried it. It was locked.

Damn. Unless he could find the owners' home address, he'd have to wait until tomorrow morning to talk to them. *Tomorrow might be too late.* A desperate urgency overtook him. Maybe somebody in the neighborhood knew where these people lived. He saw a place selling Thai pottery midway down the block. Mac hurried there. He tried English and French. But the clerk spoke only Thai.

Mac brushed past her to the rear exit and went outside. No lights lit the darkness, but a full moon beamed overhead, turning the drab square buildings into silver. A paved alley ran along the back of the shops. The Vietnamese place had been five doors down. Counting, Mac jogged the few steps to it and tried the door.

It was open. Mac paused. *Open? What shop owner would leave his back door open?* Ignoring two children squatting across the alley, Mac went in and closed the door behind him.

There's got to be an address or phone number, some-where I can reach the owners. He forced himself to think clearly. Was it possible somebody lived on the premises and had left on an errand? Was that why the door was open? God, he hoped so.

Inside, the place was dark as dirt. Through the silence he heard the buzzing of flies. He felt them flying near his face and swatted at them, but the pesky creatures refused to leave him alone. They seemed to be everywhere.

A sliver of light showed under a curtain dividing the shop's rear from its retail area. Cautiously moving across the floor, Mac went to the curtain and drew it open part-way, enough to provide meager illumination to the rear without alarming anyone peering into the shop through the front window. In the dim light he made out the body of a woman lying facedown on the floor.

My God! It's Marilyn! His heart pounding crazily in his throat, he knelt beside the body. It took only half a second to see that this was somebody else. But that half second seemed an eternity. This woman had the same flowing black hair, the same petite figure. But she was wearing a loose silk garment with baggy white pants underneath instead of Marilyn's pink dress. Blood from a gunshot wound covered the woman's back. She'd been shot through the heart.

Mac didn't have to touch the body to know the woman was dead. He felt an overpowering sadness. He supposed he'd never get used to death, even if he'd worked for the bureau until he retired.

A faint rattling sound from the retail part of the shop put every nerve in his body on full alert. Somebody was jig-gling the front door, trying to get in. Was it the killer? Or someone with a key?

Mac remained motionless, crouching by the body where he couldn't be seen. If someone came in, he mustn't be found here with a corpse. Poised for a quick exit out the rear door, he didn't move until the only sound was the buzzing of the flies. Whoever it was had left.

Cautiously he got to his feet and glanced around the dingy windowless room. He saw a desk in one corner, a counter with painted ceramics on top, a hot plate on a low table, a lumpy upholstered couch. He went to the desk hoping to find a clue that would tell him where Marilyn was. She'd been here. He didn't doubt that. This murder had to be connected in some way to her brother. And to Marilyn herself. Both this address and the one of the murdered man in Manila had been on envelopes in her handbag, envelopes addressed to Van Wainwright. Both murders had occurred within hours of Marilyn's arrival in each of the two cities. He was shuffling through a stack of papers—invoices for merchandise delivered—when the door to the alley creaked open. Mac dropped to the floor.

Dan Moschella stood framed in the doorway, the luminescent glow from the moon behind him. Mac couldn't believe his eyes. How had the agent found him? He hesitated, then stood up. "If I didn't know better, I'd say you were following me, Moschella." Mac's voice was dangerously quiet.

The agent pushed the door shut. "Wouldn't want you to feel neglected, Mac. Mind explaining what you're doing here?" An unspoken threat lingered in Dan Moschella's easy tone.

In the darkness, Mac felt his face burn with anger. "It's none of your damned business what I'm doing here, Moschella. But for your information, we've got a corpse on the floor."

"Who is it?" Moschella didn't sound surprised.

"How the hell should I know?" Mac shot back. "Some woman in a Vietnamese outfit."

"You owe me one, MacIntyre. If I hadn't come along, the Thais would probably be after you for murder, the way the Filipinos nailed your girlfriend. As it is, we'll go through channels and get this all cleaned up, nice and neat." Moschella paused. "Say, it's an interesting coincidence that people seem to get murdered every time you two show up. Any explanation for that?"

Mac swore under his breath. "Just do your duty and report the murder, Moschella."

The agent picked up a phone on the desk and dialed a number. "This is Dan Moschella, Sam. Since I'm out of the bureau's jurisdiction here in Bangkok, I wonder if your boys could give me a hand with a corpse I've just found?"

Mac could hear the other voice, but couldn't make out the words. Moschella must be talking to the CIA station chief.

"If you could keep me out of this, I'd appreciate it. I stumbled on the body during my—uh—unofficial investigation of the Wainwright case."

There was an answering buzz, then Moschella laughed out loud. "Don't worry. You boys will get all the credit, when this case is solved."

He paused and stared straight at Mac. "Where's the woman?" he asked into the receiver.

Mac felt his heart lurch. *He knows where Marilyn is.*

With a sinking feeling he remembered the agent's interest in her picture. *It was taken when she was disguised as Li LaFitte.* Mac also remembered the telephone call Moschella had made from Manila's airport before their flight left for Bangkok. He'd said it was to Neil Warner in the U.S. Embassy. Instead, it had probably been to the CIA station chief in Bangkok. CIA agents had probably been tailing Marilyn ever since she got here. And the first place she went was the little shop off Tri Petch Road. No wonder Moschella found Mac so easily. He'd guessed Mac knew the address.

"Fine," Moschella said into the phone. "Keep her under surveillance." He hung up with a smug smile.

"Take me to her or I'll throttle you." Mac's voice vibrated with barely controlled fury.

Moschella took a step backward. "Take it easy, Mac-Intyre. I'm on your side, remember?"

"This is your chance to prove it." Mac headed for the door.

In the shadow of the wall around the temple compound, Marilyn waited for an unknown someone to appear. Anxious and a little frightened, she deliberately concentrated on Mac and how he'd betrayed her. Somehow, standing alone in the dark in this strange place, anger was easier to handle than fear. How could she have been so wrong about him?

Across the top of the wall, Marilyn could see pointed spires and the steep, three-tiered roof of the Emerald Buddha's chapel. It shone white-gold in the moonlight. The chapel and grand palace were closed now, but the street outside the wall was still crowded with restless people. *Didn't anyone ever sleep in Southeast Asia?*

Who would come for her? She examined the faces of the people who passed by. Would it be a man? A woman? A child? Would they take her to Van, or was this another deception in a cruel game of lies? Her heart dropped. Would she still be alive on Christmas Day?

For at least the hundredth time, Marilyn studied her watch. She had only minutes to wait until ten o'clock. The past three hours had inched by with snail-like slowness. She'd sipped tea at the Chitr Pochana for half an hour until, intimidated by the solicitous attention of the waiter, she'd paid her bill and gone to the Oriental Hotel. There she'd fidgeted for another hour in the elegant lobby.

She'd arrived at Wat Phrakaeo half an hour early and had paced up and down along one of the temple compound's outside walls. Now she watched and waited near the front entrance. Would anybody come? Someone touched her arm. Marilyn whirled.

A woman stood in the shadows. "I am the one you wait for." Her voice was high-pitched and musical, and somehow vaguely familiar.

Marilyn strained to see more clearly through her dark glasses. About Marilyn's height, the woman was dressed in a dark flowing garment that was belted at the waist. Her face was shadowed by the wall. Marilyn stepped away from it. "Thank God, you've come."

The woman moved toward Marilyn. As she left the shadows, moonlight illuminated her features.

Marilyn gasped with disbelief. This wasn't possible. The terrifying events of the past few days must have driven her mad. She grabbed at the wall to steady herself.

"Mother?" she whispered. "Can it really be you?"

Chapter Seventeen

"Your mother?"

Her words jerked Marilyn back to reality. The earth stopped spinning beneath her feet.

"Take a close look."

Marilyn heard a hint of irritation in the woman's lyrical voice.

"I am Madame Vinh."

Still not over her initial shock, Marilyn yanked off her dark glasses and peered at the woman's face. It was remarkably like her mother's, before the stroke. The woman who called herself Madame Vinh had the same high cheekbones, the same heart-shaped countenance, the same delicate features. She, too, wore thick glasses. Her black hair was tied in back in a chignon. Even their voices sounded similar.

But there were significant differences. Marilyn's mother had round violet eyes. This woman's were dark and almond-shaped. And where her mother's forehead and brows were creased with deep lines, Madame Vinh's were smooth, at least insofar as Marilyn could make out in the moonlight.

"I'm sorry," she mumbled, feeling foolish. She drew a deep breath. "Even though you're Vietnamese, you look enough like my mother to be her sister."

The woman smiled enigmatically. "I know." She turned and began walking quickly toward the river. The humid night air smelled fecund and ripe, like the life-giving Chao Phraya. Contrasting with the river scent was the lingering fragrance of frangipani.

Marilyn, in high-heeled sandals, had to lengthen her stride to keep up. "How do you know you look like my mother?" she asked, astounded. "Have you met her?"

"No, but I have heard much about her. I feel as though I know her personally." Her English was grammar-school perfect with only a faint accent.

Marilyn's breath caught in her lungs. "You—you're Van's mother." Astonishment caused the words to wedge in her throat.

Madame Vinh smiled and nodded. "Yes. Van is my son."

"Where is he? Is he all right?" Marilyn wanted to stop, to talk to this woman face-to-face. But Madame Vinh maintained her fast pace toward the river.

"You will see him soon," she said.

Leaving the shadow of the wall, they crossed a broad street and started down a narrower one. Marshy ground along the sidewalk was inundated with standing water.

"I can't believe you look so much like my mother," Marilyn blurted out, still struggling to recover her composure.

"That's what Van said, too." Madame Vinh's voice was quiet.

Marilyn was grateful to her for not stating the obvious: that her father had married her mother because she reminded him of this woman. Marilyn's throat tightened as she remembered the pain her father had caused her mother. It wasn't fair. He should have realized that, inside, his young bride was nothing like the woman he'd left behind in Vietnam, the woman who was probably the love of his life.

"Why didn't you come home with Van's...with my...father when he left Vietnam?" Marilyn's matter-of-fact question concealed the jumbled emotions she was feeling.

"I couldn't face permanent separation from my family and my country." Madame Vinh left the sidewalk and started toward a small round-bottomed boat pulled up at a wooden dock.

Marilyn's heels sank into the marshy grass. Her sandals were soaking wet after a couple of steps. The wide Chao Phraya River seemed to melt into the grassy bank.

"Your father didn't find out about Van until he returned to Vietnam three years later," Madame Vinh explained. "He was shocked at the discrimination against the child because he was part Caucasian. I knew Van would have more advantages in the States, so I let Van's father take our child."

Marilyn heard the anguish in her voice.

Turning, Madame Vinh shoved the boat into the water. "Get in," she said, over her shoulder.

Removing her shoes so she'd have better balance, Marilyn clambered to a seat at the boat's center. There was brackish water in the bottom. She squirmed as it sloshed over her bare feet. Judging from the smell, the craft had recently been used to carry a load of raw fish. Marilyn didn't let herself think about what might be crawling in the dirty water.

Madame Vinh picked up a paddle. Standing in the rear but facing toward the front, she gently propelled the small boat out into the Chao Phraya. The river's surface looked glassy black, like obsidian, in the pale moonlight.

Somewhere nearby, an outboard engine turned over. For a brief moment, the acrid smell of gasoline and exhaust fumes mingled with the pungent raw fish odor. Marilyn peered toward the dock trying to see the other boat, but like this one, it had no lights. Other small craft paddled past them, shadows in the moonlit darkness. She heard a subdued murmur of voices as one went by. Strangely, the boat with the outboard seemed to stay about the same distance behind them. But sounds across water were deceiving. Perhaps it was headed across the wide river, toward one of the luxury hotels on the opposite shore.

"Are you taking me to Van?" Marilyn asked.

"Yes, but we've got to be careful." Madame's voice was low, tense. With her head inclined to one side, she, too, seemed to be aware of the whine of the outboard engine behind them. "Meeting you was risky. A small group of internal security officers in Vietnam—known as the police cadre—is trying to kill both Van and me."

Even in the semidarkness, Marilyn could see the worry lines on her face. Marilyn gasped. "They must be the ones who've been after me. Why, for God's sake? What have we done to them?"

Madame Vinh wielded her oar expertly, guiding their small craft downstream. "The cadre works with an American syndicate controlling Vietnamese gangs in the States. In addition to many other crimes, the syndicate extorts money from the refugees who have left Vietnam. In exchange, family members who remain behind aren't hurt by the police."

Marilyn caught her breath. "The FBI thinks Van is the one who organized that syndicate. The bureau claims to have substantial evidence to prove it."

Madame Vinh laughed bitterly. "Someone in your Federal Bureau of Investigation is working for the police cadre. He is the one who organized the syndicate. That so-called *evidence* against Van is false. Lies, all of it."

Mac. Marilyn felt her heart thumping wildly, out of control. "An FBI agent would never organize a crime syndicate," she said, her voice shaky. "It's simply not possible." But her mind was screaming Mac's name. Was this his ultimate betrayal? Was he framing Van to divert suspicion from himself?

"It is indeed possible that an FBI agent would organize a crime syndicate," Madame Vinh said. "I know because I was an informer for the cadre and learned of many of their activities."

"You? An informer?" Marilyn could barely force the words out.

"As a government clerk, I was able to supply some of the names the cadre wanted. I'm ashamed of what I did, but I had no choice. They threatened to kill my son in America if I didn't cooperate."

Struggling to understand, Marilyn settled back on the hard wooden seat. "And I suppose the syndicate was getting money from him to protect you?"

"Exactly so." Madame Vinh's voice broke painfully. "Neither of us knew about the other's problem until I learned of the plan to trap him. I fled Vietnam to warn him."

So that's why Van was having so much financial trouble with his little business, Marilyn thought. He was paying extortion money to protect his mother.

"Is this cadre of police officers backed by the Vietnamese government?" In her eagerness to know everything, Marilyn leaned toward Van's mother, and the boat tipped. The foul-smelling water sloshed over her bare feet again, but she hardly felt it.

"Only a small percentage of police officers belong to the cadre. Officially, the government is not aware of their activities." Madame Vinh shrugged. "Unofficially, who knows?"

Behind them, the outboard engine whined steadily, an omnipresent companion. A whisper of fear crept down Marilyn's backbone. Why didn't the boat pass? The sound was drowned out as an open motor launch, one of Bangkok's water buses, chugged past, its tassels swinging from its flat roof. It was half full of Thai passengers seated side by side on benchlike seats.

Madame Vinh stopped paddling until the rolling waves left in its wake had past. Obviously at home on the river, she did not sit down.

"They're accusing Van to protect the FBI agent who organized the gangs in the States into a syndicate." She glanced down at Marilyn from her standing position at the boat's rear. "That's why they want Van dead. With him out of the way, the real leader escapes detection."

"Why Van?" Marilyn cried.

Now that the noise from the water bus's engine had faded, the buzzing of the outboard engine seemed louder. From the landing they'd left only minutes ago, someone turned on a powerful flashlight. There was an answering flash from the boat.

Suddenly Marilyn felt weak, defenseless. If the police cadre described by Madame Vinh was after them, what could they do to protect themselves? She forced herself to concentrate on her brother so she wouldn't give way to her fear.

"Why did they pick Van to frame?" she asked again. Maybe the answer would help her understand why she and her brother had suddenly become targets.

"Several logical reasons," Madame replied. "Van worked with the refugees in the Los Angeles area and was well-known in the community—probably as well-known as any other single individual. Also, he'd made a trip to Vietnam two years ago, about the time the syndicate was organized."

"But that was to find you," Marilyn said. "He had no political reasons for going."

"Tell that to American authorities who know his birth mother was a Vietnamese government employee with access to information helpful to the cadre. Consider, too, that his sister had a top secret clearance, and could be drawn in as a collaborator. Consider that he had his own business, and conceivably could be running the syndicate from there." She lifted a shoulder. "For all these reasons, he was the perfect candidate for the cadre's trap."

Madame Vinh guided their craft closer to the shore, where a row of ramshackle houses lined a long wooden dock. The houses squatted on stilts above the river's smooth black surface. Through open doors, Marilyn saw the flickering lights of television sets.

"If you were providing such valuable information for the cadre, wouldn't they think twice about involving Van?" Marilyn asked. "Surely they knew you'd quit as soon as you found out."

"I was what you call small potatoes. I was of more value to them as a deceased, former government employee—the birth mother of the accused syndicate leader—than as an informant." Her voice was bitter. "They did not guess I would find out the truth about the syndicate and its FBI leader or that I would manage to flee Vietnam and warn my son."

The roar of the motorboat grew louder. Madame Vinh's expression turned anxious. "Were you followed to the Emerald Buddha, Marilyn?"

Marilyn frowned, listening to the persistent buzz. "I don't think so. I'm in disguise, you know."

"Thuy—Mrs. Phoung—told me you were pretending to be Vietnamese."

"What is Mrs. Phoung's role in all this?" Marilyn asked. "And poor Mr. Nguyen?"

"They are agents who oppose the communist regime in Vietnam. When I fled, Mrs. Phoung helped me escape. She found a refuge for me in the city so I wouldn't have to stay in one of the detention camps. Van knew of her and Mr. Nguyen because they had helped many of the refugees who resettled in the States."

"Did you hear of Mr. Nguyen's murder?" Marilyn shivered, remembering that horrible afternoon.

"Yes. We heard that you found the body." Madame Vinh's voice was sympathetic. "Thuy—Mrs. Phoung—thinks he was killed by the assassin hired by those Vietnamese refugees in California. Fools, all of them. Blind, stupid fools, to believe the disinformation put out by the real syndicate leader."

In the distance, Marilyn heard the subdued roar of another outboard engine starting up. Flashlight beams stabbed the night darkness, forming a pathway between the two motorboats. The lights were switched off almost immediately.

Watching, Marilyn felt the beginnings of the same panic she'd known in Manila. Was it all starting again? The fear? The dreadful waiting for something awful to happen? She'd felt reasonably secure as Li LaFitte. Was that security gone?

"CAN'T THIS THING GO any faster, Moschella?" Mac's voice simmered with barely controlled rage. "The company boys are way ahead of us." Fear tore at his insides like a million tiny worms gnawing at his gut. If Dan Moschella knew where Marilyn was, maybe the killer did, too.

Moschella, operating the outboard engine at the boat's rear, threw him an A-Okay sign with his circled thumb and forefinger. "Don't worry, Mac. Your girlfriend's not going to get away."

"Damn the CIA!" Mac fumed. "Finnegan's right. They're all a bunch of stumblebums who don't know their tail sections from a hole in the wall. Why didn't they stop her? How they could let an American woman by herself paddle away from them on this filthy river in the middle of the night?"

"She's probably not by herself," Moschella broke in. "She was waiting for someone by the temple."

"Her brother?" Mac guessed.

"Or someone sent to lead her to him. He's around here somewhere, Mac. We'll have him in custody before the night is over." Moschella's voice fairly bubbled with good spirits.

"So that's why you let her get away." Mac could feel himself hurting inside. "You wanted her to lure her brother out of hiding."

"Can you think of a safer way to nail the leader of a big crime syndicate?" Moschella grinned in the moonlight. "He's probably got firepower. Lots of it. But we might be able to take him by surprise, if he thinks he's meeting his sister."

Mac stared at the big man opposite him. Moschella's mention of a possible gunfight triggered his sensitive alert system. "The sister better not get hurt. I'm warning you, Moschella. If those company boys have itchy trigger fingers, they'd better be damned careful who they're aiming at."

For the first time since he'd shown up in Manila, Moschella seemed somewhat unsure of himself. "I've got a confession to make, Mac."

A premonition of impending disaster settled on Mac like a dirty oil slick.

"The men in that other boat aren't CIA."

"Not CIA!" Mac couldn't believe what he'd heard. He jumped to his feet and the small boat tipped crazily. "Then who the hell are they?"

MADAME VINH stopped her paddling and sat down. "If no one knows your disguise, it's not likely you were followed. We'll remain motionless for a few minutes to see if the other boat passes us."

The buzzing of the outboard continued, neither farther away nor closer, as though the boat were turning in a big circle behind them.

"Someone knows my disguise." Marilyn felt her eyes filling with tears. "An FBI agent followed me to Manila. He's the one who made up this disguise for me, who got me the false passport."

"Was this man the one who controlled you when you worked as a double agent in San Diego?" Madame Vinh's voice sharpened with alarm.

Marilyn's mouth dropped open. "No. How in the world did you know about that?"

"My sources in Vietnam told me. Remember, the police cadre controls the Vietnamese syndicate in the States. As soon as Van and I learned you'd gone to the Federal Bureau of Investigation, we feared for your safety. The cadre didn't want you to find your brother and me because then you would know the truth. You'd know that the syndicate's leader is an agent with the United States Federal Bureau of Investigation, that the syndicate itself is controlled from Hanoi."

Marilyn struggled to make sense of what she'd learned. "But the attacks on my life didn't start until I got to Manila."

Until I got to Manila. Marilyn repeated the words in her mind. The attempts on her life hadn't occurred immediately upon her arrival in the Philippine capital either. *Only after Mac got there.* She stiffened on the boat's hard wooden seat. A very large lump formed in her throat. Could Mac, the syndicate's leader, have ordered her assassination after he arrived?

Don't be an idiot, she told herself, swallowing hard. *The man saved your life three times.* In the distance, Marilyn heard the whine of a second outboard. As she listened, it came closer. The boat near them turned off its engine. Telling herself not to borrow trouble, she focused on Van's mother's startling revelations.

"What's wrong, Marilyn?" Madame Vinh's voice was worried.

"Something doesn't add up," Marilyn said. "Mac—the FBI agent—lied to me about quitting the bureau, so he must be connected to the syndicate. Also, the attempts on my life began after he arrived in Manila. But after we disguised ourselves, the attacks stopped."

Madame Vinh paddled to the edge of a dock. "Your friend may be the one the cadre wish to stop from seeing Van."

Her words jarred Marilyn. "What do you mean?"

Madame Vinh nodded thoughtfully. "As long as you were with your friend, there was a good chance he, too, would make contact with Van. So they had to do away with you. Once you were disguised, they didn't recognize you and the attacks stopped. Are you certain your friend lied to you about leaving the FBI?"

"When I saw him with Agent Smith, I was positive he'd lied." Marilyn frowned, picturing Mac in Rizal Park. There was something wrong with the picture.

"You mean there were two agents with you in Manila?"

Marilyn heard a new urgency in the woman's voice.

"Yes—no. Agent Smith is the one I worked with in San Diego. I saw him with my friend in . . ." Marilyn stopped in mid sentence. She hadn't seen the two men together, she realized suddenly. She'd seen Smith and then Mac, by himself, obviously hunting for someone. She'd thought Mac was looking for Smith. Maybe she'd been wrong. Lately she seemed to be wrong about a lot of things. *Maybe Mac was hunting for me.*

"HEY, SIT DOWN," Moschella snapped. "These round-bottomed boats tip easily. You'll dump us over."

Impatiently Mac sat, facing forward so he wouldn't have to look at Moschella in the rear with the engine.

"Mr. Finnegan didn't want to use the company boys for this job," Moschella went on. "He said to hire some local talent. All I have to do is get Van Wainwright to the Thai police. Mr. Finnegan will arrange for his extradition."

"So now the bureau's hiring thugs to do its dirty work. Somebody ought to tell Finnegan that's illegal." Mac's breath was coming in explosive little gasps. "Are they carrying weapons?"

"They wouldn't agree to do the job otherwise." Moschella paused while he turned the boat into the swells left by a passing water bus. "Don't worry, Mac. They're professionals, ex-military officers. Your girlfriend's not going to get hurt."

Mac intended to make damn sure of that. This whole setup made him nervous. The CIA would have been bad enough, but at least the company was halfway predictable. Who could tell what Moschella's thugs would do? Mac had never trusted Dan Moschella. There was no way he intended to leave Marilyn's fate in his hands. He heard the buzz of an outboard motor kicking over. At last they'd caught up with Moschella's "local talent."

A few minutes later, the two boats were about fifty yards from the craft they were following. It remained motionless near a wooden dock. In the moonlight Mac could make out a woman in a light-colored dress sitting at the boat's center. He was certain it was Marilyn. Another figure, he couldn't tell whether a man or woman, was huddled in the stern.

Unobtrusively Mac untied his shoelaces. Then, using his feet, he pushed his shoes off. A second later he propelled himself over the boat's gunwale with one arm and slid into the water, feet first.

Moschella made a grab for him. Mac felt the agent's hand on his arm. Quickly, he twisted away.

"Fool," Moschella snarled. "Now we'll have to kill you, too."

What does he mean? Before Mac had a chance to think about it, the tepid water closed over him. Rising to the surface he took a great gulp of air and sighted toward Marilyn's boat. Then he dived downward. Swimming underwater, he headed for it. He surfaced twice for air in his long swim. The second time he heard the pop-popping sound of small arms fire. What was Moschella up to? The gunfire lent fresh power to his legs, already well-muscled from years of swimming.

He reached Marilyn's boat. Instead of surfacing, he swam under it to the dock side, where he couldn't be seen from the other two boats. Grabbing the gunwale, he pulled himself up. The craft rocked dangerously, but he heard no cry of protest. Cautiously he peered inside.

Marilyn's sandals were thrown carelessly on the wooden seat across the bow. Her bag lay on the center seat, where Mac had seen her sitting only minutes ago. But Marilyn herself was gone.

TREADING WATER under the dock, Marilyn peered through gaps in the structure's wooden frame, her eyes only inches from Mac's T-shirt-clad back. Somebody was firing at him. She didn't stop to question why. Grabbing the dock's frame, she pushed herself down under it, and surfaced beside him half a second later.

"Quick. Under the dock." She tugged at his shirt. "There's a tiny air space between the river and the deck."

"Marilyn! Thank God you're okay!" He reached for her, as though to clutch her to him.

She shoved him away. This wasn't the time or place for a loving embrace. Staring at him, she blinked. The silly man looked as though he were about to cry. She must be mistaken. Cynical Mac MacIntyre was the last man in the world to cry about anybody or anything. The polluted water must be affecting his eyes.

"Quick," she said again. "Get under the dock."

"No. That's exactly where they'll look. I've got to get you away from here." She heard fear in his voice and realized it was for her. There was still a chance for them, she thought. If they could just get out of here in one piece. Flashlight beams probed the darkness around the boat.

"Keep looking. They've got to be there." It was Agent Smith's voice.

Marilyn stared at Mac's face. He looked mad enough to strangle the agent. If there'd been any doubt in her mind about Mac's loyalties, they vanished at that moment.

"Bring the boats in closer," Smith said.

Marilyn heard a man in the second boat repeat the order in Vietnamese. *So Agent Smith is working with the Vietnamese. And he's after me, Mac, Van, and Madame Vinh.*

With a flash of insight, she realized who the real leader of the syndicate was. Twisting her head toward the dock under which Madame Vinh waited, she said, "He's the one, *madame*. The man in that boat is an FBI agent. He's the head of the syndicate."

Marilyn knew Madame Vinh couldn't answer without swallowing a mouthful of water. But madame must have heard.

A terrible fury engulfed Marilyn. An FBI agent, who was supposed to protect innocent civilians, was behind all the awful things that had happened.

"Who're you talking to?" Mac sounded confused.

"Van's mother is hiding under the dock," Marilyn said through clenched teeth. Though submerged in the water, she felt hot with anger. "I just told her who the head of the syndicate is. It's not Van. It's Agent Smith."

"You can't be serious." Mac sounded more perplexed than doubtful.

There was no time to explain what Madame Vinh had told her. Marilyn's anger turned to scalding fury. "He's firing at us, Mac." Some of the rage she felt crept into her voice.

How dare Smith do this to her and her family? *How dare he?*

"Let's dump him and his Vietnamese cronies in the river," she whispered, breathless with wrath. "We'll see what water does to their damned bullets."

"Don't be stupid!" Mac's voice was uncharacteristically sharp. "You'd drown trying!"

The dull whine of the outboard engines began again. Slowly the two boats moved toward them.

"We've got to get out of here," Mac said.

Marilyn saw the alarm on his face and knew he'd try to stop her. She didn't intend to let him.

"Follow me," she cried.

He grabbed for her, but, with a kick of her heels, she moved easily out of his reach.

"We'll dump them when they get close to the dock," she said, seething with an unholy rage.

Before Mac could move, she took a great lungful of air and plunged downward, keeping her eyes tightly closed to protect her contacts.

"Hey, you can't..." Mac said. His words fell on empty air. Black water covered the space where she'd been.

Chapter Eighteen

Twisting, Mac forced his body down through the murky waters. Suddenly a beam of light passed above him. For a brief instant he saw Marilyn's slender form ahead of him, her black hair fanned out around her shoulders, her pink dress rippling through the water like the fins of some exotic fish.

The light vanished and darkness returned. But that one short glimpse had been enough to show him that Marilyn was an excellent swimmer. She moved through the depths like a professional. And he'd been afraid she might drown! If Mac hadn't been underwater, he would've laughed out loud.

Lungs bursting, he broke to the surface and surveyed the area around him. There was no sign of her. A second later he spotted her head coming up not six feet away. She'd actually stayed under longer than he had. Mac wouldn't have believed it if he hadn't seen it with his own eyes.

She turned her head and saw him. With one fluid motion, she swam to him. "As soon as they cut their engines, we'll dump both boats." She wasn't even breathing hard. "They've got round bottoms. They'll tip right over."

"It's too dangerous," he protested. "Those men have guns."

"Van's mother is under the dock," she whispered. "If we don't dump them, they'll shoot her. C'mon Mac. We'll do the two-man boat first."

The outboards cut off.

Marilyn's head went down and her pretty little bottom came up. Then she was gone, leaving ripples behind her. Mac followed. When he surfaced he was close to the bow. The boat's two occupants were standing up, flashlights and weapons in their hands. He saw Marilyn's head next to the stern. While he watched, she reached up and grabbed the gunwale. He did likewise.

This is going to be like shooting fish in a barrel. He nodded at Marilyn. Then, lifting himself half out of the water, he yanked at the gunwale with all his strength. The boat didn't tip over, but the sudden motion sent the two men inside toppling into the water.

Suddenly lighter, the little craft righted itself. He gave it a mighty shove downstream. If the boat's former occupants wanted to swim after it, more power to them. Without weapons they weren't a threat. He could hear them jabbering in a foreign tongue as they flailed around in the water. From the dock came the sound of running feet and excited voices.

He looked for Marilyn. She was gone. Quickly he sighted the remaining boat. In it, Dan Moschella was peering toward the men in the water. Mac knew the agent couldn't risk hitting his two comrades by firing random shots at him and Marilyn.

Moschella was scanning the river's surface.

"MacIntyre, I'm going to get you," Moschella said.

Grinning, Mac plunged downward again and swam underwater to Moschella's boat. When he came up, he saw no sign of Marilyn. She must not have surfaced yet.

Mac grabbed the gunwale and tensed himself for the move that would topple Moschella into the water.

There was a bone-breaking crack across the top of his knuckles. With an explosive grunt, he released his hold.

Moschella stared down at him from a seat at the boat's stern. A revolver in his hand was pointed at Mac's head.

"Say your prayers, you self-righteous SOB."

Nearby Mac heard a tiny splash and then a piercing scream. It was a high keen, so full of fury and anguish that it raised the bristles on his shaved head.

Moschella jerked toward the sound.

An instant was all Mac needed. With the speed of a striking snake, he reached up and yanked the revolver from the agent's hand. Before Marilyn could swim to the boat, he'd grabbed the gunwale and tipped it. Moschella fell into the river. Then Mac stretched upward, caught the other side, and turned the craft completely over. The falling boat hit Moschella on the head. Facedown in the water, most of his body was hidden under the small craft.

Bracing his feet against the side of the boat, Mac caught the agent under the arms and struggled to pull him free. His clothes seemed to be caught on something. Mac couldn't budge him. Marilyn was a few feet away.

"Grab him and turn him over while I lift the boat," he said urgently, releasing his hold on Moschella's arms.

Marilyn ignored Mac's order. The man she knew as Agent Smith was the incarnation of evil. He'd been responsible for many deaths and much misery. Why not let him drown here in the Chao Phraya River, a million miles from home?

"Marilyn?" Mac said.

She caught the agent under the arms. But she didn't turn him over or pull him away from the boat. Her fury burned hot and bright inside her, a poisonous rage that threatened to consume her. This man had come close to ruining her life. And Mac's life. And Van's life. He didn't deserve to live.

"My God, Marilyn. He's going to drown. Let's not have him on our consciences for the rest of our lives. He's not worth it."

Mac's voice jerked her back to reality. Suddenly Marilyn realized what she was doing. She was letting a helpless man die, a human being who no longer posed a threat to her or anybody else. Her rage dissolved and bitter tears of remorse for what she'd almost done streamed down her face.

Quickly she pulled Moschella away from the boat, turned him over, and grasping him firmly under the chin, started toward the dock. With her experience as a competitive swimmer, her movements were automatic.

What's happening to me? she wondered, frightened at the raw emotion that had swept over her. *I never used to feel things the way I do now.* The thought scared her. Her innocence had been sacrificed on this mad search for Van. What else had she lost? She began to shiver, uncontrollable tremors that shook her whole body.

Mac appeared beside her and gently removed her fingers from the unconscious man's chin. On Mac's face, Marilyn could see his concern for her.

"Only a few more feet to the dock," he said gently.

Shaking, Marilyn followed him. At last, strong arms reached down to help her out of the water. Someone wrapped a blanket around her shaking shoulders. Marilyn looked up at her benefactor.

Van! It was Van!

"Well, little sister, you've done it now," her brother said, grinning.

"Van!" Marilyn felt as though her heart would burst. "Thank God you're all right." She glanced from him to Madame Vinh, standing behind him, her clothes dripping. "Why didn't you tell me more about your beautiful mother? She looks so much like mine that I thought I'd gone mad when I got my first glimpse of her."

LATER, AFTER Dan Moschella had been revived and taken into custody by the Thai police, Marilyn—a blanket around her—lay on cushions on the floor of the river house on stilts, the house where Van had hidden for the past month. Van sat on a cushion near her. Madame Vinh, also wrapped in a blanket, was facing them.

They were waiting for Mac, who had gone to the U.S. embassy to make a priority call to FBI headquarters in Washington.

Their clothes hung on a rod attached to one wall. Dripping water stained the planked floor underneath. A single bare bulb hung from the topmost beam supporting the steeply slanted roof. The light cast shadows on the bare walls. The house had no plumbing. Drinking water was supplied to river dwellers by boat.

A square, apartment-style refrigerator sat on the floor in one corner. Next to it, a hot plate rested on a low table. A pot of hot water simmered on one of the two burners.

Before Mac left, he'd explained how Moschella had followed him from Rizal Park, that the bureau had pinpointed the park from the classified ad Marilyn had placed. Marilyn, Van and Madame Vinh spent the two hours Mac had been gone catching up on what had happened to each of them in their frantic escapes.

Van recounted his shock at hearing his mother's voice on the telephone from Bangkok. "When you said a hit man was gunning for me, I couldn't believe it." He smiled at his mother, the generous open smile that Marilyn loved. "That same night, somebody took a shot at me when I was watering the yard." He grinned at Marilyn. "It took me about two seconds to make up my mind to leave San Diego."

Marilyn grinned back at him. "That's about how long it took me when I saw my bombed apartment. The assassin was responsible for that, too. Only he wasn't trying to kill me, only scare me so that I'd lure you out of hiding." She leaned back against the cushions, absorbing the happiness of this moment. "Even though the Vietnamese community thought you were the syndicate's leader, I knew you couldn't do all those awful things the FBI was accusing you of."

How good it felt to know the people she loved were safe and well. If only Mac would get here...

As if in answer to her wish, he strode through the back door. He was wearing tan pants and an aqua T-shirt. Marilyn noticed that he'd removed the fake sideburns and washed the gray out of the fringe of hair around his ears. Faint red fuzz showed on the top of his head where the rest of his hair was starting to grow back. Before long he'd look like his old self again. She wondered if she ever would—if, indeed, she wanted to.

Mac dropped the shopping bag he was carrying on the floor. Marilyn barely glanced at it, looking at him expectantly. Van and Madame Vinh were also watching him.

"My old boss offered me my job back," he told them. "When I told him he could shove it, he said to take Moschella's place in San Diego." Mac grabbed a cushion and, tossing it on the floor next to Marilyn, sat down beside her. "He seemed to think I might have personal reasons for wanting a San Diego assignment." He looked at Marilyn for a long moment.

"What did you tell him?" Marilyn tried to keep her voice steady.

Mac put his arm around her blanket-clad shoulder and squeezed. "I told him I was going to move to San Diego, but not as an FBI agent. If I'm going to be a family man, I don't want to be involved in that business any longer. A certain lady I know said she'd be happy to let me move in until I set up my own law practice." He gazed at Marilyn, a sudden tenderness and vulnerability on his face. "I hope she still feels that way." His voice ground to a stop.

Marilyn's heart was pounding so loudly she felt as though everybody in the room could hear it. She wanted to throw her arms around him to reassure him. "She...she still does." Then, with a mock sigh of resignation, "If she still has an apartment, that is."

Mac's face lit up. An infectious grin spread from ear to ear. "We'll find you another apartment, if yours isn't fixed when we get back." He turned toward Van. "Before I met your sister, I thought having a family was about the worst thing that could happen to a man. Thanks to her, I've learned a thing or two. Her faith in you was something to behold."

"I know." Van smiled affectionately at his sister. "We trust each other, Mac. And we watch out for each other." He glanced from Marilyn to his mother. "Isn't that what families are all about?"

Mac nodded slowly. "A month ago, I wouldn't have agreed with you. Today I do. That's why I turned down

Finnegan's offer. From now on, I want to be able to tell Marilyn everything that happens in my life. No more secrets. No more games." He paused. "No more FBI."

At his words, an incredible joy swept over Marilyn. Too filled with emotion to speak, she touched her lips to his cheek. Looking around her, she felt a bottomless sense of peace and satisfaction.

Madame Vinh broke the comfortable silence. "Would you like some tea, Mac? We have a pot of water boiling on the stove."

"That would be nice, *madame.* Mac pulled Marilyn's head to his lap and stroked her hair. She found the touch of his hand stimulating and soothing at the same time. For a moment she wished they were alone. Then, glancing at the radiant faces of Van and his mother, she gave silent thanks that the four of them were here, together.

Hugging her blanket around her, Madame Vinh started to rise. Van touched her shoulder. "I'll get it, Mother," he said.

Van had always been immaculate. Tonight, in spite of his primitive living conditions, his jeans and white short-sleeved shirt looked freshly laundered.

When he'd returned with steaming hot cups for everyone, Marilyn sat up to drink hers. "You know, Mac," she said thoughtfully, after she'd taken a sip, "we've agreed that Benson, the assassin, killed poor Mr. Nguyen. But do you have any idea how he found the address? We know he didn't follow me. I got it from the envelopes in the back of Van's stamp albums. But nobody else saw them."

Mac focused on Van. "Was Toan Nguyen's name and address anywhere in your album besides on those envelopes?"

Van nodded, his face troubled. "It might have been. I've got a bad habit of jotting information down in margins. Toan was someone I corresponded with frequently about the refugee assistance program."

"Then that's where he got the address." Mac frowned, trying to recall his conversation with Moschella and Finnegan at San Diego's Old Town. "My ex-boss said Benson broke into that old BMW of yours, Marilyn, and stole some books from the back seat. If I remember rightly, you put the stamp albums there when we left Van's house. Benson must have figured they held the answer to where Van was since they were the only things you took."

"Why did you tell me to call Mr. Nguyen in Manila instead of Mrs. Phoung here in Bangkok?" Marilyn asked her brother.

Van smiled at her fondly. "I thought you'd be safer in Manila." His mouth curved in a wry grin. "I sure figured wrong on that one."

"What's going to happen to Benson, Mac?" Her mind fastened on the awful sights and smells in Mr. Nguyen's library. Deliberately, she stared at Mac's profile, letting his image replace the hellish memory.

"Benson?" Mac smiled apologetically. "I should have told you as soon as I came in. The Philippine police have him in custody, along with enough eyewitnesses to put him away for the next fifty years. Finnegan told me that just now." He kept stroking Marilyn's hair. "So you're off the hook, as long as you let the police know where you are. You might have to make a trip out there when the bas... when Benson goes to trial."

Mac glanced at Van. "He's already given the embassy the names of the Vietnamese in Orange County who hired him to kill you. He's trying to save his own skin, of course. They'll be brought to trial, too." A frown creased his brow. "That explains Nguyen's murder, but it doesn't account for the woman at the little shop on Tri Petch Road. I suppose the cadre..."

Horrified, Marilyn stiffened with shock. She saw the same horror she felt reflected on the faces of Van and his mother.

Mac stopped speaking when he heard Marilyn's gasp and the stunned silence that followed.

"I'm sorry," he said quietly. "Was she a friend?"

Madame Vinh found her voice first. "The owners of the shop are friends of mine. What did the woman look like?"

"She was a tiny woman not much more than five feet tall."

A look of indescribable sorrow touched Madame Vinh's face. "Then my dear friend, Thuy, is dead." Tears filled her eyes. "I owe her my life."

"She was alive this afternoon," Marilyn said stubbornly. "I don't see how you can sit here and tell us she's dead. Who told you?"

Mac chose his words carefully. "I know she's dead because I found the body."

Marilyn sat up and swung around, facing him. "That's not possible. You had no way of knowing who or where Madame Phoung was."

Mac took both her hands in his. They were cold and unresponsive. He wanted to hug her to him, to comfort her, but he knew she wouldn't let him.

"Please don't take this the wrong way," he began slowly. "When it happened, when I did what I did—remember, you'd just been wounded by a killer and you were being very mysterious about what you were up to—I was afraid you were doing something to put yourself in danger...."

She jerked her hands out of his. "You searched my handbag and found the envelopes. How could you, Mac?"

He heard a thin thread of hysteria in her tone. Something inside him sank like a stone. Was he going to lose her now, after they'd survived all this?

"He was only trying to protect you, Little One," Van said. "In his place, I'd have done the same thing."

"It was wrong. He shouldn't have done it." Marilyn's chin jutted out angrily.

"I know it was wrong, but I couldn't risk losing you." Mac struggled to keep the fear from his voice. "It was the only thing I could think of to do."

"I suppose you followed me, too. After you said you'd respect my privacy." She gave him a hostile glare.

"I'll get down on my knees and beg forgiveness, if it will help. As God is my witness, I did it only because I care for you and wanted to be sure nothing happened to you." His eyes pleaded with her. During that moment, he was unaware of anyone else in the room.

Madame Vinh eyed the two of them. "Mac loves you, Marilyn." Her eyes took on a far-away look. "Men don't always use good judgment when women they love are in danger."

Marilyn seemed to wilt right before Mac's eyes.

"I'm sorry, Mac." Her voice trembled. She seemed on the verge of tears. "I guess I was trying to put some of the blame on you."

"Blame?" Mac asked, trying to figure out what she meant. "Blame for what?"

Her eyes were starred with tears. "For the murders. First Mr. Nguyen is tortured because of those albums I stupidly left in my car. And, now, Mrs. Phoung is murdered within hours of the time I talked to her. Somebody must have followed me to her shop. That's how they found her."

"It's not your fault, Marilyn." Mac tried to pull her to him, but she pushed him away.

"Somebody *did* follow me, didn't they, Mac? If I mean anything to you, you'll tell me the truth." She bit her lip, and Mac knew she was trying to control her sobs.

"Moschella saw the picture of us together, so he knew your disguise," he said slowly. "He told the police cadre. They had you followed as soon as you arrived in Bangkok."

Tears rolled down Marilyn's cheeks. "Then, I *am* to blame." She wept, rocking back and forth.

Madame Vinh wrapped her blanket closely around herself and glided across the floor. Kneeling, she grabbed Marilyn by the shoulder with one hand and shook her.

"Mac's right," she said firmly. "It wasn't your fault. Those two people were agents working to overthrow the government of Vietnam. Much as I loved them both, I must tell you that they knew the risks of such a dangerous pur-

suit and were well prepared to protect themselves. You have
accomplished something they were not able to do—you have
put the police cadre's American arm—the syndicate—out of
business."

Marilyn's weeping came to a slow halt. "The gangs are
still there, *madame*. They will continue to harass the Vietnamese communities."

"Ah, but the organizational leadership is gone," Madame Vinh replied. "By themselves, the gang members in
America are little more than teenage thugs. They intimidate. They cause trouble. But nothing like the trouble of a
syndicate with an FBI agent at its head, a syndicate that's
controlled from Hanoi."

Behind her thick lenses, Madame Vinh's eyes narrowed.
"And you have helped do something else important, Marilyn. Thai authorities have two members of the Vietnamese
police cadre in custody, the two who were in the other boat.
When I return to my country, the government will no longer
be able to ignore the group's existence. I intend to do my
best to expose them."

"I'm going with you when you go home," Van said unexpectedly.

Intense astonishment flashed across his mother's heart-
shaped face. "Vietnam is very different from the States, my
son. Your life will not be easy."

"At least in Vietnam my so-called friends won't hire an
assassin to come gunning for me." He smiled at his mother.
"Maybe the government can use a good PR man to attract
tourists and U.S. business to the country."

With gratitude, Mac noticed that Marilyn was listening
alertly to their conversation. Her tears were gone. He put his
arm around her waist. She moved closer to him.

"Are you serious about leaving San Diego, Van?" she
asked, frowning.

He nodded. "I've given it a lot of thought during this past
month. I'll stay in Vietnam awhile, give it a look, get to
know my heritage. Maybe you could sell the business for me

and the houses. That should be enough to keep me going for a while."

Her frown deepened. "It sounds like you're not coming back."

He grinned at his sister. "I'm like the bad penny, Little One. I'll turn up again. In the meantime, you must come see us in Saigon—excuse me—Ho Chi Minh City. Before long Vietnam will be on every American tourist's wish list."

"Damned if I don't believe you," Mac said. He turned to Marilyn, who was eyeing him quizzically.

"You know, Mac," she said thoughtfully, "all this talk about Vietnam and the police cadre reminds me of something. If they were following me from the time I got off the airplane at Bangkok, why didn't they kill me? After trying three times in Manila, why didn't they finish what they started?

Mac shrugged matter-of-factly. "Because they weren't trying to stop you from getting together with Van. Moschella admitted I was the one they were worried about. By getting you out of the way, they prevented me from finding your brother."

With a triumphant look, Marilyn glanced toward Madame Vinh. "That's just what you suggested."

"Moschella knew that if I heard Van's story, I'd move heaven and earth to find out the truth." Mac took a deep breath. "After you and I separated, he decided to use me as a witness. He intended to have both you and Van killed by those Vietnamese thugs, and wanted to be sure it looked like self-defense. The scumbag thought I wouldn't see through his little game."

Marilyn threw him an innocent smile. "Maybe he thought that because you were so convinced Van was guilty."

Mac shifted uncomfortably on his cushion. Squeezing her waist, he whispered, "Why'd you have to bring that up?" To Van he said, "All the evidence was stacked against you. I didn't realize I might be wrong, not until Moschella threatened to kill me and started firing. Even then, I wasn't positive, not until I saw that loaded revolver pointed at my head.''

Mac turned back to Marilyn. "Incidentally, you saved my life. If you hadn't popped out of the water and screamed when you did, he would have shot me. Where'd you learn to swim like that?''

"She's like a fish in the water," Van answered for her. "When we were growing up, one wall of our house was lined with her trophies.''

"Why didn't you tell me?'' Mac studied her face, so close to his that her pale skin seemed to shimmer in the light from the bare bulb.

Marilyn grinned mischievously. "You were so proud of your beachboy life-style that I didn't want to deflate your ego by showing you my awards.''

Mac grimaced. "Ouch. I deserved that.''

Outside, the sky was lightening with the beginning of dawn. Hugging her blanket around her, Marilyn stood up and went to the door. Mac followed her onto the dock.

Mist was rising from the Chao Phraya, where boats piled high with produce were headed upstream to participate in the daily floating market.

"Do you know what today is?'' she asked him softly.

Mac thought for a moment. Then his face brightened. "Merry Christmas, darling.''

He cupped her face with his hands. As his lips touched hers, Mac knew that never again would the ghost of Christmases past make him lonely or unhappy. Since he'd found Marilyn, his world had changed. The endless days alone, playing shadowy games where no one could be trusted, were behind him. For the rest of his life, Marilyn—and, later, their children and grandchildren—would be with him to warm his holiday seasons.

ROMANCE IS A YEARLONG EVENT!

FEBRUARY
S M T W T F S
1 2 3 4 5 6

MARCH
S M T W T F S
1 2 3 4 5 6

APRIL
S M T W T F S
1 2 3

JULY
S M T W T F S
1 2 3

AUGUST
S M T W T F S
1

SEPTEMBER
S M T W T F S
1 2 3 4

OCTOBER
S M T W T F S
1 2

NOVEMBER
S M T W T F S
1 2 3 4 5 6
7 8 9 10 11 12 13
14 15 16 17 18 19 20
21 22 23 24 25 26 27
28 29 30

Celebrate the most romantic day of the year with MY VALENTINE! (February)

CRYSTAL CREEK
When you come for a visit Texas-style, you won't want to leave! (March)

Celebrate the joy, excitement and adjustment that comes with being JUST MARRIED! (April)

Go back in time and discover the West as it was meant to be . . . UNTAMED—Maverick Hearts! (July)

LINGERING SHADOWS
New York Times bestselling author Penny Jordan brings you her latest blockbuster. Don't miss it! (August)

BACK BY POPULAR DEMAND!!!
Calloway Corners, involving stories of four sisters coping with family, business and romance! (September)

FRIENDS, FAMILIES, LOVERS
Join us for these heartwarming love stories that evoke memories of family and friends. (October)

Capture the magic and romance of Christmas past with HARLEQUIN HISTORICAL CHRISTMAS STORIES! (November)

WATCH FOR FURTHER DETAILS IN ALL HARLEQUIN BOOKS!

CALEND

HAPPY VALENTINE'S DAY

James Rafferty had only forty-eight hours, and he wanted to make the most of them.... Helen Emerson had never had a Valentine's Day like this before!

Celebrate this special day for lovers, with a very special book from American Romance!

#473   ONE MORE VALENTINE
by Anne Stuart

Next month, Anne Stuart and American Romance have a delightful Valentine's Day surprise in store just for you. All the passion, drama—even a touch of mystery—you expect from this award-winning author.

Don't miss American Romance
#473   ONE MORE VALENTINE!

Also look for Anne Stuart's short story, "Saints Alive," in Harlequin's MY VALENTINE 1993 collection.

Take 4 bestselling love stories FREE

Plus get a FREE surprise gift!

WELCOME TO

The quintessential small town,
where everyone knows everybody else!

Each book set in Tyler is a self-contained love story; together,
the twelve novels stitch the fabric of the community.

"The small town warmth and friendliness shine through."
Rendezvous

Join your friends in Tyler for the twelfth book,
LOVEKNOT by Marisa Carroll, available in February.

Does Alyssa Baron really hold the key to Margaret's death?
Will Alyssa and Edward consummate the romance they began more than
thirty years ago?

GREAT READING...GREAT SAVINGS...AND A
FABULOUS FREE GIFT!

With Tyler you can receive a fabulous gift, ABSOLUTELY FREE,
by collecting proofs-of-purchase found in each Tyler book.
And use our special Tyler coupons to save on your next
TYLER book purchase.
